A. M. MATTHEWS

BODY

OF

KNOWLEDGE

A NOVEL

Piggyback Press

Printed in the United States of America

Print ISBN 978-1-7320841-0-0

E-ISBN 978-1-7320841-1-7

Library of Congress Control Number: 2018940062

Piggyback Press

Mill Valley, CA 94941

Email: PiggybackPress@hotmail.com

Cover and Interior: Design Damonza

www.ammatthews.com

For Randy, Mallory and Shana

Body Found in Emeryville Laboratory

EMERYVILLE, Calif. – Police are investigating what they're calling a suspicious death after a body was found yesterday at a laboratory near Powell and Hollis Streets. The body was discovered when officers responded to an activated alarm at approximately 2:30 p.m. The manner and time of death have yet to be determined. Authorities have not released the identity of the deceased.

CHAPTER 1

THE LATE AFTERNOON sun poured through the slats in the blinds, filling the office with bands of light. Sitting with her back to the windows, Susan moved her arms up and down, playing with the stripes of light and shadow. This was her favorite time of day, her work at the lab finished and everyone else having left. But today something was troubling her.

The office was orderly and well decorated. The wood trim on black-and-gray-tweed upholstered chairs matched the dark walnut furniture and bookcases. With its cream-colored walls and gray carpeting, the space was serene, almost Zen-like, yet Susan felt uneasy. Typically, by concentrating she could pinpoint what was bothering her and then lay it to rest through careful reasoning. It was only later, when she had begun to think about other things, that her anxiety might rise again. Once more, it would require concentration to retrace her thoughts and recall the source of her disquiet.

As she continued playing with the strips of light, she tried to bring into focus what was bothering her. Nothing came to mind. In fact, her day had gone surprisingly well, far better than she had expected. Lifting the top paper from the single neat stack on her desktop—*Investing in Biotechnology, The Security Analysts of San Francisco, Tuesday, September 21*—she smiled, astonished that she had actually ended up speaking at the conference today. When Russell had suggested she give a speech as a way of attracting investors, she had been reluctant to even consider it.

Three months ago, Miles Edwards, her former attorney, had retired abruptly, and Susan had turned to Russell Harris until she could find a suitable replacement. Since Russell had been adequately handling her mother's rather basic legal needs, Susan had thought that he might be useful in the interim. To her surprise, Russell had quickly begun familiarizing himself with her business and advising her. This was quite different from her previous experience. Once her company had incorporated, Miles had answered her questions and looked over her contracts, but he had never delved into its operations or suggested any changes. Russell, on the other hand, had immediately started asking questions and making suggestions.

At first, Susan had found this behavior intrusive. Russell had no specific knowledge about her industry, and she had limited faith in his abilities. Still, some of his suggestions had proven helpful. He had pointed out that she needed publicity if she wanted to increase her laboratory's visibility to the financial community. At his repeated urging, she had agreed to think about speaking at the security analysts' conference and ultimately accepted the invitation.

When informed that she'd been selected as the keynote speaker, Susan had fervently regretted her decision. Speaking about her own research would not be difficult for her, but delivering the main address to a large audience about the industry in general, while attempting to interject bits of humor, was not something she could do well. Unable to decline at that point, she had spent considerable time preparing her speech and practicing her delivery. Earlier today when she had stood to deliver her talk, she had not needed notes.

And the very first question, from a young financial professional, had opened the door to discussing her company. "Dr. Glasser, I was wondering if you would tell us what types of research your company is conducting?"

It was the very question she had been hoping for. "At Glass Biotechnology, we are currently investigating immune-response enhancement. The specific area we are researching is anti-idiotypic antibodies. Let me explain briefly. Anti-idiotypic antibodies occur in normal blood. When our bodies mount an immune response to something, we not only develop antibodies against that specific antigen, we also develop antibodies against those original antibodies, and further antibodies to those antibodies. These finely tuned networks ensure the robustness of the body's immune capabilities. Understanding and ultimately impacting these networks should enable us to fight a variety of diseases."

The next two questions had been more general but also easily answered. The last question had come from a member of the press attempting, Susan felt, to stir up controversy.

"Doctor Glasser, don't you think that the potential for biotechnology misuse should be a major consideration?"

It was a question she'd been expecting, and she had addressed her response to the entire group. "Of course any technology can be mishandled and misappropriated, but my training is in biochemistry, not in psychic predictions."

A murmur of laughter had run through the hall, and she had continued, "From my present vantage point, I see this body of knowledge continuing to benefit people all over the world."

Relieved that her portion of the program had concluded and anxious to avoid the afternoon traffic, Susan had hurried through the lobby and out onto the sidewalk. San Francisco's fall weather had been bright and cool, and it had felt refreshing to be outside. As she fumbled through her handbag for her parking ticket and a twenty-dollar bill for the garage, something had caught her eye. In the passing crowd, she had noticed…something…and had instantly felt a twinge of recognition. Trying to determine what had grabbed her attention, she had scanned the sidewalk. Not finding the answer, she promptly forgot about this fleeting impression. When the light changed, Susan had hurried to cross with a large group of pedestrians.

Now, alone in her quiet office and finally able to pinpoint the source of her unease, Susan was annoyed with herself for once again ruminating about nothing. She hadn't seen anything on the sidewalk that afternoon and was sitting safely in her workplace across the bay.

She needed to make one call before leaving Emeryville. Lifting the telephone, she heard a deep rumbling, then the building creaked and made a wheezing sound. Trying to connect the sound with its source, she saw the stripes of light and shadow vibrating. She felt the side of her desk pushing against her leg just as items began cascading from the bookcases. Books, journals and papers, award plaques and framed photographs flew from the shelves. The glass bottle on the water cooler swayed from side to side before crashing to the floor, spraying water everywhere. Her heart racing, Susan realized it was an earthquake.

Pushing back her chair, she tumbled to the floor and crawled uncomfortably under the desk. As she did, she heard a tall bookcase crash loudly onto her desk, which shuddered violently from the impact. Susan's first thought in the midst of this mayhem was to notice how clumsy she felt. The business suit with its fitted skirt made it hard to move easily, but even so, she felt slow and stiff. It struck her as odd that while experiencing one of nature's great forces, her initial thought was how cumbersome and old she felt.

Susan could not determine if this was a large tremor or a major quake. The shallow edges of San Francisco Bay had been filled in for urban development, and much of Emeryville was built on this bayfill, so seismic episodes were likely to be magnified. As the shaking continued, she crouched under her desk, waiting for the movement to subside. Finally, the fear that had evaded her flooded her mind; her heart pounded wildly, and she felt herself breathing rapidly. Her hands and legs were trembling.

Once the quaking subsided, she waited to see if there would be more movement, an aftershock. It was only then that she realized she was wet. Cold water had seeped onto the carpet under the desk, and her knees, hands, and feet were soaked. Noting large pieces of glass shelving next to her hand, she was grateful her back had been to the windows. Not sensing any more quaking, she began to calm down. When she started feeling foolish crouched on the floor, she climbed out from under the desk.

Once on her feet, she checked the windows, relieved to find none of the glass had broken. When Susan had moved into this building, she'd been advised to have the glass coated on the inside with a plastic film as an additional security measure. She was glad now that she had done this; it was likely the film that had kept the windows from shattering.

In stark contrast to its former state, however, the office was a mess. The one bookcase that remained standing was empty. The items that had been placed so meticulously on its shelves were strewn on the floor. The toppled bookcase was resting face down on her desk; its glass shelves, having fallen out, were now shattered and lying on top of a wet jumble of books and papers. So much for the peace and quiet of being alone at the end of the day. It would have been far better if someone had stayed late. Now she would have to clean everything up herself.

Walking carefully to avoid the glass, she heard the crunch of shards under her sodden shoes. How ironic that her company was named Glass Biotechnology. How fitting that she, the president and sole owner, should be the only one available to clean up this mess.

Proceeding down the hallway past the bathroom and the locked storage cabinet, she pulled open one of the double doors to the laboratory. An empty laboratory is always a strange place, but in the evening or nighttime when deserted, the space seemed especially eerie. It always felt as if people had just been there but mysteriously disappeared the moment she entered. Everything was oddly silent.

All the company's research was conducted in this large, high-ceilinged room, divided into six main workstations and four areas for specialized tasks. Every square inch of surface and wall space was used for work or material. Above each workstation, crammed shelves reached up to the ceiling. At the ends of each aisle were sinks. Between each station were computers and other equipment shared by the researchers; some of the larger equipment was on rollers, so it could be moved from station to station. On one wall close to the ceiling was a row of windows made of thick metal-reinforced glass.

These panes did not open and were for light only. Since the plate-glass windows in the office had not shattered, Susan was sure these much smaller and sturdier panes would be unscathed.

The workbenches were so cluttered, it was not immediately apparent if anything had been overturned by the tremor. Gloves, lab coats, protective eyewear, and work in progress were strewn on every flat surface. Susan carefully examined the first workstation she came to. Across the fume hood, used to protect scientists from volatile chemicals and to keep their experiments sterile, someone had scribbled a complicated diagram for a chemical reaction. Food wrappers, a disposable cup, a soda can, and the remains of a sandwich were left on a workbench, along with papers, paraffin, and slide trays. Two boxes of old slides were on the workbench as well. Susan was sure these belonged on one of the high shelves above. From their position and intact condition, it did not appear they had fallen; more likely, no one had bothered to return them after finding the specimens they'd been seeking.

Looking at this first workbench, Susan thought it did not appear noticeably altered from its normal state. Research scientists are notoriously messy and seem to work most comfortably in cluttered, crowded spaces. Still, Susan could not help feeling that in this regard, her employees were in a class by themselves. Why on earth did she have to have such sloppy employees? Each new person she added to her staff was more careless about maintaining the workspace than the one who'd come before. Even if she hired someone tidy and organized, it was only a matter of a week, two at the most, until he or she became as messy as the rest of her researchers. Maybe it was viral, she thought. Or maybe it was because she was so neat and precise that she was a human magnet for the terminally disorganized. Gary had been terribly messy, and a packrat to boot. How could anyone as fastidious as she was ever have been married to him?

As she continued checking for damage, Susan reflected that she had spent thirty-three years working in research laboratories, and every one had looked like this. When people were done working, eating, drinking, or whatever, they either went on to something else or left for the day. Perhaps when someone ordered a pizza, they threw out an old box to make way for the new one. The level of debris and disorganization was constant, never getting worse but never getting better.

Scattered about was the odd newspaper, a jacket, an old sweater. Susan stopped to pick up a baseball cap and an empty coffee cup. Likely all had recently fallen.

Moving on, she was relieved to find the second workbench also seemed undisturbed by the quake. A lucky thing, too, since most of the caustic and dangerous chemicals were used at this station. Still, messy as the station was, it was difficult to know for certain if anything had been disturbed. Just ahead, a pile of papers and notebooks were on the floor. These had obviously fallen from the temblor. Better to leave them—Wolf or Mandy would know what was work in progress and what should be returned to the file boxes overhead.

Susan looked above the workbench hood to shelves that reached to the ceiling. Boxes upon boxes of old lab results and records had stayed in place, thank goodness. Her office was such a mess, she had been sure she'd find papers and broken glass on the workbenches and all over the floor. On closer inspection, this station, too, appeared to be in good shape. Perhaps she would have an easy time of it, and only her office would need to be cleaned up today.

But at the next workstation, broken beakers and the remains of specimen slides were scattered all over the floor. The fragments of glass twinkled in the fluorescent light. She was sure nothing here could be salvaged. How much work would they have to repeat because of this? The time that would be lost and the expense she would incur in repeating these trials were certain to cause significant setbacks.

Discouraged, Susan moved out of the work area to the animal room. First checking the rodent cages, which were closest to the door, she was relieved to see all were still neatly lined up on their shelves. Each of the thirty-two rodents had its own cage, and every one of them seemed alert.

It was mandated by law that laboratory animals be well cared for at all times. Susan made sure their water supplies were intact and did not need refilling. The specially constructed water bottles used a valve and sipping straw that had survived the seismic episode. The food pellets were undisturbed as well.

On the opposite wall were small cages that weren't being used; these, too, were neatly lined up. On the back wall, six large cages designed to hold primates were precisely placed on a wide counter. Only two were occupied, by two fully mature female *Macaca mulata*, or rhesus monkeys. Had someone actually followed up when she'd mentioned that everything in the animal room had to be securely anchored? She would have to find out who had secured the primate cages and thank him or her with a gift card.

Speaking to the primates, Susan said, "Gigi, how are you, girl? Did you get frightened by the earthquake? You look fine to me, wide awake. And what about you, Gina? Did you get scared? I'll tell you a secret, but you mustn't tell anyone: I was scared, too. But we're all safe now."

Both had adequate amounts of water and food. With a sigh of relief, she said goodnight to Gina and Gigi and left the animal room, closing the door softly behind her.

Once back in the laboratory work area, Susan went to the storage closet. Research labs need significant cleaning equipment, and the closet was loaded with supplies. None of her staff ever bothered to close the closet door once they found what they were looking for; if the door was closed, it was only because she had been the last one to go in there. Susan took out a shop-vac, a bucket, a pair of heavy work gloves, and a broom. Things could have been much worse. She'd have to leave the broken glass on the laboratory floor; there just wasn't enough time to deal with it now. She still needed to sweep up her office and get the shards out of the carpet. Then she would have to dry things as best she could before she checked the walls and the outside of the building for cracks or other visible damage. And she would need to hurry. She couldn't be too late to meet Rosa, not tonight.

CHAPTER 2

As ALWAYS, ROSA greeted her with a beautiful smile. Smiling back at her best friend, Susan stepped on the treadmill next to her friend, who was already jogging, and punched in her weight (135 pounds), age (53), and speed (4.2 miles per hour). Getting side-by-side treadmills truly was fortuitous.

Rosa motioned with her chin. "Look who's here."

Standing by the rack of dumbbells were the gym buffs Susan and Rosa called GG and BB. Rosa had dubbed the local Adonis God's Gift. According to her, GG had briefly played professional football, although these days he seemed to spend most of his time working out and impressing himself and his friends with his good looks and athletic credentials. GG did not talk to just anyone. Tonight, he was conversing with his favorite workout partner, whom Rosa had nicknamed the Body Beautiful. BB was tall, late-fortyish, and state-of-the-art surgically enhanced. She was married to a plastic surgeon, and both he and she took great pride in her appearance. Standing together, BB and GG looked like blond Barbie and Ken dolls brought to life. Susan and Rosa found them very entertaining.

Susan had never spoken with either of them and didn't think Rosa had, either. The conversations they overheard were confined to very few topics. First and most important was physical appearance, in all its permutations. This included their own looks, which they deemed most excellent, and the looks of other members, which generally were not up to their standards. They also discussed exercise, weight, diet, plastic surgery, and, on occasion, weekend plans.

"I wonder what they are talking about tonight," Rosa said, jogging her few last steps before slowing to a brisk walk.

"Anti-idiotypic antibodies and affinity chromatography, no doubt," Susan replied, deadpan. Rosa responded with exaggerated eye rolling and a giggle.

"How many years since we first met?" Rosa asked, her voice revealing her fatigue.

"At least twenty. I was still married when I joined FitMarin, and we were still young and beautiful."

"But were we up to their standards?" Rosa asked with a nod toward BB and GG.

"Well, of course we were," Susan said facetiously.

"Too bad they weren't members then, because we could have all become bosom buddies," Rosa chuckled.

The demands of starting and running her own laboratory, combined with increasing responsibilities for her aging mother, had left Susan little time for other things. Going to her gym remained a priority, especially when she was able to see Rosa almost every time she went. When Susan had joined FitMarin, she and Rosa had become close almost immediately. After all this time, Susan was still in awe of her talkative, intelligent, and always highly amusing friend. Susan had other friends, of course, but she saw them infrequently.

"I have some pictures to show you," Rosa said. "There are some good ones of our new house."

Rosa had never wanted to move out of the Bay Area. But her husband was twelve years older and had been talking about retiring as long as Susan could remember. When he had announced his official retirement, Susan had been dismayed.

"Idaho? Whatever are you going to do in Idaho?" she had asked Rosa.

"I will do what I do here but on a smaller scale, or run an art gallery or two. If that doesn't work out, I can join a right-wing militia," Rosa had joked. "I think Ray just likes the idea of Idaho. Hopefully, when he sees what living there is like, he'll want to move back."

The treadmill stopped, and Susan looked at her friend. Rosa had never said anything, but Susan felt that being married to Ray had aged her as much as the years had. Although she dyed her hair brown to cover the gray, when Rosa was quiet her face looked tired and drawn. Ray was, from all Susan knew, a decent man, but he was difficult, and Rosa was the one who made the accommodations in their relationship. Susan could only hope that living in Idaho with a retired, older husband would not weigh her best friend down further.

"What do I know? I've never even been to Idaho," she had commented, trying to sound lighthearted. Really, what did she know? She certainly had not chosen well when she married. She had been thirty-two and ready to settle down when she began dating Gary, who was about the same age. He had two degrees from Stanford and was nice looking, with a trim physique and regular, rather small facial features. Impressed with himself, he had exuded confidence, intelligence, and charm. But the façade was a thin one, and it didn't take long for her to realize the kind of man she had married. Every conversation they had was either about money or centered on Gary. If Susan expressed anything other than total admiration, her husband became cold and distant.

After they had been married a year, Gary had started a hedge fund with two partners, renting a fancy office in a prestigious building. A short time later, he purchased an expensive foreign sports car. One night after they returned home from a party, Susan came down with a fever and chills. The medication she needed was downstairs in the kitchen, but she hadn't felt well enough to get it. Gary had told her he didn't want to be bothered and was going to bed.

When Susan had filed for divorce, his primary concern had been to keep his business and all his assets for himself. Under California law, she was entitled to share in the profits and equity of his management company, but she'd been so anxious to get out of the marriage, she agreed to the terms he wanted.

Susan had begun working for Avery Biogenetics Corporation right out of graduate school. During her twenty-four years there, she became the head of its most prestigious and profitable research unit. From the start, her compensation had been a combination of salary and equity. The terms of their divorce left her all her stock and options, in return for allowing Gary to keep his business as his personal property. Since Avery had been privately held then, the stock had no market value. When the company went public five years later, Susan's stock had been worth a considerable amount. And once she had exercised the last of her options, her total payout was more than two and a half million dollars after taxes.

Not long after the IPO, Susan had run into one of Gary's partners. Dan had told her how angry Gary was that his share of the divorce settlement had not included any of her stock or options; apparently, this was a major thorn in Gary's side. The next time Susan ran into Dan, he had informed her that Gary had taken excessively risky positions and refused to listen to either him or Larry, their partner, when they had tried to rein in his behavior. He continued to blame him and Larry for the mistakes Gary himself had insisted on making. The professional reputations of all three had been severely damaged when the hedge fund folded. Dan and Larry had recovered and were once again doing well, but Gary had lost his last two jobs and was currently unemployed.

Dan had also gleefully reported that her ex-husband had lost much of his hair and most of his looks, saying that Gary had turned into a regular Pillsbury Doughboy.

Susan's mother had never been fond of Gary. Early in their relationship, Bunny had pointed out that, while she had no specific complaints, there was something about Gary she did not like. After their separation, she revealed that the first time she'd met him, he made her skin crawl. Looking back, Susan realized her mother did have good instincts. At least she had been right about Gary.

Though Susan would have liked to have children, she was grateful that she never had any with Gary. She hadn't seen him in fifteen years, and other than those two encounters with Dan, she hadn't heard anything about him. He was long out of her life, and she rarely thought about him; so it was surprising that twice today, at the laboratory and now at the gym, he had crossed her mind.

Done working out, Susan and Rosa walked to the ladies' locker room. Susan's locker was near the front on the right side of the aisle; Rosa's locker was at the back on the left. As a result, in all these years they never dressed or undressed together. As always, Rosa continued down the aisle. Susan opened her locker and undressed quickly, then neatly folded her gym clothes and placed them in the locker. Slipping into her rubber flip-flops, she took a towel, shampoo, and conditioner from her locker and headed to the showers.

On most nights, she and Rosa would sit in the sauna and chat after their showers, then dry their hair and put on their makeup together, but the earthquake had made that impossible. Such bad timing! It was likely Susan would never work out or sit in the sauna with Rosa again.

Susan and Rosa never used the private stall showers, preferring to use adjacent shower heads. Realizing this was probably the last of many such evenings, they took their time showering and washing their hair.

As they dried off across from the sauna, Susan looked at their reflections in the mirror. The two were about the same height, five feet five inches, and moderately overweight. The main difference in their appearance was that Rosa had darker skin and hair. In the florescent lighting, they looked awful, but everyone looked terrible under these lights. Without their regular workouts, Susan thought, they would probably look scary, not just old.

Back at her locker, Susan quickly put on a pair of cotton pants, a T-shirt, and a cardigan sweatshirt, glad she had remembered to bring a change of clothes so that she didn't have to put her business suit back on. As she dried her hair, she studied her reflection again.

It wasn't only Rosa who had grown older. There were deep wrinkles around Susan's hazel eyes. Though her hair still looked okay, it was thinning at the temples. She kept it a medium blond with lighter highlights, in a bob ending an inch above her shoulders, virtually a uniform for middle-aged women of high status. The style, along with the expensive-to-maintain color, was dated. Susan felt she looked exactly what she was: a middle-aged scientist seriously lacking in flair. Her teeth were probably her best feature. She had whitened them just yesterday, to look her best for her speech today.

Standing next to her, Rosa was almost done drying her hair and would soon begin applying an astounding array of hair and skin products. Susan smiled to herself. Rosa sure knew her cosmetics, and when she put them all on, she certainly did look good, even if she was getting fixed up just to drive home.

"Here," Rosa said as she handed Susan two small jars. "Take these; I am not going to use them, and you might like them." Once Rosa found something superior, she could no longer abide using the old product.

"Thanks."

In the mirror, Susan could see Crazy Rene at the sink behind them. Rene was probably eight or ten years younger than Susan and Rosa. Every time Susan saw her, with her dark hair, dark eyes, and tan skin, she thought of the color brown. Rene occasionally attempted to be friendly, but there was something off-kilter about her. After her evening shower, she sometimes put on pajamas, flossed and brushed her teeth in the gym sink, and went home ready for bed. Tonight she was wearing oversized flannel pajamas printed with pumpkins of various sizes.

On one occasion, Rene left her athletic shoes in the sauna overnight to dry, and the shoes overheated and combusted, starting a fire. It had not been easy to get workmen into the ladies' locker room to make the repairs; because of the extensive damage, the sauna had been closed for three months. Susan and Rosa had been so happy when the sauna finally reopened, Rosa had declared it

National Local Sauna Day. After their workout and sauna, they had gone out for drinks to celebrate.

Rene was always on warning at the health club for something or other, constantly on the brink of losing her membership. Her locker was right next to Rosa's, and Rene always talked to Rosa while she was changing her clothes. Later, doing an excellent imitation, Rosa would report Rene's latest news. Susan had often thought they could make a sitcom based on Rene's life. Now, without Rosa, Susan would no longer know about Rene's latest mishaps or her membership status.

Back at Rosa's locker, Rosa took out her phone and showed Susan her latest photographs.

"This is the house we bought," Rosa told her, displaying a photo of an attractive two-story wood-framed structure with a massive stone fireplace. "Here's one of the view from the master bedroom. You can see the mountains in the distance. This is a picture of Dave and his family. The children are good-looking, as you can see. I wish I had a new picture of Tyler to show you. He's so tall now, and still such a nice boy. With that mother, it's hard to believe he turned out so well."

Ray had married right out of college and had had two children, Dave and Lauren. When Susan had first met Rosa, Lauren and her son, Tyler, had been living with Rosa and Ray. Lauren had always been troubled and lacked direction—like her mother, Rosa had said—and Rosa, who never had children of her own, had tried to help with Tyler; Susan recalled her bringing the child to FitMarin for swimming lessons. Rosa had been crushed when Lauren found a new boyfriend and moved with him to Idaho, taking the boy with her. The boyfriend was no longer in the picture, but Lauren must have liked Idaho or met someone else, because she had stayed. Rosa had been elated when Tyler returned to the Bay Area to attend college. Living closer to Lauren, especially now that Tyler was in Berkeley, was not at all appealing.

"I won't need this locker any longer," Rosa said as she took out her possessions and put them into her gym bag. It looked like a mini locker itself. With a place for everything, it was a portable cosmetics store. "I paid for a year and still have eight months left. You can have it," she added, zipping up her bag.

Trying to sound more jovial than she felt, Susan replied, "I don't have all the cosmetics you do—one locker is just fine for me, thank you. Anyway, my locker is up front, and yours is all the way back here. I'll never use it."

"You might. Twenty-five-seventeen-thirty-four," Rosa said, whispering the locker's combination. "If you forget the numbers, you can email me. But you're a computer brain. You never forget anything. And don't forget, it's near Rene's locker, in case you feel like talking," Rosa said, winking at Susan.

CHAPTER 3

"MAMA, ARE YOU here?" Susan unlocked the door and let herself in. Bunny lived in a seniors-only complex in San Rafael, but since she was frequently out at activities or visiting neighbors, Susan often had to track her down. It was still early in the morning, so that was not necessary today. Bunny was seated on her couch, visibly happy to see her daughter. In dark blue slacks and a light blue sweater that looked hand-crocheted, the collar and cuffs of a well-tailored cream cotton blouse peeking out from under the sweater, her mother was her usual elegant self. Susan had not seen this outfit before. As always, Bunny had *put on her face*, as she put it. Carefully applying makeup was the first thing she did every day. Her given name was Bernice, but her family and dearest friends called her Bunny, a nickname that, with her crown of naturally wavy white hair, suited her well. She had never asked Gary to call her Bunny.

"Come give me a kiss. You look nice today. I like your shoes with that sweater," Bunny said, referencing Susan's dark gray suede shoes and charcoal gray and powder blue sweater.

Susan leaned over and gave her mother a kiss on the cheek. "Glad you approve. I bought the shoes awhile ago, but this is the first time I've worn them."

The living room was smartly furnished in an eclectic mix of rustic Italian and English country-style furnishings. The sofa was a comfortable overstuffed piece with rolled arms, covered in beautiful floral chintz. All the other furniture had different fabrics and wood tones. Her mother had enough style and confidence that nothing matched exactly.

"It doesn't look like anything fell yesterday," Susan said.

At a wall of distressed-wood bookcases, Susan paused to look at the framed photographs her mother had placed in front of the books. Many were of her, including an entire shelf with her school pictures. Beginning with Susan in kindergarten, missing two front teeth, the photos progressed year by year to her high school graduation portrait. Above that was Susan's college graduation portrait, followed by two more formal shots of her in graduate school. On the higher shelves were pictures of Bunny and David's parents and other relatives. Lower shelves held photos of Bunny and David on their wedding day and at other events, alone as well as together and with Susan. Bunny arranged her photos in chronological order, so if you looked at them one by one moving from left to right, you could see each person age as your eyes moved down the row. The last picture of David showed how frail he was, still making an effort to smile for the camera.

Returning to the couch, Susan sat down close to her mother and lifted her mother's hand. "We have to get your ring cleaned next time we go out."

A cameo surrounded by diamonds, it had been a unique choice for an engagement ring. Her wedding ring fit against it perfectly. Early in their courtship, David had bought both rings, sure about Bunny and their life together. They were the first and most treasured of many beautiful pieces of jewelry David had selected for his wife over the years.

Instead of responding, Bunny changed the subject.

"You work too much," she told her daughter. "With your training, you could design cosmetics, and you wouldn't have to spend so much time in the lab."

Seeing the look of annoyance on Susan's face, Bunny added, "Cosmetics help people, too. The next time you're feeling sad or disappointed, put on some new makeup, and you'll feel better. I always do. You know, dear," she went on, touching Susan on the cheek, "since we are discussing cosmetics, you really need to change your makeup. Everyone should update their look every year or two at the very least."

"So I work too hard and should have gone into the cosmetics industry. Where have I heard that before? And now I have to completely change my makeup?"

Bunny laughed. "As I always say, *If something is worth saying, it's worth repeating.* And where have you heard that before?"

Susan thought of Rosa and her cosmetics bag. No one could ever fault Rosa for not having an updated look.

"Rosa is moving to Idaho," Susan told her mother with a sigh. "Would you like to go there for our vacation next year? We'd wait until the weather is warmer."

"I don't want to miss the ballet."

"You won't miss any performances. When did you ever miss the ballet? The season is over in May. We won't go before then," Susan told her, trying not to let her irritation show.

"I'll be eighty-one in May. I hope I'm still able to travel."

Immediately, Susan felt a wave of sadness. Her mother was getting old; she wouldn't have her forever. Susan could not imagine life without her mother. Before she was born, Bunny had had two miscarriages. Her parents had wanted more children, but after Susan's birth, her mother never got pregnant again. Fifty years ago, infertility was not easily remedied. It had been the three of them when she was growing up. Now it was just the two of them.

"What are you doing today?" Susan asked.

"Well, since you asked, Florence and I are going to Choga class. I'm getting quite good at it, if I do say so myself."

"Choga? What's Choga? Do you mean yoga?"

"No, not yoga, Choga. It's a special set of exercises you do in a chair. Shirley and Doris only go once a week, but Florence and I go to every class. I'm going today even though I have to be at the doctor at eleven."

Susan smiled at the thought of her mother and Florence in a Choga class and wondered what outfits they wore. Bunny surely wore something special to do chair exercises.

"You didn't mention you had the doctor today. If you tell me about these things in advance, I can take you."

"I don't need you to take me. I'm going on the shuttle. It's only for a blood test. You can't possibly take me to every appointment; you wouldn't have time to do anything else. My life is medicalized, dear girl. The golden years aren't so golden."

"Well, I have to Choga on out of here," Susan said. "I need to stop in the city to see Russ before work."

"So that's why you look so nice today. Russ, is it? You know, I like Russell, and I think he likes you."

"Mother! Russell? He's your lawyer, and for the time being, he's my lawyer, too, and probably not a very good one, at that."

Russell had called and asked her to come in about something that needed to be dealt with as soon as possible. He had recently switched law firms, for reasons he did not disclose. This was his second change since her mother had started using him. What was pressing was probably his need to increase his billable hours. What was Bunny thinking, saying Russ liked her? Sometimes her mother said outrageous things just to get a reaction.

Enough of this, Susan thought. I need to get out to the real world.

CHAPTER 4

RUSSELL STOOD BY the window, reading her latest financial statements. Sunlight poured into the office. Looking at him in the natural light, Susan wondered whether his looks would hold up as he aged. She guessed him to be in his late thirties, though it was possible he was already in his forties. He was of average height and attractive, with thick dark brown hair, dark blue eyes, and very fair skin. No, on second thought, it was unlikely he would still look this good at forty. Fair skin typically ages early.

Susan had seen him out of a business suit on one occasion. Russell had drawn up Bunny's will, revocable trust, and healthcare directives and come by her mother's apartment to drop off the paperwork. It was a Saturday, and he'd been wearing slacks and a polo shirt. In that outfit, Susan could tell that he was fit and well built.

He should be trim and fit, she'd thought; he's single, and men take care of their appearance when they're young and unmarried. At least she thought he was single. Russell didn't wear a wedding ring, and once he'd mentioned that he lived alone. But things could have changed. Susan wondered if he had ever been married, but the subject had never come up, and, of course, she had never asked.

This was the first time she had been in this office. It was so small, it barely had room for two client chairs. His last office had been almost three times as large and much better appointed.

Susan was unprepared for what her lawyer had to say. "The

bottom line is, you are spending more than you are taking in. You don't have the resources for this to continue, Susan. All of your personal assets are tied up in your business. I don't know how your last advisor let your finances get to this point. If things continue as they are, in six weeks you won't be able to make your payroll or pay your rent."

Susan was aghast. She'd known that money was tight but had no idea things were this dire. Maybe Russell was mistaken—how much did he know about finances, anyway? Apparently, more than she did.

"As I see it, you have the following choices," he continued. "You can look for additional capital. You have one hundred percent ownership of Glass Biotech, which is highly unusual, and if you choose to go this route, you will sacrifice considerable control. Even a minority investor will want protections. Your other option is to do more contract work. Currently, you're doing, what is it…sixty percent contract work and forty percent proprietary?"

Susan nodded.

"To avoid selling equity, you'll need to start doing at least eighty-five percent contract work. I know this means limited time and resources for your own research. But this is the quickest route, and there are no additional legal or financial-reporting costs."

Susan looked down at the floor. It seemed the real world wasn't so great lately, either.

When she looked up at Russell again, he said, "There is one more option. You could sell your business and go back to working for another company, or retire. I bring up this because it is a viable option, unlike going public at this time, which is not. Glass Biotech would need at least one fairly significant drug to make an IPO practicable. I'm sorry; I realize these are difficult choices, but you will need to decide quickly. I'll work on getting you a home-equity loan to tide you over until your cash flow improves."

"Yes, please look into raising some capital," Susan told him. "In the meantime, I'll try to find additional contract work that can be done with our present equipment. In fact, I have an appointment with ABC today, and I'll see if I can pick up some more work from them."

"ABC?"

"That's Avery. When I worked there, we called it ABC among ourselves," Susan explained.

"Is there anything else you want to discuss?" Russell asked.

Susan shook her head.

"Well, then, we're off the clock. How is your mother doing?" Russell seemed to be fond of Bunny and always asked about her. But then, everyone liked Bunny. Even at eighty, she was still making friends.

"I was over there this morning. She's fine, all dressed up with nowhere to go. Actually, she did have somewhere to go. She's taking Choga classes."

"Choga classes? Is that some kind of dance lesson? Sounds like it would be done in a conga line."

"No," Susan said with a chuckle, "from what I can tell, it's a kind of exercise, some kind of yoga done in a chair. My mother is almost ready to turn pro, if I have the story right."

Russell was smiling at her. "Susan, I'm sorry I have to be such an ogre when it comes to your business. We've just started working together, and already I am harassing and nagging. But I would be remiss if I didn't help you keep your finances in good order."

"And I appreciate it. The more you nag, the more I know I am getting my money's worth," Susan responded, attempting to inject humor into a dismal situation.

Russell laughed, clearly in a good mood. "Susan, do you…."

Before he could finish, Susan heard her cell phone ring. She opened her handbag, saying, "Sorry, I always pick up if it is my mother. Oh, it's the lab. Hello…. Yes, I'm leaving the city now. I'll be there soon. Probably twenty minutes, twenty-five at most.

"Something's come up at the office," she told Russell. "I have no idea what it is, but they want me to come in immediately."

"Too bad; I wanted to invite you to lunch. Perhaps we can do it another time. At least let me walk you out."

"That's so nice. Yes, please do invite me another time," Susan said as they walked out of the office into the reception area.

Russell proceeded to walk with her down the long hallway to the elevator. Susan was surprised when he got in with her. Maybe he doesn't have much work, she thought. His latest firm was in an older building, and the elevator creaked and moved slowly down the four floors to the ground level.

In the lobby, Russell motioned to the stairwell door next to the entrance, saying to the security guard, "Gus, are you having a problem with those kids again?"

Susan had not even noticed the door, which had been closed when she arrived. Gus grunted and nodded vigorously.

As they stepped outside, Russell explained, "The bike messengers that come to deliver documents are always in a big hurry, and the elevator is so slow, they take the stairs. The problem is, every so often one of them will urinate in the stairwell. By the time Gus realizes it, the stairwell is reeking, and he has to leave the door open for a couple of days to air it out. There seems to be no way around it, as the fire code mandates that stairwell doors be unlocked, and the restrooms are always locked."

"So you can understand why those bike messengers are in such a hurry," Susan said.

Her comment struck them as funny, and she and Russell laughed. It felt good to laugh with him, and yet concern gnawed at her. Why had Wolf called her from the lab? What was so urgent? Bidding her attorney goodbye, her anxiety rising, she hurried to her car.

CHAPTER 5

DRIVING OVER THE Bay Bridge to Emeryville, Susan thought about what Russ had said to her. His third option, selling her business, did not appeal to her at all. Glass Biotechnology was the center of her life. Susan had been in college when her father received his diagnosis. As his cancer ran its course, David had suffered horribly, and Susan and her mother suffered along with him. In the midst of their anguish, Susan had decided to go into medical research, thinking she might mend her heart by helping others find the happy outcome she and Bunny were denied. For more than thirty years now, her dream had been to develop products that could help other families stay whole.

Once Susan began doing laboratory research, she realized that she was remarkably well suited to this field. Looking at things at the micro level felt more real to her than anything outside the lab. The larger world was not as easy for her. Differences were greater and people were more complicated than the molecules they were made of. Working with minute differences that she could isolate, analyze, and control was where she felt most competent and at ease.

After three decades, Susan was still excited by her work. When she first began her career, she had worked exclusively on creating small-molecule therapeutics, inorganic particles that act on targets within cells. The main problem with these drugs is that they often have side effects, due to a lack of specificity for where they bind within the cell. Later in her career and since starting her own company, her research had been exclusively into biologics. Biologics are a class of therapeutics made from large molecules, usually antibodies, that are able to link with great specificity to desired targets on the outside of cells. While less prone to unwanted results, the manufacture of biologics was far more complicated than synthesizing therapeutics.

Currently, Glass Biotech was evaluating two biologics, GI-79 and GI-80. GI stood for Glass Immunoreaction, and Susan numbered her trials consecutively. These therapeutics were not intended to target any particular disease. Rather, they were attempts to improve a body's general immune response so that it could better defend against a variety of diseases.

The formulas Susan used were enormously complex. While some earlier formulations had shown promise, none had proven successful enough for higher-level trials, let alone for human testing. Now, unless she made the changes her attorney had recommended, Susan could not afford to continue her research. Her current financial situation was unsustainable—Russ was surely right about that.

Twenty minutes after leaving San Francisco, she pulled into the parking lot her building shared with two three-story office buildings and parked her silver Infinity in front of her building. Glass Biotech was in a modern, single-story stucco structure whose plate-glass windows faced the parking lot. The company was all hers, its logo proudly displayed over the door. Every time she walked in, Susan admired that logo: **Glass Biotechnology Company** in a rounded font below an italicized arc spelling out the slogan *The Future Is Clear*. The building was only large enough to house her current laboratory. If business grew significantly, she would have to look for a larger space. As things stood, this was unlikely to be a problem.

Grabbing her purse and tote bag, she hurried to the front door, walking across the adjoining parking space to shorten the distance. Oh, no! Looking down, she realized she had stepped in a puddle of something that had leaked from a car. What was it? Transmission fluid? It was a viscous solution, she knew that much. Susan's left shoe was covered with the gooey substance and was surely ruined. Why on earth had she worn her new shoes today?

The building was always kept locked, even when fully staffed. Susan took off her shoe, unlocked the door, stepped inside, and hobbled down the hall to the laboratory. It had a different feel to it than it had last night; now it was filled with life. She heard voices coming from the back and could see Wolf, Kevin, and Jess in their white lab coats in the animal room. When she got close enough to see what they were looking at, Susan stopped walking, amazed at what she saw.

On the wall with the small cages, sixteen of the rodents were unusually active, scurrying around in their individual cages, while the other sixteen were behaving normally. The difference between the two groups was striking.

"They were like this when we got here this morning," Wolf said. "At first, we thought it was from the earthquake—you know those theories about animals predicting quakes. We thought maybe they were sensing aftershocks, or perhaps were still on edge from last night. We didn't feel any aftershocks, so we thought they might be noticing something we can't. But clearly, only half of the rodents are affected.

"And look here," he added, pointing to the primates, across the room.

Gina's behavior was unremarkable, but Gigi was most certainly not her usual self. She lay on her back at the bottom of the cage, rocking her wiry body back and forth and emitting cooing sounds. When Susan approached her cage, Gigi jumped up, held onto the bars, and began moving her head from side to side, all the while looking at Susan and continuing her vocalizing.

When Gina and Gigi had arrived at the lab two months ago, the crew had made extensive notes, photographs, and video recordings to document their ordinary behavior and biometric markings.

Susan was positive she had not seen this behavior before today. Now was the time to start recording these activities.

"Have you been documenting these behaviors?" Susan asked.

Three heads nodded simultaneously. She really hadn't needed to ask that question. Her staff was well trained and conscientious.

"And as soon as we determined that the behavior was not diminishing but increasing, Wolf called you," Kevin said. "But look at what—"

Before he could finish, Wolf broke in. "We haven't even told you why we knew you had to come in immediately."

Wolf was the first person Susan had hired when she opened Glass Biotechnology, and of her four researchers, he was her favorite. Tall and lanky, with a laidback personality, and just out of UC Berkeley with a doctoral degree in molecular cell biology, he had become her team leader and laboratory manager. Many evenings after the others had left, Susan and Wolf would go over work sheets and discuss results. When that was done, if neither was in a hurry to leave, they sometimes just hung out and talked.

Wolf's real name was Walter, but he never used it; Susan knew his given name only because he had put it on the W-2 form he filled out for employment tax. It was easy to see where he got the nickname. He had dark eyes and straight dark hair that fell onto his forehead and the sides of his long face. When he smiled, his eyeteeth were sharp and prominent. Susan thought that some of his ancestors were Native American. Wolf played guitar, piano, and electric keyboard and was humming what seemed a different tune every time she heard him. When he was alone in the laboratory, Susan could hear him singing. He had desperately wanted to become a professional musician, but his mother had opposed it. Mother Wolf had felt the arts were too uncertain and pushed her son to major in science.

Waving his large hand around the animal room, Wolf said, "Gigi and the active rats over there are on GI-80. Gina and the other rats are on GI-79!"

Before she could stop herself, Susan exclaimed, "Well, Howdy Doody, what do we have here?"

Wolf, Jess, and Kevin repeated in unison, "Howdy Doody?"

Smiling, Susan just shook her head. There was no explaining Howdy Doody to three kids in their twenties, and right now she had more important things to discuss, anyway. What was happening in her lab was certainly interesting. Increased energy was a known symptom of immune-system stimulation. Further tests would have to be done to determine if the animals' immune systems were activated or if only their nervous systems had been affected. Susan would need to go over the differences between GI-79 and GI-80 in minute detail, since the antibodies were similar. She also needed to ascertain exactly when the doses had been administered. Only after a careful review of the lab notes could she formulate any theories.

Still, two species were showing effects simultaneously. This was extremely interesting and likely to prove significant.

The TV marionette's name must have distracted her crew, because before Susan had a chance to ask for the lab notes, the three looked down at her feet and back up to the shoe in her hand. "Did something happen to your foot?" Jess asked.

The youngest of the three, Jess was a tall blond with a beautiful face and terrific figure, always fashionably dressed. She looked more like a beauty pageant contestant than a scientist. Still an undergraduate student—only a month into her senior year—Jess had already been unofficially guaranteed a spot in the university's PhD program. (All PhD programs make offers in the early spring so that students can compare the financial offers from different programs.) Her potential was evident not just to Susan but to the academic community as well.

Susan had been concerned that Jess's beauty could be a distraction to her male co-workers. She was glad she had decided not to worry about it, since this turned out not to be the case. Wolf and Kevin seemed unaware of her physical appearance. She got along well with everyone, and Susan frequently heard her chatting happily with her co-workers about her sorority and active social life.

Susan told them about stepping in the automotive fluid.

"That's from Mandy's car," Kevin explained. "She can't get it fixed, because it doesn't make sense. It will cost eighteen hundred and ninety-five dollars to repair, and the car is only worth three thousand four hundred dollars."

Just at that moment, the door to the lab opened and Mandy walked in, carrying a cardboard tray with five cups of coffee and a bakery box. "What about my car?" she asked.

"I just stepped in the mess that it caused in the parking lot. You need to get that leak fixed," Susan told her.

"*Leaks*, not leak, I'm afraid. There is more than one. I'm just a poor lab researcher. When you start paying me more, I'll be able to get it fixed." Mandy's tone indicated that she was in high spirits. This was unusual for her. She was by nature the least jovial member of the team. Susan did not view her serious disposition as a negative; quite the opposite—Mandy was a good addition to the team precisely because she provided balance.

Mandy had gleaming black hair, almond-shaped eyes, and a pointy chin and was the same height as Susan. She often referred to herself as an ABC, for American-Born Chinese. According to Mandy, ABCs were different from Chinese born in China, though Susan had not overheard enough conversation to know just how these groups differed. "I brought snacks," she announced.

Eating in the laboratory was technically against the rules, so the five retreated to Susan's office. Because of the long hours her researchers put in, Susan tended to ignore the pizzas and snacks they brought into the lab. Still, in her presence, they ate at the table in her office.

The staff seemed more focused on the food than on the behavior of the lab subjects. Everything was beautifully boxed and looked scrumptious. Selecting a large pastry, Kevin looked at it admiringly before biting into it. "This is primo—you can't find these for less than six dollars anywhere. Way to go, Mandy."

Taking a cup of the coffee, Susan thanked Mandy but declined a pastry. It would not go uneaten. All her staffers had great appetites. When Susan was in her twenties, she, too, could eat whatever she chose. Too bad those days were gone forever.

"If I hadn't stepped into that mess, I would have thought this was my lucky day," Susan said.

Mandy nodded. "There's a famous Chinese proverb, and it goes like this: *It is impossible to know if luck is good or bad.* There's a story they always tell to go along with it. A man in a small Chinese village finds a horse. Horses are very valuable and few villagers have one, because they are so poor. All his neighbors tell him, 'My, you have good luck.' The man replies, '*It is impossible to know if luck is good or bad.*' The next day, his son rides the horse and is thrown off and breaks his leg. The horse is injured as well, and now the man has no one to help him take care of the crops. The neighbors say, 'My, you have bad luck.' The man replies, '*It is impossible to know if luck is good or bad.*' The very next day, the Chinese army comes and takes all the horses and all the able-bodied men to be in the army. They do not take the man's horse because it is injured, and do not take his son because he cannot walk."

Mandy was not usually so talkative. And Susan was too steeped in science and research methodology to believe in luck. She did, however, believe in coincidence. When two things happen at the same time, the human mind will often interpret this as cause and effect. She knew this is not necessarily the case, and that much scientific experimentation was devoted to separating the two.

For instance, yesterday's earthquake and the increased activity of the GI-80 lab animals was most likely a coincidence, particularly since the GI-79 specimens were unaffected. Also, just this morning she and her attorney had been discussing how much easier it would be to get funding if she had a drug that might be ready for clinical trials. Now, less than an hour later, it appeared Glass Biotech might be close to that very thing.

Almost immediately, Susan recognized a third coincidence. Because of this development, she needed to meet with her researchers, and all were present. This was unusual because of their schedules. She could not remember the last time she had needed to have a meeting and they had all been in the lab together.

Addressing her team, Susan said, "This behavioral change is very interesting. I will have to write up new lab assignments. I have an appointment that I need to keep, but I should be back in an hour and a half, and I'll do that today. I also plan to formulate more GI-80 as soon as possible. We will be doubling up on those trials. Wolf, we'll need more rodents. Will you see to that?"

"I can order them today if you want, but I have bad news, too. All the specimen slides from the GI-79 and GI-80 trials broke yesterday. When I came in this morning, they were all over the laboratory floor. Nothing could be salvaged. All the GI-80 trials will have to be redone, and if you want the results for comparison, we will need to repeat the GI-79 trials as well."

Since she no longer had those specimens, Susan would have to think about the best way to structure the next round of trials. She couldn't afford any unnecessary duplication.

Susan kept a pair of black flats in a desk drawer to wear in case of rain. They were shabby but would go well enough with her outfit. Whether they went well or not, she had no alternative. Slipping into the flats, she took her tote and handbag and headed out the door. It was more crucial than ever that this meeting go well.

CHAPTER 6

AVERY BIOGENETICS CORPORATION was in Alameda, only a short drive from Emeryville. The mid-day traffic was flowing well, and soon after she left Glass Biotech, Susan pulled into Avery's big parking lot and drove around to the back of the building.

Unlike the visitor parking in the front, the back lot had tall trees and shady spots for cars. Most important, this side of the parking lot was not prone to flooding when it rained. When she had worked at Avery, she had always parked in the back and entered through the back door, which meant she was right by her car when she came out each evening. Though she no longer had a key for the back door, she still parked in the back lot, whether or not it looked like rain.

Susan had a few minutes before her appointment, so she called Bunny. When she heard her mother's voicemail message, she assumed Bunny might be with Florence at Choga class and did not leave a message. She would telephone her mother later.

Heading to the front of the building, she saw a small puddle of what looked like automotive fluid. Another coincidence? This time, she carefully avoided it. She had no more shoes at the office, and if she ruined another pair, she would go barefoot until she got home. Susan smiled to herself, first from picturing herself walking around like a hippie and then from thinking Avery Biogenetics Corporation apparently did not pay its employees any better than she did. Susan wondered if her lab researchers knew that hippies didn't wear shoes. Maybe they didn't know anything about hippies. Laughing to herself, she supposed they were more likely to know about hippies than about Howdy Doody. Susan recognized that she was in high spirits today.

While waiting to be escorted into her appointment, she could not help but notice the beautiful lobby. Although she had been in Avery's lobby many times since it was redecorated, it never ceased to impress her. Everything was professionally designed and highly luxurious. The floor was of cream-colored marble, and the caramel-colored leather furniture was of the highest quality. Lush plants in antiqued brass containers were placed strategically throughout the space. The walls displayed mahogany-framed news articles on Avery's successes from publications including the *Wall Street Journal*, *Barron's*, *The Financial Times*, and others.

Susan was surprised to see Christian Dietz coming toward her. On her past visits, his administrative assistant had come down to the lobby to escort her upstairs. Susan noted the close cut of his suit. Just by looking at him, it was clear that Christian was European. Susan supposed a sophisticated observer could identify him as German.

Last year, Avery had been acquired by a big German drug manufacturer. The company had sent its own team to California to run the company and merge their operations. The team she had worked with was losing influence in the newly combined organization. Today, only one person Susan knew attended the meeting, and he did not speak a single word after saying hello.

Susan provided updates on the research her lab was conducting for Avery, and went on to inform the group that she was actively seeking additional contract work. She did not discuss her own research, well aware that the large biotechnology companies kept an eye on their competitors, however small. Anxious to return to her lab, Susan was glad the meeting was a fairly short one.

Just as she sat down at her desk, Kevin popped his head into her office. "Jess won't be back today," he told her. "She lost her student ID again and said she had to get a new one before the student services office closed. She said to say she was sorry she had to leave, but if she didn't go today, she wouldn't be able to get into the library this weekend."

Kevin shook his head. "More likely, she was worried she wouldn't be able to get into the fraternity parties. That's where she loses them. This is the second ID she's lost already this term."

"But who's counting?" Susan said softly after Kevin left.

She could not help smiling as she thought about Kevin. At some five feet, seven inches, he was not much taller than she was. Fair skinned, with light brown hair, a young-looking face, and a crooked smile, Kevin always wore hooded sweatshirts and loose-fitting pants with pockets on the legs. His appearance, along with his boyish demeanor, made him appear much younger than he was.

The guy could quantify anything. Susan had known he played poker online, but during one of their evening chats, Wolf had told her that Kevin usually made money. He always played the odds and did not let emotions influence his decisions—in the online-poker world, he was known as The Kevinator. Not only did he gamble himself, he bought stakes in other players. Susan had overheard him negotiating on his cell phone. "I need an edge. I won't buy at 1.3, but I will at 1.25. Shoot me the details on Two Plus Two."

Kevin rode his bicycle to work, and on the last Friday of each month, he would leave early to ride over to the BART station to take a train to San Francisco, taking his bike with him. He and several thousand other bikers would meet in Justin Herman Plaza, a large open space across from the San Francisco Embarcadero. Cycling together, they would form Critical Mass, whose stated goal was to bring attention to cyclers' rights and environmental concerns. The group attempted to accomplish this by tying up the evening commute.

Critical Mass had originated in San Francisco and spread to other cities; Kevin had once bragged that the largest ride ever had been eighty thousand bikers in Hungary. The San Francisco ride, however, was typically a big one. Only just prior to the five-thirty p.m. start would ad hoc leaders determine the route. Since the course was not predetermined, commuters could not avoid getting caught in traffic jams, and the police seemed helpless in their attempts to control the riders. The Critical Mass cyclists proudly obeyed no traffic rules. They rode through red lights and dominated the road.

With traffic snarled, altercations routinely broke out between riders and drivers. Normally, profanities were shouted, though occasionally pedestrians were struck and property damaged. The most frequent victims were side mirrors, but more serious injuries and damage were not unheard of. Most of the community despised the group.

Although he had tried repeatedly, Kevin had yet to get Wolf or any of the other lab staff to ride with him—or to play poker, for that matter. None of Kevin's outside activities affected his work in the laboratory. Methodical and observant, he was an excellent researcher.

CHAPTER 7

TYPICALLY, SUSAN ATE breakfast at home or with her mother before going to work. Today, however, she picked up a cup of coffee and a bagel at a drive-through kiosk. There was only a small amount of the GI-80 left, and she wanted to start a new batch. She made all of the therapeutics when no one was present. Now that this formulation had shown promise, she wanted to create a large amount so that they could run several trials simultaneously.

The manufacturing of antibodies is a highly complicated process. It requires growing the antibodies in a living cell, such as bacteria or yeast. To harvest the antibodies, the cells have to be lysed, or broken down, in such a way that they release their contents into a heterogeneous soup containing not only the antibodies but all the cell machinery that grew them. Then, using a process called affinity chromatography, the desired biologic had to be separated from the rest of the cellular material.

Extracting molecules of purified antibody was like passing a fine-toothed comb through hair to remove impurities. The difference is that what sticks to a comb is usually the grime and dead hair that one wants to discard, whereas with affinity chromatography, the unwanted proteins and impurities are washed through the column while the desired molecules stick to an immobilized ligand. The process was intricate and time consuming, requiring several different washes to remove impurities and finally an elution to extract the purified antibody. Susan took great care during the purification process so that she could control the dose and make sure her therapeutic did not contain additional substances that could accidentally trigger an unwanted immune response.

When she first started this research, she could have worked with enzymes instead of antibodies. This would have been easier and more direct, especially since she had no reason to think one approach was more likely to succeed than the other. She had chosen to start with the more difficult path only because, in her experience, things rarely turned out to be easier than expected.

Susan kept her test formulas, carefully recorded and annotated, in a small, handwritten notebook with lavender flowers on the cover. Though she used abbreviations, she was well aware that someone with scientific training could decipher her notes. Using codes to keep research secrets was nothing new to scientists. In the late fifteenth and early sixteenth centuries, Galileo had used reverse writing and coded notebooks. He had even mailed sealed dated letters with a brief summary of his latest discovery: for example, *I, Galileo, have discovered a fourth moon orbiting Jupiter*. That way, if someone beat him to publication, he could ask to have the letter opened and prove his precedence. Interestingly, one of these letters was not opened until the 1980s. It turned out to be a test letter Galileo had sent to see if his system would work.

One of the reasons Susan was so adamant about retaining control of Glass Biotech was to maintain the secrecy of her formulations. She alone knew the exact recipe for the therapeutics they were testing; none of her staff had knowledge of the specific molecules or combinations they were administering or exactly how they were produced. Anyone putting up funding would be unlikely to allow this level of privacy.

Susan carried the coded notebook at all times and took it home every evening. She could not remember ever forgetting it or misplacing it. Secrecy and confidentiality did not come naturally to her, but she had grown accustomed to this particular industry requirement. Maintaining proprietary information was a major part of the biotech industry. Whether her flowered, coded notebook constituted an acceptable level of security was questionable, but it had proved adequate for her needs. She only hoped anyone trying to steal her research would look on her computers or search for a flash drive. If anyone did think to look in her purse, she hoped he or she would never notice a little notebook with lavender flowers that looked like an overgrown address book.

Susan had called her mother as soon as she'd gotten home from work. If the increased activity of the GI-80 subjects was the result of increased immune function, the potential was enormous. Even if the increased response was minuscule, it might be the gateway to enhancing the immune system that she'd been trying to find.

Usually, it was Bunny who did most of the talking. Her mother had been delighted to find her so animated, even though Bunny, who never took a science class after high school, did not really understand her daughter's work.

When Susan finished explaining what the developments could mean, Bunny had replied, "My dear, you know what they say: *Be careful what you ask for; you might get it.*"

They both had a good laugh over this comment.

It was just six-thirty when Susan pulled into the parking lot that morning, stopping directly in front of the main door. Just as she turned off the ignition, she saw two uniformed police officers walking around the side of the building. Quickly getting out of her car, she approached the men.

"Good morning, I'm Officer Morales," said one, "and this is Officer Brennan. May I ask who you are? We need to ask because there's been a forced entry and, we believe, a burglary."

"A break-in? A burglary?" Susan repeated.

Worried, she showed her driver's license to the younger officer, who wrote down her name and other information.

"If you walk around to the back with us, I'll show you what we found," Officer Morales said.

Susan saw an Emeryville police car parked near the laboratory's back door. As they drew closer, she saw that the top right side of the door frame was bent inward, and a sizable chunk of metal was missing below the doorknob. Susan's heart was racing and she felt faint. She leaned against the building to steady herself.

Officer Brennan began photographing the door and surrounding area. As the younger officer worked, Officer Morales explained that it hadn't been easy to break open the heavy metal door, especially since the doorjamb and frame were metal as well. This had been a sophisticated break-in, he told her, not some random crime.

"It takes equipment and know-how to do this. A lab on Halleck Street was broken into last week. It's too early to say for sure, but this might be FAN's work."

Before Susan could ask any questions, he asked her to step inside. Officer Morales requested that she not touch anything, just to show him where the light switch was, and to let him know if anything was missing or damaged. Officer Brennan continued taking photographs.

In the animal room, the doors to all the cages were open, and all of the animals were gone. It struck Susan that she and the two officers were the only remaining life forms in the lab. Officer Morales told her that what had happened here seemed analogous to the crime at the other lab. *Analogous* was an odd word for a police officer to use, Susan thought; she would have expected him to use the word *similar*. What did it matter? She was feeling lightheaded and wondered if she was in shock.

In both labs, he explained, there had reason to believe that a fanatical animal rights group was responsible. The police were aware of a number of such groups operating in California, and FAN—which stood for Free Animals Now—was known to be active in Berkeley. It was committed to preventing animal experimentation and had repeatedly declared its willingness to do "whatever it takes" to protect lab animals.

"I would take them at their word," Officer Morales added. "You and everyone who works for you needs to be very careful."

At the Halleck Street laboratory, the animals had also been missing. He did not know if they had been set free or taken to another location. Susan had no idea where Halleck Street was.

Susan and Officer Morales looked around the rest of the lab and in her office. All the computers and laboratory equipment were there. Her supply of GI-79 and GI-80 was untouched. A tremendous feeling of relief flooded through her, and she felt her mood begin to change.

Nothing seemed to be missing other than every single one of her animals. Officer Morales gave her a number that would correspond with the police report, which she would need for any insurance claims, handed her a card, and told her to contact him if she discovered anything else missing.

After the officers left, Susan did her best to cover the back door. Then she walked down the hallway into her office and sank into her chair. She sat for a moment with her face in her hands. Only a moment ago, she had been relieved; now she was overcome with despair. Suddenly, she dropped her hands and looked up. The police had said nothing about her alarm. Why had it not gone off? Had someone forgotten to set it before leaving?

Wolf, Mandy, and Kevin had still been in the lab when she'd left yesterday. Had one of them neglected to activate the alarm? She would have to call the security company, and she needed a locksmith. She hurriedly typed out a text message telling her staff there was no need to rush in to work today. Then she revised her message, saying that except for Wolf, they could all take the day off.

The laboratory rodents she used came all the way from Jackson Lab, in northern Maine. Replacing the rodents would be simple, if inconvenient. Getting new primates would not be as easy or quickly done; it could take three weeks to replace Gigi and Gina. Susan had no hope that her original subjects would be found. Even if they were and returned to the lab, they would no longer be suitable for research, as they'd been in an uncontrolled environment.

It seemed odd that whoever broke into her laboratory would not try to access the supply cabinet. The chemicals stored there were valuable, controlled substances not easily obtainable. Was it because they were in a hurry, or did they really care only about the animals? If they cared so much about the animals, how could they just free them to a certain death? If they took them somewhere, why didn't they take any cages? How could they transport the rodents and two monkeys if they didn't have cages?

When she had more time, she could think this through, but right now, she had to secure the lab. The chemicals in the locked supply cabinet were replaceable, but it was too risky to leave the supply of antibodies in the lab. She would have to take the therapeutics with her until the back entrance was secured and the locksmith and alarm company had increased security.

How could she wait to continue her trials? Russ had just pointed out that she needed to focus on contract work. Devoting just fifteen percent of the lab work to proprietary research did not give her much time to work on GI-80. These were setbacks she couldn't afford. She needed to run trials *now*, and she needed a subject that could not be stolen or set loose in the middle of the night.

Although not exactly encouraged, self-experimentation is relatively common in the world of science. In the 1950s, Jonas Salk tested the polio vaccine on himself, his wife, and his children before testing it on a wider group and making it available to the public. In 1984, when the Australian researcher Barry Marshall wanted to prove that the bacterium *H. pylori* causes ulcers, he drank a Petri dish containing a culture, and won a Nobel Prize in 2005.

The chemist Albert Hofmann made a famous discovery by accident in 1938. He had been seeking a general stimulant that would work on the central nervous system, hoping his discovery could be used to stimulate respiration and have more general effects as well. By chance, he ingested some of his drug formulation. Immediately noticing something unusual, Hofmann took the substance again three days later, this time intentionally, and recorded its effects. He had discovered LSD.

Other examples flooded into Susan's mind. She recalled reading about a researcher at UCSF who had found that restricting the caloric intake of mice dramatically increased their lifespan. He was now following a calorically restricted diet. Other researchers had injected themselves with the blood of diseased patients to prove that diseases were or were not communicable.

Her self-experimentation would be less dangerous. She would start with a low dose of GI-80 and see if she felt any immune effects. If necessary, she could increase later doses.

At the supply cabinet, Susan took out several hypodermic needles, along with the remaining vials of GI-79 and GI-80, and placed them in a small white metal box. Once the door was repaired and security ramped up, she would return everything to the cabinet. Then she went into the lab's small bathroom, carefully washed her hands, and filled half a syringe with GI-80. An intramuscular injection would probably be best. That's how they had administered the therapeutic to the animals. She pulled her trousers down to her knees and shoved the needle into her thigh. Immediately she felt curiously calm, relieved that her research was moving forward.

Heading into the lab to dispose of the syringe in the Sharps Container, where used needles were left for special disposal, she passed the back door, still partially open and now covered with tape and butcher paper. At that moment, she thought of Gina and Gigi. Was it possible the animal rights fanatics had taken them home to be pets? Releasing them would be too cruel; the Bay Area was not their natural habitat, and they could never survive here. Wherever they were, she wished them well and hoped they were together.

Chapter 8

Susan hoped that getting some exercise and spending time in the sauna would help her relax. She missed Rosa more than ever. It would have felt good to tell her what had happened today. She had few friends, and even if she had been able to reach Bunny—Susan knew her mother was playing bridge with Florence and Shirley—she would not have told her mother about the break-in on the phone.

There was less reason for Bunny to worry now, anyway. The locksmith and alarm-company technician had come soon after the police had left. The locksmith had found someone to fix the back door, and the technician had made some temporary modifications to the alarm system. Since he had been unable to explain why the alarm had failed to work, Susan had asked him to upgrade the security system.

When Susan walked into the gym, the lavender-flowered notebook and the white metal box were in her oversize plum-colored tote. Since buying it on impulse, she was rarely without it. It was her signature item, an expensive bag that held everything. She generally left this bag in the car, but thought it best to bring it in with her while she worked out. For most biologics, constant temperature was important for maintaining consistency and potency; allowing antibodies to freeze and thaw, especially more than once, was one of the surest ways to denature them. It was unlikely to get that cold tonight, but it was better not to take any risks until she understood how stable her formulations were.

Wolf was already arranging for the delivery of new lab animals. The rodents could arrive as early as next week. It felt as if things were already getting back to normal.

Heading toward the locker room, Susan saw GG and BB conversing as they watched themselves in the mirror. They were doing arm curls, GG with heavy black iron weights and BB with small, lighter silver ones. She promised herself to call Rosa as soon as things settled down.

Since she had brought not only a change of clothes but the big leather tote, the only way Susan could get her locker to close was to take out two of her gym towels and leave them on top of the cabinet. She hoped her beautiful plum bag would not be damaged.

As she walked to the restroom before starting her workout, Susan passed Crazy Rene, heading toward the sauna and shower area wearing only a towel wrapped into a turban and rubber flip-flops. Susan smiled and shook her head. She was glad she didn't have a locker next to Rene's. If she did, she'd have to listen to nonstop stories about Rene's self-created problems.

Susan stopped. She did have a locker next to Rene's—she had Rosa's locker. It would be the perfect place to store the GI-79 and GI-80 until the lab's new security system was in place. She hurried back to her own locker, took out the white metal box, and grabbed the two towels.

Back at Rosa's locker, she tried to recall the combination: twenty-five, seventeen, thirty-four. The lock opened immediately. Maybe she did have a computer brain. She was certainly better with numbers than with people.

Susan put the box in the locker and covered it neatly with the gym towels. She wanted to be gone before Rene returned. She did not feel like talking and certainly did not want to explain why she was using Rosa's locker.

Walking back down the center aisle, she passed the scale. Best to start keeping a record of her vital signs. Susan slid the weights until the scale was in balance and saw that, as expected, she weighed one hundred thirty-five pounds and five ounces. Ideally, she'd weigh fifteen pounds less, but she hadn't been that light since she was in college. She'd need to pick up a thermometer and an electronic cuff to keep track of her blood pressure and pulse.

A gym was the perfect place to test an immune system, she thought. She'd heard anecdotal stories of people picking up methicillin-resistant *Staphylococcus aureus*, or MRSA, from the communal gym equipment, and dying from the difficult-to-treat infection when otherwise in the prime of health. It was likely her immune system would get a better workout here than her muscles.

CHAPTER 9

STARING AT HER log, Susan was utterly disappointed. It had been twenty-one days since she had injected herself with the GI-80, and nothing she had recorded was the least bit unusual. She was glad she hadn't gotten sick, but her weight, body temperature, and blood pressure were unchanged. Actually, something had happened that morning that was out of the ordinary, and she wondered if she should make note of it. To be consistent and complete, she wrote it down. *October 13, 07:15 Argument with Mother.* Suddenly feeling foolish, Susan debated crossing out this entry. Though it was obviously not of any significance, she let it remain.

Letting herself into Bunny's apartment about seven, she'd found her mother in a straight-back chair in the middle of the living room. Susan had no idea where her mother had gotten this chair; it did not match the décor of the living room or bedroom. She appeared to be in the middle of some exercise or meditation. Susan had been anxious to get into the lab and did not want to get stuck in the heaviest part of the morning traffic. Bunny could have waited to do her silly routine until after breakfast. Finally, after fifteen minutes, she came to the table. By then, the toast Susan had made was cold.

"You know, dear, you are built like me. When I was your age, I had precisely the same figure you do now." Her mother's tone made it sound as if she was surprised her daughter had inherited her genetics. "I don't think that outfit does anything for you," she continued. "A loose-fitting top doesn't go with pleated pants."

Susan had not been in the mood for unsolicited fashion advice. She'd be working alone in the laboratory and wearing a lab coat over her clothes, so what did it matter? She had changed the subject and told her mother she was disappointed that her latest experiment wasn't showing any results. She had not mentioned that the key subject was sitting across the table having breakfast.

Bunny had listened and then shared some of her kitchen-table philosophy. "Well, dear, one thing I have learned is that *things happen when you least expect it.*"

For some reason, this annoyed Susan even more than the remark about her clothes. "Mother, you are so irritating when you make comments that have nothing to do with the conversation."

Bunny had looked at her daughter in surprise. Though the two had different temperaments, they had not quarreled in years.

"Excuse me, I was just trying to be helpful," said Bunny, emphasizing the words *excuse* and *me.*

"Well, you are not being helpful when you say things like that," Susan had replied with emphasis of her own.

"Someone's sure PMSing," Bunny said. "You haven't been this cranky in years."

Susan had gotten up, perfunctorily kissed Bunny goodbye, and left without another word.

Bunny hadn't done anything to deserve this kind of attitude; her mother was just being herself. Susan told herself to call at lunch-time to say she was sorry.

Her journal updated, she walked back into the laboratory. It was the second Wednesday of the month, when the biohazard waste was scheduled to be picked up, and the special container had to be moved next to the back door. Her staffers usually did this, but Susan wanted to make sure the waste was collected. The red container was unusually weighty, so she dragged it across the floor and then, wondering what made it so heavy, checked the contents. Mixed in with the medical waste were paper cups and discarded food.

Her staff were all well aware that laboratories paid by the pound for hazardous waste to be picked up, crated, and carted off for incineration. Why didn't they use the trash can for their garbage? They all had brains; why didn't they use them?

Susan attempted to cool down by focusing on what was going right. Though macaques need considerable care, she had ordered four monkeys rather than two, and two of the primates, both males, would be delivered next week. The females would arrive soon after. The four cost more than twelve thousand dollars. The males were more expensive because they were older. Susan did not know if the females were fully mature and had been able to get them for a good price primarily because they were young; if necessary, she would wait to begin experimentation on them. She had already decided to delay delivery of the rodents until they were closer to starting trials.

In an ideal world, she would have ordered mature females and started testing them along with the males, but the ninety-thousand-dollar loan Russell had arranged was already exhausted. Susan planned to ask if he could arrange with the bank to increase her line of credit. She was still awaiting money from her insurance company and barely had enough to make the next payroll. And since she'd been forced to stop all contract work, her business was not generating any income.

Surprisingly, Christian Dietz at Avery Biogenetics had been very understanding, probably because the company kept its most important research in house. Apparently, the problems caused by the animal rights activists were something Avery was willing to accept. Maybe the larger labs were familiar with this sort of thing. In all Susan's years in the industry, she had never been affected by these activists. Possibly, as the police had suggested, they were getting more aggressive.

In the first two weeks after the break-in, Susan had talked to the police several times. When she had last spoken with Officer Morales, he had told her that the police had not found any useful fingerprints and had not identified any suspects. The only good news he had to report was that there had been no more break-ins in Emeryville. When he had suggested that she stay in touch, the comment struck Susan as oddly humorous. Maybe she should send a Christmas card.

With no animals in the lab to monitor or care for, Susan had asked her staff to use their paid vacation days while the security work was being done. Over the past three weeks, only Wolf had come into the lab, and only when she needed help advising the technicians or ordering supplies. She still had no definitive answer as to why her alarm had not functioned properly. According to the technicians, it could have been any number of things, including human error. In any event, the improved security system had been installed, and the door locks had been upgraded as well.

When everyone returned, Susan hoped they would be able to work steadily and without interruption. Once the contract work was progressing, they'd start generating income, and needless to say, she was anxious to restart testing the GI-80. She was extremely disappointed that the test she had done on herself was not showing any results, especially when the GI-80 research on the animals would be starting all over again. Their work had been set back well over a month. When all was said and done, it would probably be more like a three-month delay.

Susan packed her tote bag, activated the new security system, and stepped outside, using the new lock on the front door. As she walked to her car, she was glad that Daylight Saving Time had been extended until November, since it was still light out. There was only one other car in the lot, a small, dark Japanese vehicle, parked directly across from hers, in front of another building. Thankful that at least she wasn't the hardest-working person in Emeryville, she got in her car and drove to her gym.

Seeing no one near Rosa's aisle, she quickly opened the locker, took out the white metal box wrapped in a towel, relocked the locker, and went into the bathroom's disabled stall, because it had a sink. She washed her hands, took out a needle, and filled the tube with the remaining GI-80. After tapping the syringe to eliminate any air, she unzipped her pants and stuck herself with the needle, this time in her left thigh. It was twice the amount she had used three weeks ago. She could only hope that this dose, or the two doses in combination, was at a therapeutic level for someone of her size and weight.

She would need to make more of the therapeutic for the animal trials. But since she had no idea how long these antibodies retained their potency, a fresh batch would be better, anyway. It would take another ten days, though; she was losing even more time. It was all very discouraging.

With all the distraction, she had not been able to reorganize the contract work she'd started before the burglary, let alone work on lab sheets for new research. She had talked to Russ several times in the past three weeks, and he had no information about equity funding. She definitely needed a better attorney, Susan thought, one who knew more about biotechnology. Somehow, she would have to make the time to find one.

As she put the metal box back in Rosa's locker, Susan realized that she still had not called her friend. Now that she thought about it, she was surprised that Rosa had not called her. Brooding about things not going well, Susan felt she definitely needed some good luck. Then again, since she didn't believe in luck, good or otherwise, it might be hard to come by.

Returning to her own locker, Susan reminded herself that at least one thing had gone well. She had successfully avoided Crazy Rene twice now—and it's not easy to avoid Crazy Rene, she thought.

Quickly changing into her gym clothes, Susan locked her locker and then remembered to weigh herself before starting her workout. With the hundred-pound weight already in place, she pushed the smaller weight to the right, as always, and was surprised to see the weight dip at one hundred and thirty-five. She moved it toward the left, and when the weight reached thirty, the scale balanced. She had lost five pounds and avoided Crazy Rene not once but twice. Now she really missed Rosa. They would surely have had a good laugh over this.

Out on the gym floor, the only available treadmill was next to the wall. It was her least favorite machine, but at least it was free. She punched in her numbers and speed—4.2 miles per hour—and started jogging. Feeling energetic, she increased her speed to 4.5.

Without Rosa to chat with, Susan ran along watching the other members work out. With their small entourage in front of a long mirror, God's Gift and Body Beautiful were always interesting. BB wore fashionable workout clothing and got new gear frequently. Tonight, she was wearing an all-black outfit with a waistband that had something written on the back in rhinestones or some other sparkly material, probably some designer name or logo. Susan thought the most appropriate slogan would be something like "Look at Me." GG, too, was pleased with his appearance. As usual, he was smiling as he viewed his physique from various angles while he worked out.

Susan's pace was not giving her any problems, so she increased her speed to 5.2 and then 5.3. As she started the cool-down phase, she realized that she had run slightly more than 3.7 miles in forty-five minutes—by far the best run she'd had in a very long time. Now she'd have something to note in her journal. Maybe the GI-80 was having an effect. More likely, she told herself, with Rosa gone she was exercising more and talking less.

Just then, Susan noticed that she was feeling queasy and her stomach was bothering her. She would need to make a note of this, too. Might this be a side effect of the GI-80? While it could be from the recent dose, it would be unusual for an injected drug to cause an abdominal reaction so quickly. She had not experienced any symptoms with her first injection, but that dose was a smaller one. Maybe it was something she ate.

CHAPTER 10

THE NEXT MORNING, Susan's stomach felt better, but even if she wasn't completely well, there was no way she would miss going into the lab today. Her staffers were all due back, and she planned a short meeting with them. Though anxious to get to work, she stopped at Bunny's first, hoping to smooth things over after yesterday's quarrel. They had such a good conversation over breakfast, she stayed on to sit on the couch with her mother, happy that things were back to normal.

Susan could hear Wolf humming when she opened the double doors to the work area. Thank heavens for Wolf. He didn't talk much but was highly efficient; Susan did not know what she would do without him. Certainly her laboratory would not run as smoothly, and she would have far less time to spend with her mother.

Though her team had been back just a couple of hours, the lab already had started to look as if the four had never been gone. It appeared all four had been eating at their workstations, and more trash would surely accrue by the end of the day. But Susan was elated to see everyone, and her researchers seemed happy to be back.

Mandy had a new look. On one side, her perfectly straight hair was cut at a sharp angle; on the other side, it was longer and highlighted in bright blue. The back was cut asymmetrically as well: longer on one side than the other. It was edgy and flattering.

Her long blond hair pulled back into a braid, Jess looked even more beautiful than Susan remembered. Or was it just that she had not seen her youngest researcher in three weeks? Searching for a scientific explanation, Susan concluded it was probably the latter. Attractive women often become even more beautiful in their twenties, when they lose some facial fullness and their bone structure becomes more visible.

To mark their first day back as a special occasion, Susan had ordered lunch. It wouldn't matter that they had just eaten; they always had room for more food. She planned to wait until after lunch to remind them not to throw trash in the biohazard waste bin.

She had telephone calls to make before lunch, but all her plans changed when she stopped in the restroom. Her panties were smeared with dark red blood. How could that be? She'd had her last period two years ago, and her gynecologist had confirmed that she was fully menopausal. Postmenopausal bleeding, she knew, was not a good sign.

When lunch was delivered, Susan set everything up on the table in her office, then took a step back to assess the array of food she had ordered from a nearby restaurant: a variety of Armenian-style rolled sandwiches, walnut cookies, and small pastries made with candied fruit and dusted in powdered sugar. She felt the meal looked appropriately celebratory and was pleased. But once everyone came into the office, Susan was too anxious to eat. She had been able to get an appointment with her gynecologist later that afternoon. Until then, she tried to enjoy socializing with her staff and hearing how they had spent the past three weeks.

While the laboratory was closed, Jess had had more time for parties. It seemed all the fellows Jess dated were in fraternities, and each fraternity and sorority house had a distinct personality. Kappa Theta, Jess's sorority, was known for having the prettiest girls, while a nearby house, Delta Delta Lambda, was filled with society girls with big allowances and generally referred to as Visa Visa MasterCard.

Susan had never dated any fraternity men herself, but even she knew the Greek houses had frequent parties. Her college boyfriend,

Stewart Serber, had been a nerd long before it was fashionable to be one. Considering how long they had dated, they had never been particularly close. After graduation, they had drifted apart. Susan was aware that Stewart currently worked at the Lawrence Livermore Laboratory, a well-respected physics research facility only an hour's drive from Emeryville, but she had no contact with him.

Kevin had spent time at the Round Up, the oldest tavern in Emeryville. It was in an old building that had been a speakeasy during Prohibition, and every few years someone threatened to tear the place down and put up something more respectable. Kevin had repeatedly invited the other staffers to go with him after work, but Susan did not think anyone had. A dive bar for bikers and cyclists did not seem to have much general appeal.

Wolf preferred a club in Berkeley that featured alternative music. All her researchers seemed to know what constituted alternative music, although Susan had no idea and didn't ask. Recently, Wolf told them, he had heard two musicians from Iceland. "I want to go to Reykjavik to see them perform at a music festival next month. Mandy, you should come with me. We can go over Thanksgiving weekend. It's supposed to be kick-ass."

"Sorry, you'll have to go by yourself. I'd love to see the Northern Lights, but my parents would think traveling to Iceland is a big waste of money. They're still recovering from my haircut," Mandy sighed.

"I like your new haircut," Susan told her. "And I love the blue highlights."

"I'm afraid my parents don't agree with you. My mother was crying when she told her sister about it on the phone."

"And you were able to buy this," said Jess, picking up the electronic gadget in front of Mandy and holding it up. "I am dying to get one of these. It's a good thing you had time to go wait in line to buy one."

"It's a better thing you had the money to buy one," Kevin said. "They cost seven hundred and forty-five dollars plus tax. You need a yearly subscription, and the apps are additional. How much did you pay for the subscription?"

Susan smiled. It was good to be back with her staff. It felt so familiar, almost like being with family. Wolf was humming as he ate, and Mandy was her usual dour self. Though Susan didn't eat anything, all the food was consumed. Before leaving for her appointment, she popped into the lab and reminded Wolf to explain to the others how the new security system operated and to give them the new alarm codes.

Chapter 11

A SMALL, THIN woman with sharp features and limp brown hair, Dr. Klein always reminded Susan of a bird. As she walked back into the examination room, the long skirt jutting out from under her lab coat swished. In her absence, Susan had gotten dressed, always more comfortable in her own clothing than in a hospital gown.

"I can't say for sure until I see your test results, but I do not think anything is abnormal," said Dr. Klein. "I am not concerned about the breast tenderness or the weight loss. A spontaneous loss of ten or more pounds is considered significant, but a five- or six-pound weight loss is merely a fluctuation. On your way out, I'd like you to stop downstairs in the lab for a blood draw. We'll be able to determine the level of hormones in your blood. If that test is not definitive, we can do a saliva test. Saliva is more accurate, but I usually prefer blood tests, because we get the results back sooner. So let's start there.

"I want to point out that hormone levels vary even in the same woman," she continued. "You are only two years into menopause, and it is not unheard of for someone your age to have these symptoms. I want to rule out ovarian problems like tumors or cysts, so I am ordering a pelvic sonogram. The imaging center is across from the lab. If your symptoms persist, I can order an MRI of your pituitary gland to look for tumors there, but I really don't think that will prove necessary. We'll wait for the blood-test results and see if this resolves on its own. I want to impress upon you that I am not overly concerned at this time."

Relieved by what her doctor had to say and by her matter-of-fact manner, Susan felt her anxiety start to decline.

"How are you doing generally?" Dr. Klein asked. "Are you experiencing any unusual stress these days?"

"Actually, yes. My research was going exceptionally well until last month, when my laboratory was broken into. We were forced to shut down for several weeks, and now our work is seriously backed up. And lately, I have other business concerns as well. Could this be causing these symptoms?" Susan asked.

"It could be connected. You need to try to find some way to reduce this stress. Running your own research laboratory is a big job. I can tell you that running my own medical practice is very hard these days. It is so difficult to find competent staff; I am working more hours than I ever have. I find comfort in my religion. I look at the trials we all must face as something God created as a means to get closer to the Divine, a path to become more godly. For me, it puts problems in a different light. When faced with challenges, instead of feeling stressed, I appreciate that I have an opportunity to do God's will."

Susan merely smiled and nodded, since she had no desire to prolong this discussion. Denise Klein often injected her religious beliefs into consultations.

After she'd given blood and had the sonogram, Susan felt extremely hungry, so she stopped at a small restaurant nearby. Everything she ate tasted delicious. Not only did she finish a thick panini sandwich and a bowl of butternut squash soup, she followed it up with dessert. This was something she rarely did, but the carrot cake on the counter looked so enticing, she bought a slice. After all, she had just lost five pounds, so she could splurge a little.

She knew she would hit a lot of traffic if she went back to her lab, but she'd get caught in commute traffic if she drove home, too. When she finally got to the lab, it was just after five o'clock. Parking her car, she looked in her rear-view mirror to see if the other late worker, the one who owned the dark Japanese car, was still at work. While she didn't see that car, quite a few others were parked in front of the building across the way. He or she had probably left at a reasonable time to have dinner with the family.

Once inside, Susan looked around the lab and the animal room. The cages were still empty, of course, but the workbenches were covered with clutter, so it already felt less lonely. Returning to her office, she quickly closed the blinds, so that no one could look inside and see she was alone. She had never worried about that before the break-in. As she started to twist the blinds shut, she noticed fewer cars were parked in the lot but the black compact was among them. No dinner with the family, then. Maybe he or she had gone to pick up something to eat and was settling in for another late night.

Susan pulled out her flowered notebook and turned to where she was keeping her journal. She had quite a few entries to make. When she got her test results back, she would record her hormone levels, too. She was, after all, a subject.

Chapter 12

The next day, a Friday, she planned to take Bunny to the dentist and then out for breakfast. Her researchers had their assignments, things seemed to be running smoothly, and she had worked late the night before. While Bunny was in the dental chair, Susan called her attorney, but the receptionist said he was not available and would call her back.

Her mother looked stunning in a pink turtleneck sweater and charcoal gray slacks. She carried a floral-patterned needlepoint handbag that picked up both colors and ankle-high boots of dark gray leather. Except for her wedding and engagement rings, she wore silver jewelry. Looking at her mother, Susan found it hard to believe that Bunny was an octogenarian.

"What an outfit. I can't believe you wore that to the dentist!" Susan told her mother.

"Where should I wear it? I don't go out much anymore, and I like to get dressed up when I do."

"Mom, you get dressed up when you are sitting in the house," Susan laughed.

"Yes, I do. What is the point of having nice clothes if you don't wear them? And I like to look nice. By the way, you look lovely today."

Appreciating the compliment, Susan smiled at her mother.

In fact, that morning as Susan was applying her makeup, she'd noticed that her skin looked smooth and her coloring less drab. Perhaps she did have some kind of hormonal imbalance. Increased estrogen levels positively affect a woman's complexion.

Susan noticed that her clothes were fitting well, too, probably because of the weight she'd lost. She had dressed with care, not only because she was going out with Bunny but because she hoped to stop in the city and see Russell. She'd finally settled on a pale green sweater set with taupe slacks and low-heeled taupe pumps two shades darker than her slacks. Bunny had given her a lot of jewelry over the years. In the last few years, Bunny had started giving her daughter pieces of her own, for birthdays and other special occasions, and Susan tried to wear some of it whenever she dressed up or was going to see her mother. Today she had on a crystal-and-gold necklace and gold earrings that had been Bunny's.

Her mother still owned a lot of jewelry, which she kept in a large velvet box on top of her dresser. On numerous occasions, Susan had asked if it would not be better to hide it or at least put the box in a dresser drawer. Bunny always refused, saying that her entire life, even when she was a little girl, she'd kept a jewelry box on her dresser. Besides, it would be too much trouble to keep it anywhere else.

"That sweater looks wonderful on you. Try to wear that shade of green more often," Bunny advised. "Your hair should be a little longer, though. Maybe it's time to try a different hairdresser."

Ignoring the comment, Susan gave Bunny a kiss and took her arm as they crossed the street and went into a fancy Italian bakery and restaurant. Decorated like an old Italian cafe, it was one of her mother's favorite places. The walls were dark wood, with black-and-white photographs of Italian street scenes. The tabletops were white marble with black and gray veins running through the stone.

Susan ordered more pastries than they would eat; what they didn't consume she would pack up for Bunny to take home. Her mother loved to have treats. Everything was delicious, and when they were ready to leave, she was surprised to find nothing left.

After dropping her mother off, Susan checked her messages; Wolf had texted that the male primates had arrived. And when she tried to reach Russell again, the receptionist put her through. Russ told her he was busy the rest of the day and couldn't see her. Disappointed, Susan was pleasantly surprised when he suggested they go out for dinner and a baseball game the following evening.

"We can have dinner near the ballpark. Can you make it?" he asked.

Susan knew that law firms typically buy season tickets for athletic events so that their attorneys could invite important clients. She smiled at the thought that Russ considered her an important client. She had not been to a baseball game in decades, and the team was playing at a new stadium that had been praised in the newspapers. The old phrase *Be there or be square* popped into her head. She did not want to be square, although she unquestionably was, and going to a ball game with a handsome young man was sure to be a change of pace. Susan accepted enthusiastically, reminding him they still had business to discuss.

They made plans for Russ to pick her up at her house and discuss her business on the ride into the city. Once the drive was over, their business conversation would be, too. Dinner, the game, and the ride home would be pure recreation. The plan sounded perfect to Susan. So much had been going on lately—a break was just what she needed. It had been a long time since her wardrobe was at the top of her thoughts, and it felt good to be thinking about something so pleasant for a change. Although this wasn't a real date, her attorney was young and nice looking, and a little fantasy on her part wouldn't hurt anyone.

So far, she was having a very good day.

When Susan arrived at her lab, she noticed the Japanese compact was not in the lot. The driver certainly kept unusual hours, but then, so did she. Her staff was hard at work in the lab area. Wolf was talking to Mandy as he organized a group of slides. Mandy seemed to prefer working closely with Wolf and she definitely communicated with him far more than she did with the other researchers. Susan had often wondered if they saw each other outside of work. It was clear that her favorite researcher liked Mandy, though she didn't know if his feelings were reciprocated.

From their conversation, Susan quickly ascertained that Wolf's mother's house was being fumigated and she was temporarily staying with him. Apparently, the visit was not going well. No matter how bad his situation was, Mandy was telling him, hers was worse. Wolf had an unusually expressive face, and it became more and more contorted as Mandy compared his situation to her plight.

Mandy's old-world mother expected her daughter to be dutiful in the traditional Chinese way. At least Wolf's mother would be moving back to her own house someday, Mandy pointed out. Her parents expected to live with her even after she married, and she would be responsible for their physical care as well as financial support. They in turn would run her life and raise her children.

Walking into the animal room, Susan was pleased to see her two new primates. The mature males looked healthy and alert; tests would start on them shortly. Because they had so much contract work to catch up on, Susan had decided to formulate a new batch of GI-80 the following week. Although anxious to start her own research, she desperately needed the income from Avery. In addition, she had to determine the proper timing and dose levels for the GI-80, which would take a considerable amount of her time. Right now, her highest priority was making her next payroll.

As she stood in front of the cages, Kevin joined her. Of all her staff, he was the most interested in animals. He seemed to have a rapport with them. After they had discussed the new arrivals, he commented, "Mandy had her car fixed. The repair cost fifty-seven percent of the car's value. I told her she should have used part of that money for the down payment on a new car. You can buy a Kia with zero percent financing."

Apparently, Mandy doesn't take financial advice from Kevin,

Susan thought as she left the lab area. Back in her office, she looked through the slats of her blinds. The parking lot was filled with cars.

As always, Susan meticulously arranged her papers in the order that she would work on them. Then she called her voicemail. Dr. Klein had left a message asking her to return the call. Her medical office was typically hard to reach, but today the receptionist put her through immediately.

"Susan, your blood test came back, and I must say I was surprised by the results," Dr. Klein said. "The sonogram didn't show anything out of the ordinary; from what I could see, your ovaries look fine. It is the blood work that I…." She hesitated. "I would like to repeat this blood test and see if we get the same results."

Overwhelmed with anxiety, Susan could hardly breathe. "What were the results?"

Dr. Klein hesitated again. "I don't want to alarm you. The results showed hormone levels higher than normal for a woman your age who is not on hormone-replacement therapy. I don't want you to worry. Hormone levels fluctuate even in women who are in menopause.

"But we'll need to repeat the test. I would like you to have blood drawn at the same lab. I am sending a requisition over now. They close early on Fridays, so it may be too late for today. Can you go in sometime Monday? There's no need to fast. Now that I think of it, I am going to ask them to take a saliva sample while you're there. I want to compare those results with the blood levels."

Her day had been so good until now. Too many things had been happening in the past few weeks. Was her life about to become medicalized?

CHAPTER 13

THE NEXT DAY, Susan decided to loosen up, have some fun, and not even think about her work or her health. She was no longer bleeding and her breasts did not feel tender. The problem was probably just a hormonal surge. Most likely, it had resolved itself and the next test would show appropriate hormone levels. Anyway, there was nothing she could do about it, so there was no need to think about it.

She planned to go to the gym and then get her hair cut, styled, maybe colored. And then—why not?—a manicure and pedicure, too. She found she was excited about her fantasy date that wasn't really a date.

Gyms are unusual places. Unlike other public settings, they have a completely different feeling depending on when you're there. Even the people you see are different. Rosa never worked out on weekends, so Susan had gotten in the habit of exercising on weekday evenings, when she could see her friend. It had been years since she'd come in on a Saturday, so she probably wouldn't see a single person she recognized. Even Crazy Rene might not be there. But that wouldn't matter, since she didn't need anything from Rosa's locker.

Inconveniently, all the treadmills were taken, so Susan walked over to the dumbbells to do some free-weight exercises until one became available. To her surprise, there were God's Gift and Body Beautiful. Susan wondered if these two dopes had anything else to do. GG was wearing sweatpants and a T-shirt with a sports logo she assumed was for the team he had played on ever so briefly. BB had on an exercise outfit Susan had not seen before, midnight blue with an iridescent tint. Her bright blue shoelaces matched her outfit, nicely accessorized with gold hoop earrings and a gold necklace.

Taking a single ten-pound dumbbell, Susan put one hand on her head and, with the weight in the other, leaned to the side to stretch her oblique muscles to warm up. As she stretched in front of a mirror-covered wall, Susan noticed GG and BB stop talking, look over at her, and then resume their conversation. When this happened again, Susan was sure they were talking about her. This did not concern her; after all, she and Rosa had always talked about them and their little group of friends.

She wondered what they could possibly find interesting about her. Maybe they were wondering what Susan was doing there on a weekend and what had happened to her friend. Perhaps they'd decided that Susan should see the Body Beautiful's husband for a little plastic surgery. On second thought, they were probably saying that she should ask for a lot of plastic surgery.

"That's good work," BB said, speaking to Susan for the first time.

"I'm not really doing much," Susan mumbled.

Continuing to look at Susan, BB added, "Your butt looks really good."

Susan stopped stretching and stood there with her mouth open. Thankfully, she saw someone getting off a treadmill. "Excuse me," she stammered, walking over to claim the machine before anyone else could.

She had finished her weight training only because she wanted to end the conversation with Body Beautiful. If Rosa were here, the two could have a good laugh over it. Without her friend, the situation was just creepy. She wondered if God's Gift also thought her butt looked really good.

Since she wasn't doing any more weights, she had a lot of time left before her hair appointment—enough to try doing a full hour on the treadmill. If she did feel fatigued after so much exercise, she could take a nap.

Susan walked rapidly for a few minutes and then began to jog. Feeling comfortable, she increased her speed to 5 miles per hour, and then to 5.5 miles per hour. Still not tiring, she moved the speed up to 6.2 miles per hour and finished the last few minutes at that speed. After sixty minutes plus a ten-minute cooldown, Susan had jogged almost six miles.

She wasn't even winded or tired as she walked into the women's locker room. When she stepped on the scale, it balanced at exactly one hundred twenty-seven pounds—more than three pounds less than the last time she'd weighed herself. She'd have to mention this to Dr. Klein. Still, it was less than a ten-pound weight loss, and she'd promised herself she would not dwell on medical problems today. She had just had a terrific run. It was unlikely anything serious could be wrong with her.

Since she didn't need to wash her hair before her hair appointment, Susan took her towel and wrapped it around her head as Crazy Rene did. As she walked into the shower, she saw her image in the mirror. Without an opposing mirror, she was unable to get a good view of her good-looking butt, though her stomach looked flatter and her midriff area slimmer. She would need to rethink her outfit for tonight.

Susan couldn't wait to tell Rosa that BB had spoken to her, and how stupid and crass her comment had been. She'd have to call when she had time for a long conversation. They had a lot of catching up to do.

As always, Susan was right on time for her hair appointment, and today Marla was ready for her. This was unusual; her hairdresser generally overbooked herself and ran late. Marla had been doing Susan's hair for ten years. She wasn't the best colorist or stylist around, but her location was convenient and the salon was very low-key. Susan didn't care for fancy hair salons with snooty stylists. Marla's was a simple neighborhood place, with three chairs for stylists and a small parking lot behind the shop. The stylists even washed their clients' hair themselves.

Marla's work was consistent and she never made Susan's hair look too contemporary. Susan wanted her hair to match her style and be appropriate for someone her age. Unlike some stylists, Marla listened and understood what she wanted.

Susan explained that she was going out to dinner and a baseball game and wanted to look her best.

"You're going to the game tonight—I'm impressed. Somebody must like you," Marla said, explaining that tonight's was a playoff game and tickets were hard to come by.

"Not really. It's a business engagement," Susan said, remembering the plan to stop talking business once she and Russ arrived in the city. "He is attractive, but unfortunately, much too young for me."

Marla was younger than Susan, divorced and actively seeking a husband. Every time Susan saw her, she had a story about the dating scene. She wore short skirts and changed her hair color frequently. Today she was a redhead.

Marla started talking about the cougar trend, older women dating younger men. Apparently, this was a big thing with celebrities and even some of her clientele. Who knew?

"I don't see much new growth," Marla said, looking at Susan's hair. "I think you could wait a little longer to color." She parted the hair with her fingers and kept looking at different sections of it, first on top and then on the back and sides. "Huh. A few strands of hair seem to be re-pigmenting."

Marla explained that hair turns gray unevenly and that sometimes hairs regain a little pigment.

"Sorry to tell you, but it's only temporary. Once hair starts to gray, the re-pigmentation lasts only a short time. It will gray again."

"Do you know what causes it?"

"Some medications can cause it to happen. I have a client who takes B-12 shots. She was a blond her entire life, and she's started getting black hairs. It looks terrible, especially in the back. Yours looks okay. I don't think we need to color today."

CHAPTER 14

AFTER TAKING THE entire day off, Susan went into the lab on Sunday afternoon. She wanted to make a supply of GI-80, and this was most conveniently done when no one was around. No other cars were in the parking lot. Once inside, Susan was careful to lock the door and to put the alarm on the Stay setting, so the internal sensors were not activated and she could move about freely.

Everything was just as her staff had left it on Friday afternoon—the usual mess. It felt good to stop in the animal room to look at the new primates. Susan whispered to them, "You'll be getting GI-80 pretty soon, so we're going to have a lot in common."

She had not written in her log for two days and needed to note her treadmill speed and weight, then she would start formulating a new batch of GI-80. Sitting at her desk, Susan began her notations, then began thinking about the previous day. She'd had no time for a nap, because it had taken her over an hour to select an outfit to wear. San Francisco gets cold at night, and she'd had a difficult time selecting something that would look good at dinner and still be casual and warm enough for the game. Growing frustrated with the process, Susan had called Bunny. Bunny had been thrilled that her daughter was asking for wardrobe tips, and equally pleased to learn that Susan was going out with Russell.

Bunny's selections had included a pair of black skinny jeans and black leather tasseled moccasins—a gift from her for Susan's birthday. She also recommended wearing a tank top under a hip-length marine blue cashmere turtleneck sweater, and a black knit hat. Her mother had gone on to suggest that Susan take her charcoal gray goose-down vest to wear at the game. When Susan called her mother early that evening to report that the outfit looked exactly right, Bunny had been overjoyed.

Susan had added gold stud earrings, a gold bracelet, and two simple gold rings on the same finger of her right hand. Looking in the mirror, she'd felt exceedingly satisfied with her appearance and concluded that she should ask her mother's advice on what to wear more often.

And Russell had said, "You look terrific."

In dark gray wool slacks, a white cotton oxford shirt, and a black crewneck sweater, Russell had looked nice himself. He was carrying a heavy Giants baseball jacket and cap. When he smiled, he looked especially handsome. Giving him a radiant smile in return, Susan had replied, "You look great, too. I didn't know you were such a sports fan." Immediately, she had chided herself for this comment. Since she knew little of his personal life, it made no sense at all.

Once in San Francisco, they did not discuss any business, as planned. Instead, they began an animated conversation that lasted the entire evening. Susan had been surprised they had so much to talk about. Russell appeared to have many interests. He read widely and was conversant about politics and other current topics.

One of the things Russell had talked about was his career. His first job after law school had been with the district attorney's office in Oakland. Things had been so bad there, he said, the criminals got out of court before the lawyers. After one arrest, Russ had been in such a hurry, he had quickly filled out the required paperwork and walked even more quickly to BART, the rapid-transit commuter rail line that ran through the San Francisco Bay Area. Getting on the train, he saw the man he had just arrested—the guy had already made bail and been released.

The restaurant Russell had selected was close to the ballpark and served eclectic California cuisine. Susan had been hungry and had thoroughly enjoyed her meal. Russ had eaten with a good appetite as well. Over dinner, he explained that he'd felt his previous firm had not been moving fast enough to make him a partner. He was convinced that his current firm, though smaller and less established, would be better for him in the long term. He had seemed sincere; Susan had detected no dissembling. Over the course of the evening, she'd concluded that he was an adequate lawyer for anything personal, but she would need a more specialized attorney for her business.

After telling him briefly about Gary and the reasons for their divorce, Susan had explained that her business and her mother took up most of her time. In her free time, she said, she went to her gym, or took walks or hikes on the weekends. "I need to get out more," she had laughed, sounding surprised.

In turn, Russ told her that he had never married but had been engaged. When his mother had died unexpectedly, he had taken the loss very hard. Leslie, his fiancée, had not been supportive.

"She was too wrapped up in herself to be there for me," he said, and eventually, he had called off the engagement.

They could not have been too close to the wedding, since no gifts had had to be returned. Susan had been unable to tell how long ago this occurred, and she hadn't asked. He was not seeing anyone, either. Like her, work was taking up too much of his time for a personal life. Smiling at her, he had said that it felt good to be out on a Saturday night, and that he was enjoying her company.

As they entered the ballpark, a man held out a baseball bat and offered it to Susan. Russ had nudged her and told her to take it.

"It's a promotion. The first two thousand fans that come in get a bat. It must be ladies' night. They're giving them out to the women."

"Here, you take it. You're the sports fan," she had said.

"No," he replied, "he gave it to you. Keep it for a souvenir of our evening."

She had no need for a baseball bat, but Jess might want it. She often talked about playing team sports with her sorority.

Susan had enjoyed the game far more than she had anticipated. Russell had explained some of the rules and provided information about the players. Baseball was far more strategic than she had realized, and by the end of the game, Susan found that she planned to watch more games, if not at the ballpark, then on television.

The Giants had played well, and Russ had been elated. Susan told him that she could not remember the last time she'd had such a good time. Russ had felt the same and said he was glad they'd had a chance to get together socially.

Thinking about last night, Susan concluded it had truly been a lovely evening, exactly the change of pace she needed. The light from the setting sun coming through the blinds formed stripes on her desk and on the opposite wall. Feeling relaxed, Susan stretched out her arms. Something was not right: The stripes did not extend fully across the desk or her arms. Something was blocking the light.

Spinning around in her chair, Susan saw the shadow of someone at the window behind her desk, attempting to look through the slats in the blind. He was so close to the glass, he must have been standing in the planter bed.

With an audible gasp, Susan jumped up and moved away from the window. Seeing her move and then look at him, the man turned around and ran. Susan rushed to the window and pushed two slats apart, through which she saw him race across the parking lot to the only other car—the black Japanese compact. Susan could hear his tires screech. Mr. Black Car had burned rubber getting out of the lot.

Frozen with shock, it took her a moment to call the police and request they send someone as soon as possible. A few minutes later, a police car pulled up, and Susan recognized Officer Brennan. Only then unlocking the front door, Susan explained what had happened and that she had reason to believe the man had been following her for some time.

No, she could not tell him the number of the license plate or the make of the car. No, she did not get a good look at the man. Yes, it was definitely a man. No, he had not done anything threatening. No, the sunlight shining into her eyes made it difficult to get a better description. Officer Brennan went outside to look around, then said that he did not see anything unusual or any signs of an attempted break-in. Leaving his card, he told Susan that he would file an incident report noting that no crime had been committed. He told her to be careful and to call if she needed anything.

Susan did not feel reassured by the officer's visit and tried to decide what to do next. There was no one she could call. She could not tell her mother, and phoning Wolf would not be of any help. She would tell him about this tomorrow, when he came into work. There was nothing even Susan could do, except....

She unlocked the front door and, after looking around carefully, went to her car and took out the baseball bat. Returning to her office, she put the bat under her desk and attempted to get back to work.

Susan was a lot like her father. Unlike Bunny, David was not affable or comfortable in social situations. Exceedingly reserved and often shy, he did not have a large group of friends. Some people, misinterpreting his aloof personality and lack of social skills, considered him distant and unfriendly, though people who knew him well understood how kindhearted he was. Growing up, Susan had wished she could be as outgoing and lively as her mother.

But Susan had inherited much of value from her father, especially her intelligence and ability to reason. Immersing herself in her work was what she did to allay any anxiety and calm down. Like David, she could maintain her focus even when under pressure or feeling stress. Susan had the ability to push everything else to the back of her mind and concentrate.

Today, however, this ability failed her. Nervous and agitated, she didn't want to remain at work a minute longer.

CHAPTER 15

SUSAN HAD PLANNED to go to the medical lab and have her blood redrawn. Once dressed and ready to leave, however, she was still on edge. She decided to go into work first and leave when her staff did so that she would not be alone in her lab. If she didn't find time to drive to the city today, she would go tomorrow.

Before she left for work, she wanted to call Russell. Since he was not likely to be in the office that early, she called his cell phone, hoping he wouldn't mind her calling before work about something that was essentially a personal matter. She had no one else to talk to and hoped that talking about what had occurred would make her feel less fearful.

Susan hesitated, then, with a large amount of trepidation, went ahead and made the call. He picked up the phone immediately.

"Russ, I'm sorry to bother you so early, but I need to talk to someone about this."

"Are you okay?" He sounded concerned. "Don't worry, you're not bothering me. Is this about your mother?"

"Bunny is fine, so far as I know. It's me that I'm worried about." Susan took a deep breath and went on to tell him about having been followed by Mr. Black Car, how he had been right up against her office window even though he'd had to stand in a planter bed. She concluded with the visit from Officer Brennan. Susan hoped she had made herself clear and was not being overly emotional.

Russ said nothing until she was finished. Now Susan hoped that he wasn't annoyed. She did not want him to think she was a foolish, anxious woman, overwrought for no reason.

His response was not at all what Susan had expected. He was unmistakably angry, very angry. He did not raise his voice but spoke slowly and deliberately.

"I don't like this, Susan. Something is not right here—the police are not handling this properly. This isn't protocol. Your building was broken into three weeks ago. You have obviously been followed and stalked. You're a business owner in their town, and they send over one junior officer who didn't even take a good look for footprints. The man was standing in a planter box, for heaven's sake. They could have gotten a footprint, even a partial.

"They should have sent over two officers, and if two were not available, they should have sent a second one later. This isn't making sense. Either the police aren't taking this seriously, or they are not trying to prevent a crime. Until it's figured out, you'll have to be careful. Being at work only when you have staff in the building is a good idea. At least *you're* showing some judgment."

When Susan heard him say this, she felt a sense of relief and even pride. Russell didn't think that she was overly emotional. Quite the contrary. He was praising her reasoning and common sense. She had someone to help, someone on her side.

"Susan, with your permission, I am going to look into this. I need to try and find out what is going on." Russell's tone changed abruptly. "Oh, I almost forgot. I was going to call *you* this morning. Something very interesting has happened."

Susan had not been the only one who'd tried to get some work done on Sunday. When Russ had checked his messages that morning, he'd found two voicemails and two emails from Avery Biogenetics.

"Christian Dietz wants to set up a meeting. Research at Avery Biogenetics Corporation, or, as you always call it, ABC, seems to be going well. Their parent corporation is looking to expand. Dietz said that, rather than simply increase the amount of contract work Glass Biotech is doing for them, they would like to acquire your business. From what I understood, this includes intellectual property as well as equipment.

"No mention was made of price, but I did not get the impression from the voicemails or the emails that it was a major concern. Dietz said something to the effect that he was positive satisfactory terms could be worked out.

"I was surprised that he would contact me over the weekend with this. Apparently, they feel some sense of urgency. I have experience with negotiations, and I can tell you one thing I know for sure: They want to move quickly."

Susan was stunned. So many things were happening at once. The expression *When it rains, it pours* came into her head. Is that how life really was, or was she was turning into Bunny?

"Russ, I don't know. Having my own research lab was always my dream. I thought the plan was to pull some money out of my business so that I could be more liquid. I'm not sure I want to go back to work for Avery, or for anyone else, for that matter. I like working for myself, and I certainly don't want to retire. I'm not sure I want to sell."

"I know that's not your intention," Russell said. "I'll phone Dietz and sound him out. Maybe we can make things work. I won't call him this morning. I want him to think we aren't anxious to make a deal. When I think I have something that will work with your goals, we'll meet and see if we can hammer something out, only on terms satisfactory to you."

This was a considerable amount to think about, and Susan already had a lot on her mind.

Chapter 16

Arriving at her office, Susan looked around the parking lot and checked once again before getting out of her car. Happily, the black car was nowhere to be seen, and Wolf and Mandy were already busy working in the lab. Wolf was humming as he looked at slides under a microscope. Mandy was loading tubes of samples into a high-speed centrifuge, her blue-highlighted hair falling forward as she bent over the equipment.

Seeing everything in order, Susan went to her office and listened to her voice messages. The police had not called her back. Her gynecologist had left a message asking Susan to call. It pleased her to feel her doctor was taking such an interest.

Dr. Klein asked Susan how she was feeling and if she had any more bleeding, breast tenderness, or other symptoms. Susan was happy to report that all her symptoms had disappeared and that she was feeling well. For some reason, she didn't say anything about the additional weight loss.

"I called the medical laboratory this morning," Dr. Klein went on, "and they told me that you hadn't come in for the tests I ordered." She was under the impression that Susan had planned to come in that morning.

"Yes, something…came up, and I needed to be at work. I'll go tomorrow, and if not, the day after that." Susan reminded her doctor that she had said it was probably nothing significant. She wondered what the rush was. When did doctors start calling medical labs to find out if a patient had had her blood drawn?

Dr. Klein sounded irritated. "Susan, I'm going to insist that you come in today to get your blood drawn."

"Excuse me? You insist what?"

Dr. Klein made a clumsy attempt to rephrase what she had said, but Susan began feeling uncomfortable. She told her doctor she'd come into the lab shortly and said goodbye.

As planned, Susan left work that afternoon when her staff did. Taking her tote bag with her flowered notebook inside, she set the alarm and locked the front door, then joined Wolf, Kevin, and Mandy in the parking lot. Jess had gone home earlier. There was no way she was going to work late alone in the building.

Looking in her rear-view mirror as she turned onto the ramp to enter the freeway, she did not see anyone following her. Things around her seemed crazy—maybe there was something she was overlooking, something she should be doing, or maybe she was doing something she shouldn't. For some reason, Susan thought of Crazy Rene. Susan was going to become crazy, too, if she did not find some peace and a chance to think things through. Rene spent a lot of time in the sauna. When she got too hot, she'd shower with cold water and return to the sauna. Susan decided to give it a try.

Thirty minutes later, Susan pulled into the FitMarin parking lot. As she entered the gym, she pulled out her ID and ran it through the magnetic-card reader. Instead of waving her in, the young girl at the desk asked her to come into the office. In all the years Susan had been coming to FitMarin, she had never even been in the office. What was going on?

CHAPTER 17

SUSAN RECOGNIZED FITMARIN's assistant manager, Alice Coughlin, only because she had seen her photograph on the health club's bulletin board a couple of years ago, above the announcement *Employee of the Month*. At the time, Alice had been wearing tiny bike shorts and a skin-tight T-shirt. Susan remembered the photo and the saccharine writeup about Alice's devotion to fitness and to members' well-being. Her reward, in addition to the posting for all to see, was a reserved parking space near the gym entrance for a month. Rosa and Susan had gotten a good laugh that evening, and after that, Rosa always referred to Alice as Sexpot of the Month.

Susan wondered what the Ex-Sexpot (Alice had gained a little weight since then), who no longer had a reserved parking space, wanted with her.

"Susan—may I call you Susan? We seem to have a small problem."

Alice went on to explain that the lock on Susan's locker had been forcibly broken. The staff had no idea just when it had occurred. Someone on the staff had gathered up the remaining contents and put them in a cardboard box. Alice got up, bent over, and handed her the box. Susan noticed that she was still wearing tight shorts.

Susan had kept nothing of value in her locker, only worn gym clothes, a pair of old athletic shoes, two old towels, and some toiletries. Everything appeared to be in the box.

"We're happy to give you a lock to replace the one that was

broken. I am relieved nothing was taken," said Alice, handing Susan a new combination lock, still in its box.

Susan found Alice unnerving. Her high-pitched voice was insincerely sweet.

"Thank you. Were any other lockers broken into?"

"No, only yours. We had some thefts five years ago, but until now, we've had no other problems."

Carrying the new lock and the box with her gym gear, Susan went into the locker room. Though she had planned only to sit in the sauna, she thought a run on the treadmill might relax her. As she tied her shoelaces, she considered herself lucky nothing had been taken. If she had lost even one item—shoes, socks, shorts, sports bra, or T-shirt—she wouldn't be able to work out. Then again, whatever the thief was looking for, it couldn't be old gym gear.

Susan peeled the combination from the back of the lock and was about to use it when she stopped, reached into her locker, and took the lavender notebook from her tote bag. Then she locked the locker and headed down the hall. She did not see anyone and checked in the toilet and shower area as well. Tonight it was not just Crazy Rene that she was avoiding.

With no one around, Susan quickly went to Rosa's locker, opened the combination lock, and slipped her notebook in under the towels and her white metal box. After her workout, she'd retrieve the notebook and the metal box. With the updated security system installed, it was safe to leave things at the lab.

Out on the exercise floor, Susan chose the closest available treadmill and started walking rapidly to warm up. She didn't see Body Beautiful and God's Gift. They always exercised on Mondays, to make up for their weekend indiscretions; their conversation was invariably about what they had eaten and had to drink. Tonight, though, they were not in their favorite spot by the dumbbells.

Susan increased her speed and started to run but almost immediately felt too fatigued to continue. She slowed the treadmill speed to a walk. Maybe her Saturday workout had been an aberration, or perhaps it had been too much for her and she was still recovering. After two minutes, she felt too exhausted to continue. Susan hit the stop button, wiped down the machine for the next person, and headed back to the locker room. She would have to revert to her original plan and do her thinking in the sauna. Now there was one more thing she would have to consider.

Susan stripped off her gym clothes and wrapped a towel around her. She took the second towel from her locker and hung it on a hook outside the sauna. As soon as her eyes adjusted to the dim light, she saw Crazy Rene lying on the top bench, naked. No one else was in the sauna. Susan silently prayed Rene would not try to start a conversation. She did not feel like talking to anyone, and she never felt like talking to Rene.

It was not easy to lie down in this sauna. The benches were made with evenly spaced, open-framed wooden armrests to prevent people from lying down, Susan assumed, and falling asleep or losing consciousness. If someone were unconscious, the other users might think she was resting. Crazy Rene had put her legs over one of the armrests and her head under another, directly below a sign that announced *Lying Down in Sauna Strictly Prohibited!*

Spreading her towel out on the lowest bench directly across the sauna from Rene, Susan sat down. Without her towel, she was nude, too. The only light came through the heavy glass window on the wall near the door. From where she was sitting, she could see a clock through the glass and made a mental note of the time. The higher benches were considerably hotter than the lower ones; if Rene did not move in eight minutes, Susan would have to make sure she was awake. Ten minutes on the top bench might be too long. Susan sincerely hoped this would not be necessary. She had had enough drama today.

The fact that her locker had been broken into was worrisome. She should probably tell Russell about it. Susan thought it unlikely that Mr. Black Car could be responsible. Even if he had tailed her to the gym, how would he have gotten into the women's locker room? A man would not be able to slip in unnoticed. Could he have a female partner? Susan thought this unlikely as well. If he had a partner, he probably wouldn't have followed her in the same car every day. Most likely, Mr. Black Car was a sexual predator. That thought elicited a shudder.

Suddenly, there was a loud cracking noise and the sauna filled up with smoke. Susan jumped up and headed for the door, her heart beating wildly. She had her hand on the wooden handle when she realized it was not smoke, it was steam. Through the haze, she could see Rene holding a bucket high over the synthetic stones of the sauna's heating element. The sign immediately to her left proclaimed *Pouring Water on Heater Prohibited!*

This was obviously not going to be a place to relax. Crazy Rene did not know or did not care that people went into a sauna for dry heat. She really was a nut case. She could have scalded herself or someone else, pouring hot water directly on the electric heating element. She could have shorted out the heater, even started another fire. She should report this to Alice Coughlin. On second thought, she'd just report it to the person at the front counter. One meeting with Alice had been enough.

Susan snatched her second towel from the hook and headed for the showers. Though she always used the open showers, she decided to use one of the private ones, hoping it would help her calm down. The hot water felt good, but almost immediately, Susan realized that her head ached, and she could feel a pain in her back when she took a breath. When she swallowed, her throat hurt. Maybe GI-80 did not boost immune function in humans. When she got home, she would have to take her temperature. She was certain she was getting sick, and whatever she had was coming on quickly.

Abruptly, the shower curtain was pulled open and she felt a blast of cold air. Susan had never seen BB in the shower area before and had no idea why she was interrupting her shower. She opened her mouth but no words came out.

BB just stood there, staring at her. When she finally spoke, in a harsh whisper, she enunciated each word. "What have you done? I want to know. Other people want to know."

Susan reached around her and grabbed one of her towels from the hook. She didn't even have the presence of mind to look for the clean towel but took the first one she touched, not knowing if she had used it to sit on in the sauna. Without saying a word, she wrapped the towel around her and walked out of the shower area. Apparently, Rene was not the only crazy person here.

Her head throbbing, Susan opened her locker. Standing nearby in the aisle, BB watched as she dried off and dressed but said nothing more.

CHAPTER 18

By the time Susan got home, she could barely stand up. She considered lying down on the entryway floor and then, looking at the cold tile, dropped her gym bag and resolved to try to make it to the living room. Holding onto the back of the couch, she was able to advance along its length. From there, supporting herself on the walls of the hallway, she made it into the bedroom. She did not even have the energy to remove her clothes or dry her hair. If she had waited five more minutes, she might not have made it into her house.

All night, she tossed in bed, her clothing tangled and her head aching. She was dreadfully thirsty but too sick to walk to the bathroom sink. When morning finally arrived, she was still unable to get up; her head was still pounding, and she was certain she was running a high fever. Susan was overcome with disappointment. That she was so sick, with an illness that had come on so suddenly, was inauspicious.

Lying in bed, Susan wondered whether her lack of energy on the treadmill was because she'd been coming down with this illness or if it could be a side effect somehow caused by GI-80. Could GI-80 actually depress an immune response rather than heighten it? Perhaps GI-80 did not affect the immune system at all but somehow increased energy levels. The animals dosed with GI-80 had certainly been active. When she felt better and had a new supply of the therapeutic, she should take another dose.

She had run so well on the treadmill just two days earlier. Just a day or two later, her locker had been broken into. Was this a random event, mere coincidence? Or did BB have something to do with it? If so, what had she been looking for? Or was she just crazy?

She'd certainly acted crazy last night, and angry, too. Was that because BB had seen the sauna filling up with steam or pouring out the door when Susan opened it? Crazy Rene had not been lying near the window; from outside, it would have looked as if Susan was the only one in the sauna. BB must have thought that Susan had been the one who poured the water on the heater. She would have no way of knowing that Susan was a scientist, although anyone with a rudimentary knowledge of physical science would know that water and electricity don't mix.

Susan supposed that BB had gone to the front counter to complain about her. In all likelihood, the next time she went to the gym, she'd be invited into the office again, or maybe Alice would suspend her membership without giving her a chance to explain what had happened.

She imagined her defense. "I happen to be a respected scientist, with doctoral degrees as well as post-docs in both physical and biological sciences. The guilty person is Crazy Rene. You know she already started one fire in the sauna, with her shoes!" But how would Susan explain why she hadn't stopped Rene, or at least reported her to the front desk? Never mind, Susan thought. I can find another place to work out. I have more serious problems.

When she felt up to it, she would have to call Russ. She wanted to hear what Christian Dietz had said. Maybe it was time to consider selling her business.

Later that morning, although still shaky, she was able to drink two glasses of tap water and swallow some aspirin. Then she took off her crumpled clothes and put on a cotton nightgown. She had just enough energy to brush her teeth. Her head was still throbbing, and she knew she looked awful. She could feel her eyes were swollen, and her face was surely puffy and flushed. She hoped the analgesics would start working soon.

Thirty-five minutes later, she called Wolf and told him that she was too sick to come in.

"Don't complain to me," Wolf replied with a lilt in his voice. "I have my own problems. My mother is staying at my apartment."

She was glad he was in good enough spirits to joke about it.

"Guess what just arrived? Our two new primates. We haven't even named the first two yet. They are beautiful; Kevin can't stop looking at them."

Susan asked about the contract work and how far along they were. Wolf informed her that all the lab sheets had just been completed and they were ready for new assignments.

"Well, then, have everyone straighten up and stay until eleven-thirty. You can tell them I will pay for a full day, so you all have the afternoon off."

"Thanks, but I am not going home at eleven-thirty, I'll tell you that right now. Home is the last place I want to be."

Susan laughed, which made her head hurt. "You know what? Take everyone out to lunch. It's on me. Have fun! I'll probably see everyone tomorrow."

She felt pleased about giving her employees time off and buying them lunch. They were a first-rate group, and they would enjoy having a good meal together. She wanted Glass Biotech to be a superior place to work. If her cash situation were better, she could do more for her staff. Never mind; she could treat them today. She knew several nice restaurants nearby and wondered which they would choose.

After the phone call, Susan dozed off, and when she awoke, she felt well enough to get up. Walking to the kitchen, she noted that except for the gym bag at the front door, the house was immaculate. Susan had bought this ranch-style home in Larkspur after her divorce. Looking around, it was obvious her furnishings were out of style. When her finances were back in order, she thought, she would redecorate. She wouldn't use a designer this time; she'd ask Bunny for ideas. That is, if her mother was still around and able to help. A wave of sadness swept over her. She wanted to call her mother, but if she did before she felt up to a real conversation, Bunny would worry.

She toasted two pieces of bread and took a can of ginger ale from the refrigerator, then picked up the two newspapers on the doormat and brought them, along with her food and a box of tissues, to the bedroom. Arranging her pillows, she put on her reading glasses and tried to read one of the papers, but her eyes were bothering her. She was so hungry and thirsty, she finished everything, though she couldn't taste much. While she ate, she glanced at the paper without her glasses on and could see more clearly, which was odd. It had been over a year since her last refraction—not that long, but her prescription must have changed. She didn't give it much thought.

After a shower, Susan felt so much better, she put on jeans and a T-shirt and wrapped her hair in a towel. It was already noon. She desperately wanted to see her two newest primates, and with her staff gone, she would not even have to style her hair or put on makeup. She'd just run over to Emeryville, see the two new macaques, and, if she felt up to it, work on lab assignments—maybe she'd even start the molecular separation to create more GI-80. On second thought, that was probably too much for today. She could take the lab sheets they'd completed home and work on the new lab assignments there and then email them to Wolf. At least the work for Avery could proceed.

Susan pulled on a sweater and covered her messy hair with a baseball cap. At the last minute, she decided to take a few cosmetics, her blow dryer, and a hairbrush with her. If she felt well enough to pick up some food on her way home, she could put on some makeup and fix her hair in the office bathroom.

Susan parked in front of her office and left the bag with her cosmetics and hair products in the trunk. Once inside, she realized she didn't have to decide about doing the molecular separation—for the first time since she'd started her company, she did not have her flowered notebook with her. It was where she had left it, in Rosa's locker.

She felt as if part of her was missing. She would have to go back to FitMarin and retrieve it. It was too important to leave in a gym locker.

Anxious to see the new primates, she went into the lab. It was the typical mess: the usual array of food containers and lab gear, as well as work in progress. Hadn't she specifically asked that they straighten up before leaving? At least someone had closed the door to the storage closet.

In the animal room, Susan saw that her two new macaques were beautiful and, assuredly, very expensive specimens. The invoice would undoubtedly be among the papers on her desk. "You are such beautiful girls," she crooned in a high-pitched voice. "I hope you're not nervous. It's hard to be in a new place, I know. We'll be nice to you. See the boys over there? They like it here."

The female primates were young, though Susan needed to look at the invoice to find out how old they were. When they heard her voice, both looked at her. One of them came over to the side of the cage and put both hands on the wires. She tilted her head and made the cutest face. Then she started rocking her head from side to side, still watching Susan. It was easy to see why Kevin liked them so much.

"Aren't you the cutest thing? You're my favorite already, and you don't even have a name. Don't tell the others, but I like you best."

The other one came to the side of her cage and looked at Susan.

"I'm sorry, did I make you jealous? I like you, too. You're the most beautiful one. You have such a pretty face."

The second female began moving her head from side to side. Susan moved closer to the cage and imitated the primate's movements with her head. When the macaque began to make cooing sounds, it reminded Susan of the sounds Gigi had made the last time she'd seen her. Thinking of Gigi, she felt a twinge of sadness.

This needs to be documented, Susan thought. She wondered if her staff had started a log. She felt well enough to start the documentation, once she found the information she needed on the invoice. Shutting off the light, she returned to her office and hit the PLAY button on her phone to retrieve her messages.

CHAPTER 19

"SUSAN, THIS IS Doctor Klein. We seem to have had some misunderstanding the last time we spoke. I see that you still have not come in for your tests yet. Please give me the benefit of the doubt here. I'd like you to call me back when you get this message and let me know when you plan on coming in."

Listening to her doctor's thin, whiny voice, Susan realized that she did not like Denise Klein. There was something unsettling and…not nice about her. Had she ever known anyone who liked or disliked their gynecologist? After years of a physician-patient relationship, Susan and her doctor were having *misunderstandings*?

This was not something she could discuss with Russell. Maybe she should call Bunny. Her mother had been so pleased when she'd asked her for wardrobe advice. Even if she didn't have anything to add, she would like to be asked about this. Bunny did have a lot of experience with gynecologists.

After three rings, Bunny picked up the phone.

"Hello, Momma. Sorry I didn't call you last night or this morning. I was sick. It's just a cold, but I didn't even feel well enough to talk on the phone. I'm much better now. I'm at the office trying to get a little work done."

"You're okay?" Bunny said a little breathlessly. "I'm so glad to hear from you. I didn't call because I didn't want to worry you, but something happened this morning."

Susan felt her entire body tense. "What happened? Are you all right?"

"I'm fine. Nothing happened to me. I went out this morning for an early class and returned home for lunch." Bunny spoke calmly and slowly.

"And?" Susan said, trying not to sound impatient.

"When I opened the front door, it was clear someone had broken into my apartment."

"Did you see who it was? Was anything stolen?"

"No, my dear girl, I did not see who it was. And yes, things were taken. They were clearly looking for something, as my drawers and shelves were emptied. All my clothes were thrown on the floor of the closet. Florence is here now, helping me put everything back."

"Mother, don't do too much. Can you get some more people to come and help? What about Shirley and Doris?"

Florence might not be enough protection or help for Bunny. Susan wondered if either of them had had the presence of mind to call the police.

Bunny explained that with Florence's help, everything was almost back in place and that Shirley was coming over shortly. "I didn't call Doris, because I don't like her anymore. Nobody does."

This was news. Susan had not known about any problems with Doris, but she was relieved two people would soon be with her mother.

"I'll be over soon to help you. Make a list of everything that's missing. You have personal-property insurance; I will help you file a claim. I told you so many times not to leave your jewelry out on the dresser."

"That's the strange part. They didn't take any of my jewels."

"They didn't take your jewelry? What did they take?"

Bunny had expensive clothing, but it would be harder to sell clothing than jewelry.

"I don't want to tell you what they took," her mother replied.

Losing patience, Susan raised her voice, something she rarely did with her mother. "What do you mean, you don't want to tell me what they took? What do you have that I can't know about?"

Her mother had a mink stole—no, she had two mink stoles, but no one wore those anymore. They'd been purchased in the nineteen-fifties, for heaven's sake. Who would steal them? Susan wracked her brain, trying to think what Bunny could have hidden from her. Love letters from David? Love letters from someone else? None of this was making any sense.

Bunny was silent.

"I will be over in less than an hour and help you clean up. I will call for the insurance forms. If you don't want to tell me what was taken, fine; as long as you aren't hurt, I really don't care. I want someone to stay with you until I get there. I would prefer it if both Florence and Shirley stay with you.

"And you know, when I get there, I will figure out what was stolen. Didn't Daddy always say that I could figure out anything?" Susan added, trying to inject a little humor into the situation while letting her mother know she was serious.

Her mother was okay and things could have been a lot worse. What if Bunny had surprised the intruder? The thought made Susan sick.

"You're right. You will figure it out when you get here. The only things that were taken were your pictures—all of them, from kindergarten through graduation."

Calmly, Susan told her mother she would be over shortly and said goodbye. Taking the baseball bat from under her desk she walked down the hall to the bathroom. Flipping on the light, she turned and looked at her reflection in the small mirror above the sink. She stood completely still taking in what she was seeing. She was not surprised. The image of herself reflected back at her confirmed her thinking. She understood what was happening and she knew what she had to do next.

She propped the bat up between the sink and the wall. Without using the toilet, Susan flushed it and then briefly turned on the water in the sink. As she shut the water off, she saw that her hands were shaking.

Leaving the bathroom door open, she returned to the hallway, shut off the lights, and set the alarm with the "away" code. Once set, the alarm and the motion detectors would activate in exactly two minutes. Susan opened and closed the front door but did not leave. Instead, she went back into the dark bathroom, picked up the bat, and waited by the open door.

CHAPTER 20

SUSAN STOOD BY the bathroom door breathing as shallowly as possible. Trying not to make a sound, she clutched the bat and waited. The minutes passed. It seemed as if she had been standing frozen in place for an hour, though she realized it was probably not more than ten minutes.

It was possible that she was mistaken and everything didn't fit together like she thought. Could it be that she was alone in the building? Maybe one of her staffers had actually closed the door to the supply closet for once. Was it possible that no one was hiding in there?

With all her senses on elevated alert, she waited. It was so quiet that she could hear her heart beating and hear the soft whoosh of air coming in and out of her nose. Silent and still as a corpse, she remained in the dark bathroom. A muffled sound broke the silence. She wasn't sure what it could be, but it sounded like some sort of movement emanating from inside the building. Still, she stood, her position unchanged.

Then one of the double doors to the laboratory opened quietly. Instinctively comprehending the peril she was in, Susan held the bat as tightly as she could and raised it high. She sensed someone starting to walk softly down the hall. Her heart was racing and her hands felt clammy as she gripped the bat. Her whole body was trembling. Then, just as someone wearing dark clothing passed the bathroom door, she took a deep breath and swung the bat down as hard as she could. She heard a loud crack, followed by a moan. Darting out from behind the bathroom door, Susan grabbed her bag from her desk and ran out of the building.

Shaking, she fumbled for her car keys until she felt them at the bottom of the bag and clicked the remote to open her car door. She jumped in, locked the doors, and backed out of the parking space as fast as she could. Looking in her rear-view mirror, she did not see anyone following her.

Susan got on the first freeway on-ramp she reached, which was heading east. Although she would have preferred to go west, she did not want to risk driving on city streets so close to her office. Glancing at the cars around her, she didn't see any that looked familiar.

She gave her cell phone the command to dial Russ's phone, and when he answered, attempted to speak as coherently and concisely as possible. This was difficult; she was breathing rapidly and her voice was trembling. She told Russ that she believed she had made a very big discovery with her latest drug, GI-80, just before her lab animals had been taken. And in the past two days, her gym locker had been broken into, Bunny's apartment had been burglarized, her gynecologist, Dr. Denise Klein, had been acting strangely, *and* she had just encountered a prowler in her lab. She believed all these events were related to her research.

Susan took a deep breath and continued. While she had not gotten a good look at the intruder, she thought it was a man. She had left immediately after hitting him with the bat. She assumed the police were there now or would arrive very soon, since the alarm would have been tripped.

Then she realized that she hadn't heard the alarm. Two minutes would surely have passed since the intruder activated the hall sensor and she'd driven out of the lot. Those alarms are so loud, she said, they can be heard from blocks away.

Russell told her he would leave for Emeryville immediately,

and that once he got to her lab, he would call her. Until then, he stressed, she should not return there.

"Russ, there is something else I need to tell you. After the break-in, when I lost my lab animals, I needed to hurry the experiment along and, um, I used myself as a subject. I believe this drug has significant effects." She hesitated, thinking how best to put it into words. "GI-80 appears to reverse aging."

Russ did not comment on her last disclosure, saying only, "Call my cell phone in an hour. I don't know what my advice will be at that time. In the meantime, be careful. I don't think you should use your cell phone again."

A few minutes later, Susan merged onto Highway 880. She had no plan and just wanted time to think until she called Russell back. This freeway would work as well as any, or better. It was highly industrial—the least scenic section of roadway in the Bay Area—and used by many trucks. If a passenger car was following her, it might stand out.

Susan reached into her bag and powered down her phone. She wished she could remove the battery but didn't think it was possible with her type of phone. Russell must have been concerned that she could be tracked. Susan knew it was possible to locate a smartphone even when it was turned off. And her Infinity had a navigation system with GPS, which might be used to track her movements.

Too agitated to think and drive safely, she wondered what to do until she could speak to Russ again. The freeway signs were reading Oakland Coliseum, Oakland Arena, and Oakland Airport. She took the airport exit and drove past several hotels and parking lots. Most of the hotels had signs saying Free Airport Shuttle. She thought about leaving her car and taking a shuttle bus to the airport. On second thought, that might not work; she might be asked for a room number or the shuttle might not be leaving immediately. Better to go into one of the remote parking lots and wait there or, better yet, in the airport. She could find a pay phone in the terminal.

Approaching the airport, she saw signs for short-term parking, remote parking, and medium/long-term parking. Susan chose the last option, took a ticket from the parking machine at the entrance, and drove into the lot. Sitting in her car and trying to stay calm, she did not think she had been followed.

She took all the coins she had in the console before getting out. In the trunk, Susan saw the canvas duffel bag with her cosmetics and hair dryer and added two old gym towels. When Russ said it was okay to return to the lab, she could wet her hair in the ladies room, towel it dry, and style it with the blow dryer. She'd need to put on some makeup, too—she didn't want Russ or anyone else who might be there to see her looking unkempt. She wished she had thought to bring a change of clothes. Her sweater looked okay, but not the old jeans she was wearing. Nothing she could do about it now.

Was she forgetting anything? Russ had said not to use her cell phone. Maybe he would tell her not to use her car. Susan looked at her plum-colored leather bag. She didn't want to put it down on the restroom floor while doing her hair and makeup. She transferred the items from the leather bag to the canvas duffel. Wearing her cap and sunglasses, she slung the duffel over her shoulder and walked toward the airport.

Once in the terminal, Susan looked for a pay phone and located two. With nothing else to do, she bought a tuna sandwich and a bottle of a flavored tea drink from a food counter. The tea was so sweet, she was surprised that anyone drank it, and the sandwich tasted like mayonnaise, not tuna. Throwing both items away, she decided to call Russ now, though an hour had not yet passed. She had plenty of coins and could call back later if necessary.

Russ picked up immediately. "I can't talk long. Listen carefully. This is a mess. The Emeryville police must have come shortly after you left. They were already here when I pulled in, but outside in the parking lot. When the police got here, they found a body in the hallway. The victim had been bludgeoned and his neck was slit at the carotid artery. The police believe he was hit with the baseball bat they found near the body, and his throat slit with a surgical scalpel.

"Sometime after the police came, three FBI agents arrived and made them leave the building. That's why they were in the parking lot. Walter got here before I did. He said he'd left his jacket in the lab, or something like that."

Susan heard the words he was saying but was having difficulty following him. She could feel that she was sweating and trembling. And who was Walter? It took a moment before she realized he was referring to Wolf.

"The FBI agents are not interested in speaking with me, at least not yet," Russ continued. "They told me to wait outside. From what I overheard when I was inside the building, Walter told the police that you gave everyone a half-day off and told them to go out to lunch so you could have the place to yourself."

Susan had to speak. "That's not how it happened."

"Just listen. I told you this is a mess. This is not a federal case. I don't know why the FBI is here. They don't have jurisdiction, but they won't even let the Emeryville police in the building. The FBI agents took all the records, computers, and files they found inside. I don't know where they're taking them. They also took all the lab animals."

"The files? The animals? Why would they take the animals?"

"Please, just listen. They identified the man they found dead in the hallway. His name is Gary Keller."

Susan held onto the top of the pay phone for support. Her head was spinning.

"Susan, are you there?"

"Gary? Russ, I…I…was married to Gary, but I haven't seen him in years."

"Listen carefully to me. The FBI agents will not talk to me. I need to find out what is going on. That will take some time. The FBI will undoubtedly want to talk to you. As a member of the bar, I cannot advise a client to hide until I have more information. Even if I thought the best and safest thing to do was to disappear, I could not give that advice. I hope to have more information by the end of the week. Goodbye."

CHAPTER 21

SUSAN STOOD STARING at the telephone receiver. She needed to think but had no idea where to start. Putting her remaining coins in her wallet, she went into the nearest ladies room. The disabled stall was empty so she went in there, locking the door behind her. Leaning against the wall, she began to breathe in and out slowly.

When Bunny had told her what had been taken from her apartment, Susan had realized it had not been a random event. This led her to recall that the supply-closet door had been closed. She had suspected someone might be hiding in there. She had just never expected it to be Gary.

"The large one is taken, honey. We'll have to use this one." The woman was obviously talking to a child. "Yes, we're going on an airplane. We're going to see Grandma and Grandpa. Aren't you excited? Here, let me help you."

Susan heard a child's voice chirp unintelligibly.

David would know what to do next. What would he tell her to do? *Daddy, please help me, I'm so alone.* At that moment, she felt her father's arm around her shoulders. Although she hadn't experienced it in years, the feeling was unmistakable. A feeling of comfort washed over her.

Taking out her cell phone, she powered it up. Where should I go, she thought. Las Vegas? Los Angeles? Susan searched for the flight schedules from Oakland to Los Angeles. Then she did the same for Las Vegas. She put the ring tone on Silent and selected the Do Not Disturb option from the phone settings before leaving the stall.

Leaving her phone on full power, Susan gave it a kiss and slipped it into one of the bags hanging on the back of a stroller loaded with gear just outside the next stall. She washed her hands and then, on her way out, turned back and mouthed the words, "Have a good trip."

She found an ATM and withdrew eight hundred dollars. Then she left the terminal building and got on the shuttle bus to BART.

Susan rode the trains, switching lines and changing direction, with no idea what she should do next. One thing was clear: She had to hide out until Russ had more information for her—three days. She had eight hundred forty dollars and some change. She could not use her credit or debit cards. She probably should have gotten more money at the airport. How much money can you get from an ATM in one day? she wondered.

Other than her cash, she had no resources. Well, that wasn't exactly true. Her mind was an asset. Could she outwit the FBI for three days? She had a chance if she could stay focused. Wasn't that what she was best at?

She wondered if her trick with the cell phone would throw the FBI off. She thought of the mother discovering she had someone's very expensive phone in her stroller. Maybe the authorities would find her before she realized she had it.

She was more worried about another mother. She had told Bunny she would come right over. Bunny was bound to call her soon, and if she couldn't reach her, would worry terribly, especially after the burglary. She should have telephoned her from the airport. Maybe she was not showing as much genius as she thought. If she wanted to stay ahead of the FBI, she'd have to do better.

Was she thinking clearly? Susan certainly had been lucid earlier today. With speed and precision, she had pieced together Dr. Klein's message, the theft at her mother's, and the conduct of the new primates. Susan had realized her new primates were exhibiting behaviors typical of youthful macaques. Although fully mature, Gigi had presented the same way the day before she'd been abducted. A glimpse of her reflection in the bathroom mirror had been all the confirmation Susan needed of GI-80's effects.

Even so, much was still unclear. What was her ex-husband doing in her laboratory? How had he gotten past the security system? Most important, how did he get his throat cut? Could he have been so disoriented from the blow to his head that he got a scalpel from the lab and accidentally slit his own throat? That was implausible. Maybe Gary had killed himself. He could have had a scalpel with him when Susan struck him. Could he have done it to get her in trouble? That did not make sense, either.

There was a third possibility. It had come into her consciousness at the airport, although it was something she did not want to consider at all. Most strongly efficacious drugs have psychotropic as well as physical effects. Could she be delusional? Was her memory affected by the antibodies? Was it possible that she had not only hit Gary but gotten a scalpel and brought it back to kill him and, because of the GI-80, had no recollection of it?

She pulled her cap down a little lower over her eyes. The hat was starting to annoy her, but, realizing it might make it harder for someone to recognize or remember her, she left it on. She did not think she had used the scalpel on Gary. She had not gotten a good look at the intruder. If she had been close enough to cut his throat, she was sure she would have recognized Gary, or at least been sure it was a man. And if she had cut his carotid artery, blood would have spurted out. Susan looked down at her sweater and pants. They were clean, and there'd been no blood on her hands when she was attempting to eat that sandwich. While she was relieved this third explanation was also improbable, it meant she had no idea what could have happened to Gary. Even more frightening, she had no idea who could have killed him, or why.

CHAPTER 22

By now, Susan had taken BART and doubled back toward Berkeley. Exiting the station at El Cerrito, she walked to the shopping plaza across the street. The Long's Drugs she remembered was now a CVS. Taking a shopping tote, she looked for the sharpest scissors she could find, then picked up a pair of rubber flip-flops, a disposable razor, a toothbrush, and a tube of toothpaste, and headed to the hair-care section.

She wanted a shampoo-in hair color that would not wash out, and it took her awhile to locate the right product line, then find the color she wanted, semi-permanent chocolate brown hair dye with highlights. As she stood in line at the checkout counter, Susan read the instructions. According to the label, everything she needed for a professional-looking job was in the box, even disposable gloves. She could use the product with or without the highlights, and could highlight as much hair as she wanted. If she wasn't happy with the results, her money would be refunded.

It took her awhile to walk over to the Willard Pool. When she'd finally had a chance to think on the BART train, Susan had attempted to devise a plan. She could not go home for a few days, which made her essentially homeless. That prompted her to remember an article she had read about homeless programs in the Bay Area. In the article it mentioned that some cities allowed indigent people to use the facilities at public pools. A month or two later,

Susan had happened to drive past Berkeley's Willard Pool, not far from the UC campus, and recalled it was part of the city's Shower Program. Now she knew exactly where to go to become a chocolate brown brunette, with or without highlights.

After paying four dollars to use the pool and the showers, Susan went into the locker room. The showers were in individual stalls, with a private changing area and bench seat adjacent to each shower. This was going to be very convenient. Susan glanced at the wall clock, went into the stall, and pushed the sliding lock closed. She was glad she had brought her gym towels with her; otherwise, she would have had to use new towels without washing them first. Susan had to laugh at herself when she remembered that she had bigger problems than towels with potentially high bacteria counts.

It felt strange to be without a cell phone. Without it, Susan had to poke her head out twice while coloring her hair to check the time. When she went to the mirrored area to dry it and put on some makeup, she took a good look at herself. Though she knew her appearance had changed, she was unprepared for what she saw.

Looking back at her was the face of a young woman. Susan tried to estimate how old she appeared—thirty, twenty-seven, possibly even younger. She was so astonished, she found it hard to maintain her gaze.

The blow dryer attached to the wall was not very powerful, nor did it stay hot. It was fortunate that she'd brought her own hair dryer with her; staying here long enough to air-dry her hair might not be safe, and walking around town with wet hair could attract attention.

Rather than look at her face any longer, Susan focused on her hair. The medium blond she'd been was popular with older women because it was attractive with fading skin tones. Now that her hair was dark brown with lighter brown highlights, Susan saw she would need to darken her eyebrows to go with this new color. As she dried her hair, she could see that she'd gotten excellent coverage with the boxed product. She could not see any areas that she'd missed.

Looking more closely, she thought her hair might be growing in thicker at the temples. She wondered if anyone could recognize her now. Her mother would. Rosa might. Russ wouldn't. Gary no longer could recognize anybody.

When her mind turned to her former husband, Susan put down the hair dryer as the reality of his death hit her. She tried to connect with her feelings. She certainly was stunned and shocked by his death, especially by the circumstances. Other than that, she was surprised to find, she felt no emotion. She didn't care at all that Gary was dead. She wondered what that said about her but had no time to think about it now.

Another question came to her: *If my face looks like this, what about my body?*

Susan had a scientifically educated and trained mind. She desperately wanted to systematically document and record these changes. She would have to make time for systematic observation and then, until it was safe to write anything down, commit as much information to memory as she could.

Leaning close to the mirror, Susan started applying eye makeup. Immediately, she noted the lack of lines around her eyes, and the surrounding tissue showed no sign of age. Turning her face to the side, she noticed that both her neck and chin were firm. She didn't see any sagging or noticeably loose skin.

It would be hard for someone who didn't know her well to recognize her, that was for sure. Susan looked at her reflection again. She had no choice but to see this through to the end, whatever that would be. Putting her cap and sunglasses on, she picked up the canvas duffel with her meager possessions and left Willard Pool.

CHAPTER 23

SUSAN CAUGHT THE public bus to the Berkeley BART station and rode the train into San Francisco. When she got to the city, the first thing she did was to throw away the plastic bag with the hair dye box and empty bottles. She ripped up her sales receipt and threw the pieces into another trash bin. At a third trash container, she threw away the towel she had used to dry her hair.

Walking down Market Street to the San Francisco Centre, a large indoor mall, she was well aware that none of her education or scientific training could help her. What Susan needed to do now was to find out the latest fashion trends. Looking so young, she had to dress the part. Her plan was to walk around the shopping area, perhaps get something to eat, and look at the young women. They would be wearing clothing appropriate for someone who looked her age, whatever that was.

Right near the door were two young women perched on high director-style chairs. Their eyes were closed and they had dark rings under their eyes, their eyebrows painted with thick black paint. The sign above them read The Beauty Bar. An unusually pretty young girl approached Susan and handed her a card, saying, "We're having a special on tinting today. Would you like to have your brows and lashes done?"

Curious to learn if this might help her achieve a trendy appearance, Susan approached the counter. The pretty girl explained that the two women were having their eyebrows and eyelashes tinted. "If you purchase an eyelash and eyebrow tint," she went on, "you can have your eyebrows waxed at no extra cost. This is your lucky day," she added. "It's a one-day special, and it has never been offered the entire time I've worked at this counter." Considering all that's happened, Susan thought, this must be my luckiest unlucky day.

"How long does the tint last?" she asked. She didn't know how long she would have to have her hair so dark. She might leave it dark for a while before going back to her own color, whatever that was now. Marla had told her that some of her hair was re-pigmenting. She wondered if it would revert to the ash brown she had been in her youth.

The girl explained that the tints last until the hair fell out, which was at least a month. Susan removed her sunglasses and sat in the chair farthest from the door to the street.

Another attractive young woman approached and spread wax on her eyebrows. Putting the warm wax on and peeling it off with a piece of gauze took only a few minutes. Then the girl put some cream under Susan's eyes. She could feel the girl spreading the dye on her eyelashes and eyebrows. As she sat there with her eyes closed, Susan thought that the last place anyone would look for her would be at a cosmetics counter, getting her lashes and brows tinted.

After about twenty minutes, the girl wiped Susan's face clean and handed her a mirror. "What do you think?"

It had been difficult enough to look at her reflection when alone at Willard Pool. The girl must have been surprised by the look on Susan's face.

"Don't you like it?" she asked. "You look beautiful."

Susan tried to look at only her eyes and eyebrows. They did look good—her brows were nicely shaped and her eyelashes looked long, thick, and dark.

"Thank you so much. You did a beautiful job." Susan stood up and reached for her wallet, then had another idea. "I see you sell cosmetics. Could you show me what I should be wearing? I think

I need to update my look." As these words came out of her mouth, she thought of her mother.

The young woman beamed. Her response confirmed that either she was pleased that Susan liked her work or that she was working on commission. Asking her to remain on the chair, she proceeded to apply cosmetics to Susan's face, telling her the order in which each was to be applied and adding some tips to improve the effect.

"I am applying a very light spray-on foundation. You can use powder with it or not. That's your choice. I like to use powder in the evening when I go out," she rattled on.

When she was finished, she handed Susan the mirror again, saying, "I gave you a more natural look than I give most of my clients. You are so pretty, you really don't need very much. This look will work for day or evening."

Susan was unprepared for what she saw. Looking back at her was a striking and very young brunette with beautiful hazel eyes. The dark brows and lashes made her eyes the most prominent feature of her face. Her naturally fair skin looked even lighter. Even her amateur dye job was flattering. Somehow Susan had managed to put highlights in the right places. At least in the department store lighting, her hair color looked natural, with a lot of color variation.

The cosmetic colors the girl had selected for her were perfect; the hint of blush on her cheeks could not have been better. The pretty girl must have agreed with Susan's assessment, as she stood next to her smiling, admiring her handiwork.

"Thank you so much. I really do appreciate it. You did a beautiful job. I think I should purchase all of the products." The young woman told Susan her name was Brittany and gave her a card with her work schedule. Susan paid and gave Brittany a ten-dollar tip. She would have liked to give her more but calculated that ten dollars was neither too much nor too little to be memorable.

Susan thought about asking Brittany if she could pay her to look at clothing with her when she had a break, but even asking the question would be risky. Brittany was certain to remember her then, and she'd know what clothes Susan was wearing.

Once out of sight of The Beauty Bar, Susan put her cap back on and walked around the mall, studying the young women and trying to determine the unifying features of their outfits. The girls wore boots, athletic shoes, or flats with round toes and puckered backs. She saw no other types of shoes, and none of the more fashionable girls wore athletic shoes. If they wore pants, they reached only to the ankle and were tailored to fit quite narrowly. When Susan was in grade school, they called these peg-leg pants. All the skirts she saw were very short and made of stretchy material. The dresses were short as well, either tightly fitted or very loose. Some of the girls wore these skirts and dresses over leggings or the fitted pants.

Susan tried to understand the aesthetics of the jewelry and accessories they wore. There was too much variation to find a trend in the jewelry, but many of the young girls wore long oblong scarves, sometimes in multiples, twisted around their necks.

With the style survey complete, it was time to find the right store. Susan looked in a few store windows, then went to the entrance of one that seemed promising to peek at the customers inside. One look confirmed that she'd found a suitable store. It carried both male and female clothing and the shoppers had the look she aspired to.

Selecting items from the racks, Susan found it was easy to find an outfit. The clothing was either made of stretchy material or designed to fit loosely. She selected a variety of garments as well as some panties and bras and went into a fitting room, though it was likely anything she selected was going to fit.

Taking off her cap, Susan shook out her hair and began removing her sweater, pants, T-shirt, bra, and panties. It had been hard enough looking at her face in a mirror, but that discomfort paled in comparison to what she felt now. The body in the mirror was one she had not seen in a very long time. She tried to remain calm and observant—she was, after all, the subject of an experiment. Every detail was relevant. She would commit them to memory until she could write them down.

Forcing herself to study her body, Susan searched for details that would confirm her physical age. Peering at herself straight on, she was sure that she had not looked this way for at least twenty years. Her stomach was flat. Her midriff was thin and taut, and her waist was narrow. Her thighs were firm; her knees showed no signs of age. The veins in her feet were not protruding, and the veins in her legs were not noticeable, either.

Even with all that, she was unprepared for what she saw next. The dressing room had a three-part mirror; if she stood in the right spot, she could see the back of her body—and from the back, she looked like a young girl. Stunned, Susan closed her eyes. She needed to focus. She needed to think like the fifty-three-year-old scientist she was.

Opening her eyes, she looked in the angled mirror again. She calculated that she looked twenty-five years younger. Susan could not refine her estimate for a closer approximation of the age her body appeared to be.

She had no idea how long this reversal would last. Could it be a permanent condition? Would additional doses of GI-80 be required to maintain the effect? If she could get into her laboratory, she could start investigating the biochemical process that had taken place. But she was stuck in a shopping mall, trying on clothes. Figuring out fashion trends was the last thing she was interested in; but finding the right clothing was an important part of what she had to do, and she would give it her very best effort.

Susan hastily tried on the bras and panties she had brought into the dressing room. They looked like the type of things a young woman would wear. She selected a white lace bra with very thin straps and cups that left more breast tissue exposed than the bras she was used to. One pair of bikini panties had a narrow string on each side to hold them together and seemed to match the material in the bra.

With the white lingerie set on, Susan forced herself to look in the mirrors again. "Mama mia," she said aloud. Looking at her rear in the skimpy panties, Susan concluded that it was possible she could have regressed in physical age as much as thirty years.

Susan began wondering if the effects of GI-80 were entirely cosmetic or if it had regenerative effects on other organs. She needed to know what her vitals were. She wondered if she could find a way to test her reaction times. If she could get to a computer, she was sure she could find some baseline data she could use for comparison. Moreover, she still had lingering concerns about possible mental effects.

"Damn it," she muttered. She needed to research and record her findings, not stand in a dressing room trying on underwear. She'd spent more than enough time looking at lingerie. Forcing herself to focus on the remaining task at hand, Susan tried on each of the clothing items in different combinations. To take this task seriously, she reminded herself that she was not shopping for clothing; she was shopping for a disguise. The better she did, the better she would be able to fit in.

She put on a pair of black knit pants that looked like leggings and were ruched at the calf and selected a loose cobalt blue dress, made of a shiny material and coming to just above her knees, to wear over them. She also decided on a cream-colored knit shirt. Finally, she chose a couple of sweaters that would go with the dress and pants. One was a pullover in charcoal gray only a couple of inches shorter than the dress. The other was a thick natural-colored wool cardigan. Susan checked the tags to make sure everything was washable and would dry easily. She would not have a lot of clothing for the next few days.

In the shoe section, she found the kind of black leather flats with a stretchy, crumpled back that she had seen girls wearing. One pair, with a gold medallion over the toe, was made of soft leather and looked comfortable. At a nearby table laden with accessories, she picked up two long muffler scarves: one a dark but bright, almost emerald green, and the other a deep purple. Holding them against the dress, she thought the colors went together well enough. She did not want to spend any more time selecting clothing.

Two attractive young people, a male and a female, were working at the counter. Susan wondered if these stores selected staff members on the basis of their looks. Judging from the two standing there, she concluded that they did. She remembered how she had hesitated to hire Jess because of her good looks. Smiling slightly, she thought that they would probably love to have Jess working here and wearing their clothing.

Next to the cash register was a small rack of clear glasses. Susan tried a pair on and found they had no vision correction. The girl who was ringing up her clothes—her name tag read Morgan—looked at her and commented, "You should get them. They're not expensive, and they look good on you. I have a pair and I wear them all the time."

Morgan wasn't wearing them now, so clearly, she didn't wear them all the time. The young man's tag said his name was Ross. Ross looked Susan in the eyes and said, "I think they look killer."

"Killer, that's me. I'll take them," Susan said, wondering if the world was always so filled with irony or if she was just noticing it now. Maybe this awareness was a mental effect of the GI-80. She did not find this thought the least bit reassuring.

Ross handed Susan her sales receipt and a fancy paper tote bag with her purchases. As he did, he said, "We're taking applications for sales associates. Do you think you'd like to work here? The employee discount is…."

Susan interrupted him. "Killer?"

Ross laughed, showing his perfect white teeth. "Yeah, killer."

Susan said she would keep it in mind, thanked them, and went out into the mall. At the directory in the middle of the aisle, scanning the floor plans for the nearest ladies room, she noticed that she was catching the interest of some young men as they passed. Then, going by a curved-glass storefront, she stopped.

CHAPTER 24

SITTING ON A stool was a girl with the oddest hair. On one side of her head, her blond hair hung down her back, reaching almost to her waist. On the other side, her hair was cropped just below the shoulder. Another young woman was attaching long strands of hair to her head.

When Susan moved closer, the girl doing the work, noticing her interest, began explaining what she was doing. These were hair extensions that clipped right into your own hair, she said. The girl told Susan how easy they were to insert, how natural they looked, and how many different styles you could create with them. Although they were top quality, she added, they were not expensive. The salesgirl could put some in her hair when she finished with this customer; if Susan didn't like them, she would take them out and there would be no obligation to purchase anything.

By this time, the girl on the stool had long hair on both sides of her head and was gazing admiringly at her reflection. After she paid and left, Susan sat down on the stool. "I don't want my hair to be as long as that girl's. It looked nice on her, but it is not right for me."

"That's fine. The shorter extensions are less expensive. Your hair is thicker than hers, so it will be easier to blend the extensions in. It's going to look terrific. I think we should use this color," the salesgirl said, showing Susan a length of dark brown hair.

Starting to feel anxious, Susan wondered if this was a good idea after all. Maybe she should keep moving rather than stay in one place so long. Was she wasting her time and limited cash on something that would not be useful or easy to put on? She decided to sit for a few more minutes and then say she didn't want to try the extensions after all and leave.

The girl continued, "It's terrific that you have highlights. They'll help blend in the extensions." Working quickly, she instructed Susan in what she was doing. "Don't worry if you can't remember. I'll give you some information on how to put them in and how to take care of them." She had her sales pitch down, and after only a few minutes, she handed Susan a mirror. "Here, look at the front. You can stand up and use that mirror to see the back."

The last thing Susan wanted to do was to look in any more mirrors today. Maybe she should just have the girl take them out so she could leave. She had a pair of scissors; she could try to cut her hair into some short style. The problem with that was that she had not seen many girls at the mall with short hair. Her observations today confirmed that her current hairstyle was exceedingly unfashionable. Unless she wore her cap constantly, her outdated hairdo could attract attention.

Forcing herself to look at her reflection, Susan raised the mirror. She did not even recognize herself. Framed now with long, dark hair, the face she saw reminded her of a baby doll: eyes made up to look large and deep-set; creamy, even skin tone; shiny sheer lips. She was sure that she had never in her life looked anything like this.

Susan paid for the hair extensions and thanked the salesgirl. No one seemed to be following her. Now if she could just get to the ladies room. A fancy specialty store would be the best place to change, she assumed, since it was likely to have oversize restroom stalls. When she located one, she saw she had been correct. The restroom had a lounge area with couches and chairs upholstered in striped fabric, with fringe along the bottom in the same two shades. The toilet and sink area, too, was luxuriously decorated in marble and luxe wallpaper. The stalls were roomy and had good locks.

Susan went to the stall farthest from the door, took off all her clothing, and folded each piece, setting them down on the pull-down shelf designed to hold packages. She removed the sales tags from everything she'd just purchased and cut them into small pieces, then she searched through each garment for sensor tags. That done, she put on a new outfit and her new shoes. She twisted the two scarves together and wrapped them around her neck and slipped on her new glasses.

She put the extra clothing, the new white bra and matching panties, and the cream shirt in her canvas bag. Then she placed her old clothing and her athletic shoes in the fancy shopping bag. She took the cap that she'd worn since she left home that morning and put it in the store bag as well. Exiting the stall, she threw all the scraps of price tags and the sensors in the wastebasket and washed her hands, keeping her eyes down. By the door, however, was a full-length, gilt-framed mirror, and Susan could not avoid looking at herself as she crossed the lounge.

How could that girl be her? Susan was sure that if Bunny had been sitting on the striped couch, she would not have recognized her daughter. Susan stopped and considered her image. *Who is this person and how long before I can be my real self?*

Chapter 25

Just before she went into the BART station, Susan saw a homeless woman sitting on the sidewalk. She was unkempt but not very old. Seated next to her was a mixed-breed dog who was so gray, it was impossible to tell what its original color had been. Given how old he was, the dog was likely to be arthritic. Susan handed the woman the shopping bag with her used clothing, shoes, and cap, then took the remaining towel out of her canvas bag.

"Here's a towel you can use for your dog. Maybe he can sit on it instead of on the ground."

Susan wanted to give her some cash but did not want to pull out her wallet, since she had so many bills in it. When she went through the ticket gate, Susan looked back and saw her rummaging through the bag. Seeing this, Susan regretted not giving the woman any money. She had never given money to homeless people, assuming there were services available to them.

Taking the train back under San Francisco Bay, Susan got off at the Berkeley station with a notion of where she might spend the night. It was a ten-block walk. She hurried along, avoiding eye contact with the people she passed and having no idea if anyone noticed her. At the end of every block, she looked behind her to see if she was being followed.

Susan had never attended the University of California at Berkeley. She had gone to the Massachusetts Institute of Technology for her undergraduate studies and done her graduate and doctoral work in a joint Harvard-M.I.T. program. Though her lab was close to the campus and her staffers were often students or graduates, she'd had no direct contact with the institution, with one exception.

Well over fifteen years ago, Susan had attended a seminar at the Faculty Club, on the Berkeley campus. A few scientists had come from China to meet with members of the faculty, and the university had invited members of the local biotechnology community to attend. Susan had been working for Avery Biogenetics then, and for some reason that was never made clear to her, the general manager of ABC had asked her to represent the company. She had attended hundreds of conferences and seminars over the years, and that particular event stayed in her mind only because it had been so incredibly boring—a complete waste of time, or so she'd thought until today.

The seminar had offered no meaningful ideas, only a lot of posturing by both the Berkeley professors and the Chinese scientists. When the Chinese spoke, Susan had difficulty understanding them. However, when she was changing her clothing in the restroom, Susan had recalled that the Chinese delegation had stayed at the Faculty Club.

Susan realized that if asked to show identification, she didn't have any with her. Using a credit card was not an option. But, thinking she might not stand out on a college campus and that the Faculty Club might take cash, she had headed toward Berkeley. She hoped the club still rented rooms and that one would be available. If not, someone there might know of someplace she could stay.

It was a little before ten p.m. now. If she had arrived much later, she doubted that anyone would have been at the front desk.

"Hi. Do you have any rooms available tonight?" Susan asked the young man behind the desk. He had a textbook open and was highlighting sections with a yellow marker.

He looked up, and Susan saw his eyes widen when he looked

at her. He smiled. "I think we do have a room. How long are you staying?"

"I'd like to stay for three nights if possible," Susan replied. "I'd like your least expensive room."

Three nights would take her to Friday, when she was supposed to contact Russell. After she talked to him, she hoped, she could go back to her real life. By Friday, surely the police would know who had killed Gary and why he had been in her lab.

It was hard to believe that it was still Tuesday. She had run out the door of Glass Biotech only seven or eight hours ago. It felt as if weeks had passed. Susan wondered if this was normal under the circumstances or a mental effect of the GI-80. The thought struck her as humorous. How was anything that had happened to her lately normal? *Normal* was no longer any part of her reality. She was standing in the Berkeley Faculty Club at ten at night with some young student making eyes at her. How was that normal?

"We do have a room for you. If you would, please fill out this form." He handed Susan a pen and a registration form. "Brittany, is it? What a pretty name."

"Glad you like it. I always have," Susan replied with a big smile.

That must have struck the young desk clerk as funny, since he gave a big laugh. "I'm Justin, by the way," he told her. "If your parents are members of the Faculty Club, I can give you a discount. Oh, I'll need a credit card."

"Justin, I was planning to pay cash. I won't have my credit card for a couple of days. I lost it. My, um, parents said they would get me a new one but it would take two days. They're both alumni. I never thought to ask if they were members of the Faculty Club." Susan wanted to flirt a little with Justin to try to get the discount, but she wasn't sure she could do it properly. Maybe it was better to play it straight.

"Okay. You can pay cash now, and when you get your credit card, be sure to show it to whoever is at the desk then. I probably won't be working again while you're here. Are you going to pay for all three nights in cash?"

Justin took the money for three nights and explained that breakfast was included with the room. Down the hall was a small business center with a computer and printer that she could use. Local calls from the telephones in the rooms were free of charge.

He handed her a room key and a paper with the breakfast times. "And here's the log-in for Air Bears. You can use this code to access the Wi-Fi anywhere on campus; you're signed in for a guest account. There are also hot spots around the campus. I'd be glad to show you some of them."

Wondering if he realized how ridiculous this sounded, Susan just smiled at him.

"If there's anything else you need, just let me know."

Susan thanked him, anxious to get to her room. She didn't think she'd need anything more, at least not from him. The campus had plenty of Justins, and from this experience, it seemed likely a lot of them would be happy to help Brittany Ross.

CHAPTER 26

THE FIRST THING she did was to remove her hair extensions. They were surprisingly easy to unclip. Susan tried to pay attention to where they were positioned so she could duplicate the placement the next day, carefully placing them on top of the dresser in the exact order they had been on her head.

Using the soap in the bathroom, she rinsed out her undergarments. When she got out of the shower, she got in bed and reached for the television remote. Maybe she could get the local news and hear a report about Gary's murder. On second thought, whatever she heard would surely upset her. It would be better to get a newspaper and read about it, or go to the business center and see what she could find on the Internet.

Anxious and frightened, she was unable to sleep. Telling herself that rest was almost as good for her as sleep, she tried to lie as still as possible, listening for footsteps or other sounds that might suggest people were coming to get her. Lying awake in the dark, she realized she had concerns about Russell Harris. What if he was involved in all of this? That seemed unlikely but not impossible. But if he was working with the FBI, wouldn't he have told her to come back to the laboratory?

What if Russell wanted her to be in more trouble than she already was? Could he have suggested she hide so that she'd look guilty? She had believed Russell was a decent person; their time together on Saturday night seemed to confirm this. But maybe taking her out was part of a plan to get her to trust him. No, he couldn't have known what was going on before today. Susan herself didn't know until about nine hours ago, when she started to piece things together at the lab. Her attorney was trying to help her.

Before all this had happened, Susan had been planning to find another attorney for her business. Now so much more was going on, and a short stint in a district attorney's office didn't qualify him for criminal defense work, so Russell wasn't the best person to be advising her. Still, what choice did she have? She could find a telephone book and phone a more qualified lawyer. But how would she know she was calling a good one? She should have done this earlier today, before everyone left their offices.

She could look for a criminal defense lawyer tomorrow—that is, unless they found her tonight. How would they do that? Two hours ago, Susan didn't know she would be here at the Faculty Club. And high-powered lawyers were very expensive. Her home was already mortgaged and she had no liquid assets. Maybe it was best to wait. In the meantime, she would trust Russ. She could only hope she was making the right decision.

When morning came, Susan was surprised that she had been able to sleep at all. She would have breakfast and, if she felt safe enough, go out, hoping the maid would be finished cleaning her room by the time she returned.

It took her quite a while to dress. The hair extensions were easy to clip into her hair, but it took a few attempts to get each piece in the right place and adjust her hair around it. That done, she put on her makeup following the instructions the real Brittany had given her. Wearing her fake glasses and the outfit she'd worn the night before, she proceeded downstairs.

The Faculty Club did not appear to have changed at all. The breakfast room was the same paneled space, with beautiful wood-cased windows that looked original. The glass was obviously old, with imperfections that distorted the view. At the top of the clear windows was a series of stained-glass panes decorated with crests.

Susan looked around carefully before getting a cup of coffee, a bagel, and a piece of fruit. The two other diners did not appear to notice her. Seeing a pile of newspapers, she took one to a table at the back of the room.

Body Found in Emeryville Laboratory

EMERYVILLE, Calif. – Police are investigating what they're calling a suspicious death after a body was found yesterday at a laboratory near Powell and Hollis Streets. The body was discovered when officers responded to an activated alarm at approximately 2:30 p.m. The manner and time of death have yet to be determined. Authorities have not released the identity of the deceased.

Susan was disappointed that there were so few details. She got up and took another newspaper. This article had an unflattering picture of her taken two years ago.

Ex-Wife Identified as "Person of Interest" in Laboratory Death

EMERYVILLE, Calif. – Law enforcement officials today named a "person of interest" in the possible homicide at Glass Biotechnology Company. The woman is identified as Susan Glasser, 53, the owner of the laboratory.

Yesterday police discovered the body of Gary Keller, 55, at the business when called to the scene by an activated alarm. Glasser and Keller divorced in 2000. Keller was a partner in the investment firm Keller, Duggan and Weaver, which dissolved in 2001.

According to the Glass Biotechnology website, Glasser earned a joint PhD in biology and chemistry at Harvard and MIT. Investigators are looking for Susan Glasser. If you have any information, call the Emeryville Police Department.

No mention was made of the FBI's involvement or the cause of death, and there was something about the articles that did not seem right. Surprised she had any appetite, Susan finished her food but was still hungry. She had lost weight spontaneously since taking the GI-80. Was the weight loss a result of the stress she'd been under and the additional anxiety of the last few weeks, or could she really have the metabolism of a twenty-seven-year-old? She was a walking experiment and had to find a way to collect and analyze her biometrics.

Once again, she wished she had access to a lab, where she could do some real analysis and get some hard data. All she had now was self-reporting, the weakest possible source of information.

Maybe it would be possible to do some lab testing. After all, she was at one of the greatest scientific research centers in academia. No, she was at the greatest scientific research center in the world.

She went up to her room to leave her sweater before going out. The housekeeper had already made the bed and left fresh towels, so she could stay longer.

Russell was right—the FBI coming to a common crime scene did not make sense, especially when the men had arrived at her lab so quickly. Why had the newspapers made no mention of them or of the cause of death? Wouldn't this be the first thing a reporter would want to know?

Hadn't Russ said that Wolf was there? Surely a reporter would have tried to talk to her staff. Why was there no mention of Wolf or of anyone else? Her lab workers were all local and may have even come to the Glass Biotech building when they'd heard what had happened. If someone had talked to Wolf, he or she could have gotten the names of the others. Why weren't they quoted in any of the articles? The news items were too brief, nondescript; too much was left out. This was a murder. Crimes sell papers. No reporter would voluntarily write an article with so little detail.

And it was odd that neither paper had said what kind of research Glass Biotechnology did. Certainly, any reporter would have included this; it might be relevant to the crime. Just last month, she had spoken about their research at a conference in San Francisco. Tech reporters had been at the conference, and she had been the keynote speaker, for heaven's sake. The speech she had delivered was probably on YouTube. Why would a reporter leave out this information?

Susan wished she could talk to Russell about this. Would he figure it out himself? It didn't matter if Russell was smart enough or not—at the moment, he was all she had. *No. Scratch that thought. I have myself. I have to figure this out myself and come up with a plan to stay hidden for three days.*

Susan didn't believe anyone could identify her from the picture in the paper. Even if the police or the FBI found her, she might be able to convince them they were mistaken. What did she have with her that could tie her to Susan Glasser? She had carried her canvas bag into the airport and could have been picked up by the surveillance cameras. She would have to get rid of it and find something else to carry around with her. Was there anything else? She could not afford to overlook anything.

Susan sat at the desk and spread out the contents of her bag, methodically going through each item. When she came to her wallet, she remembered that she had taken it out at the airport when she'd bought food. She began cutting her driver's license and credit cards into small pieces. Once she finished, the only things left were her keys and Brittany's card from The Beauty Bar, which she cut up as well.

She put the canvas tote, her wallet, and the cut-up cards in the shopping bag that her cosmetics had come in. With no tote bag or wallet, Susan put her money, keys, and sunglasses into her pockets and left the Faculty Club, exiting by the back stairs so as not to pass the front desk. As she walked out, she wondered if she would need to dispose of her sunglasses as well.

Once on campus, Susan headed toward the main plaza. It was filled with students and tables set up by about two dozen groups. Susan stopped close to one promoting animal rights. Hoping to hear something about FAN or other radical groups, she pretended to look at the literature on the adjacent table as the girl manning the animal rights table tried to talk a student into attending a meeting. Hearing nothing of interest, she moved on.

Signs indicated that she was close to the student union. In the student store, she purchased a tote bag with the university logo, an inexpensive canvas wallet, a pair of sunglasses, a notebook, and a pen. Heading down Telegraph Avenue, she started throwing the cut-up cards, a few pieces at a time, into the trash cans she passed. Street merchants selling items from tables lined several blocks, and the avenue was crowded with an interesting array of people. The weather was warm and the atmosphere festive. Susan began feeling more relaxed.

Just as she reached the last of the street merchants, she saw two police officers walking toward her.

Chapter 27

Each policeman was holding a piece of paper, and as they walked, they looked carefully at the people they passed. In her gut, Susan knew they were looking for her. Her first impulse was to turn around and run, but the sidewalk was packed with people. There was no way she could move quickly through the crowd. She wanted to cross the street but was in the middle of the block, and Berkeley was notoriously tough on jaywalkers. Getting stopped by the police for that was the last thing she wanted.

They were only five or six feet away now. Susan could see them looking down at the papers they held and back up at the nearest people. In a few moments, they would be looking at her. With no place to hide, she turned abruptly. She wanted to reverse her direction and walk away from them, but the avenue was so densely populated, she bumped into a table. She was wedged between the crowd of pedestrians and the display. Overwhelmed with anxiety, she felt ready to faint and leaned on the table to steady herself. As she did, her long hair extensions fell forward, covering the sides of her face.

"How much is this one?" she asked.

Her hands were shaking so violently, the seller had no idea which item she was indicating. The police officers would be just a few feet from her. She was panting from nerves and fear.

"Can you tell me about these?" She tried to focus on the

merchandise. By now, the officers were likely just behind her. She felt someone's arm brush against her back.

Hearing her trembling voice, the street vendor looked up at her. His pale eyes had a blank look. "Uh, those are earrings."

Forcing herself to look at his wares, Susan noticed for the first time that he was selling jewelry. *Think about the jewelry. Ask about the jewelry.* She could barely stand up. She had to lean on his table for support.

"Are they silver?"

The vendor was looking at her quizzically. "Yes. Do you want to try them on?"

Susan could only reply with a nod. The man pointed to a mirror on a post. Both officers were directly behind her; she could see the face of one of them in the glass. Not wanting her face reflected in the mirror, she looked down immediately. She was panting from anxiety.

The street merchant was staring at her. Susan moved to the side and stared back. He was not much older than she was, with long gray hair pulled back into a ponytail. *Think about the jewelry. Ask about the jewelry.* "Are these handmade?"

Still looking at her intently, the man explained that he made all the items himself. Glancing over her shoulder, Susan saw the police officers' backs as they walked down the avenue away from her. She held one of the earrings up to her ear. It was teardrop-shaped and two inches long. These earrings had saved her; she had to buy them. She paid the old hippie for the jewelry and, once he cleaned them with an alcohol wipe, put them on. After taking one more look in the mirror, she crossed the street at the corner and headed back toward the campus. As she walked, the earrings swayed. She'd never owned jewelry this flashy, but she was pleased to have these. If she believed in luck, these earrings would make first-rate amulets.

Confident she was not being followed, she stopped at the next trash can and threw out her duffel bag, wallet, and sunglasses. Other than her keys, she had no possessions left to tie her to Susan Glasser.

If necessary, she could find a place to hide her keys and retrieve them later.

Back on the main campus, she saw a large number of students exiting a building, signaling that classes had just ended. Thinking it might not be wise to return to the guest house yet, Susan thought she might sit in on a class. A big lecture room would be the safest. She selected a hall on the main floor and slouched down in a seat at the back of the room close to the door. Taking out her notebook and pen, she wondered if she actually did look like a college student.

As she waited for the class to begin, a young girl in a Cal T-shirt went up to the front of the room and announced in an overly animated tone, "Hey y'all, we're having a dance-a-thon this Saturday. Be sure to bring your friends and come on out. It'll be a lot of fun."

A notice taped to the back of the seat in front of her advertised class notes for many classes, available at great prices. Susan had no need for class notes and no friends to go with her to a dance-a-thon.

To her surprise, the scheduled class was about "Drugs and the Brain." Maybe she would learn something useful. Unfortunately, the day's topic was caffeine, chocolate, and nicotine and their effects on the central nervous system. The lecturer was engaging and his presentation entertaining, but none of the material was new to her or relevant to her circumstances.

As she walked to the door, two young men came over to her. "Hey, I haven't seen you here before," said one.

Susan felt her anxiety escalating. "Is this the first time you've come to class?" he continued, smiling eagerly at her. Recognizing his buddy's shy grin, she relaxed. She remembered that look from college mixers years ago. Would these kids even know what a mixer was? She did not have a story to explain why she was on campus or at that particular class. She wracked her brains thinking how Brittany Ross would reply, but the best she could do on such short notice was to smile back. She was finally able to respond, "I'm flattered that you noticed."

This response was likely not what a student would typically

reply, but it seemed all the encouragement needed. The boy proceeded to introduce himself and his shy friend. They were Steven and Jeff. Steven asked if she wanted to go for coffee or get something to eat and talk about the class. Susan glanced around and didn't see anyone looking at her. Then again, she hadn't seen these two fellows watching her. Nodding her head, she agreed to go.

The three walked to a restaurant across the street from the campus. Both boys were surprised she had never eaten at the place before and told her she had to have the soup, as it was the best in Berkeley. Jeff left to save a table while Susan and Steven went to the counter to order. Steven ordered chili, sandwiches, and drinks for himself and Jeff. Susan ordered a bowl of soup as well as a sandwich and a drink. Steven insisted on paying for her food. He had a card the cashier stamped when he paid, he explained, and after ten items, he got a free burger or bowl of soup. Susan planned to find out if other places had this type of program. If she went out on her own, she didn't want to be the only person not getting a card stamped.

The soup, as promised, was tasty, and the sandwiches were enormous and equally good. Susan tried to tell the boys as little about herself as possible, encouraging them to talk about themselves and student life. The more she knew, the easier it would be to fit in over the next two days.

Both boys seemed to be trying hard to make a good impression on her. She asked them about the lecture and what they thought of points the instructor had made, listening carefully to the adjectives they used to describe things they liked. Susan asked about other classes or professors that they did not like. Happy to talk about bad classes and unpopular instructors in detail, the two did not disappoint.

Steven and Jeff were fraternity brothers. Their house, Zeta Kappa Pi, was having a small party on Friday night and a bigger party and barbeque on Saturday. Susan thanked them for the invitations and the delicious meal. She'd had a wonderful time with them, she said, but was behind in her reading. Normally, she would have said *work*. She loved parties, though, and would try to come if she could catch up.

Although nothing she said was the least bit true, her reply seemed to satisfy them. Steven wrote down their names and cell phone numbers for her. They walked two blocks up the street with her before saying goodbye and that they hoped they would see her at the parties.

Once they were out of sight, Susan took a circuitous route to the Faculty Club, looking back at each turn. An Asian girl was seated at the front desk; like Justin, she had her head in a textbook. She did not look up when Susan walked by her and into the business center.

The room was unoccupied, probably because most guests had their own devices. In the room were two computers and a printer. Susan clicked on the icon to connect to the Internet and got on immediately; apparently, she didn't need to use a code to connect from here. That was good. She could research whatever she wanted without its being traceable to her. Still, she would need to be careful.

First, she looked at the local news and, after reading random articles, searched to see if anything else had been reported about the murder in Emeryville, finding nothing more informative than she had read earlier. She would have liked to do some scientific searches but feared certain key words might somehow be traced back to her. She didn't think the major search engines shared their data with the government but couldn't be sure. With the FBI involved in the case, she had to be very cautious.

Next, she looked to see what she could find out about her two new friends. Steven and Jeff's names came up in several places, including one with their fraternity picture. Other than Jess, she couldn't think of anyone else she knew who lived on campus. On second thought, there was another person. Trying to bring his surname to mind, Susan realized she could not recall the family name because she might never have known it.

She had another idea. An inquiry for current athletic teams at the University of California, Berkeley brought up a number of links. She looked at the various sites and scanned the names on the teams. On her fifth team roster, she found what she was looking for. He was on the swim team and a member of Beta Sigma Chi. No matter; tomorrow night would be her last night on campus. When she spoke with Russ on Friday, he would have news for her and she could resume her real life.

CHAPTER 28

SUSAN DOWNLOADED THE university's class schedule and jotted down the schedules and room numbers for classes she might want to attend. No more random classes for her—if she was going to attend lectures, she wanted to know what they were. Maybe if she sat in on some science classes, she could meet someone and get access to a research laboratory.

Not for the first time, Susan wished she had her own computer or at least her own phone with her. But maybe it was better this way. Using a public computer might make her searches harder to trace. Frustrated by her lack of scientific resources, Susan deleted her search history, left the business center, and went upstairs.

There was so much she would need to do once she went home. She'd have to get new credit cards and a copy of her driver's license. Susan thought she might have been too hasty cutting everything up. She regretted it now, but at least these things were replaceable. She could use one of Bunny's credit cards until she got her new ones. If she had to go to the Department of Motor Vehicles to replace her license, the picture on file, of course, wouldn't match her current appearance. Perhaps Russell could help her out with the DMV. Maybe it was good that her lawyer was a generalist after all. She'd need a ride to the airport to retrieve her car, or she could just go on BART. Susan was glad that she hadn't parked in short-term parking.

She'd cut up her FitMarin membership card, too, but other than getting into Rosa's locker to retrieve her things, she didn't need to go there again. She could find a new gym easily enough. It would be better to join a new one, anyway, where the change in her appearance would not be noticed.

Susan still had no idea how GI-80 functioned. With everything she was trying to deal with, she had not had a moment to think about it. It appeared likely that aging was tied to the body's immune system. It was possible, however, that the immune system was not involved at all, and the GI-80 biologic was working through a different pathway. This was all speculation, of course—until she could begin real testing, it was impossible to know how aging was controlled. If she could get to a laboratory, she could run some tests on herself and try to determine what changes had taken place at the cellular level.

There was nothing she could do about it today, so she tried to stop thinking and get some sleep.

Susan walked through her laboratory. She was the only member of her species present. Once in the animal room, she saw the doors to all the cages were open. They were all empty. To Susan's surprise, Gina and Gigi were sitting on top of their cages. Speaking to the macaques in a high-pitched, sing-song voice, she said, "I'm happy to see you're both okay."

Hearing her voice, Gina and Gigi turned and looked at her.

Gigi said, "We sent you a message. You needed to take better care of us."

Gina said, "You've changed. You are not the same anymore."

Though intelligible, the sounds they made were unnatural and strange, resonating with an otherworldly hum and reverberation. Susan hadn't known that her macaques could speak. "How can you talk? Is this from the drug?"

"You already know all the answers," Gina told her.

"You knew it was Gary you saw in the crowd when you left the conference. That's why you were thinking about him," Gigi said, looking away from her.

"That's the reason you were so upset the day of the earthquake," Gina added, turning away from Susan and facing the wall.

Susan wanted to continue speaking with them, but they didn't say anything more. She felt so isolated, and she had no one to help her.

Susan sat up in her bed, her heart pounding. Fumbling for a light, she switched on the lamp by her bed. She was in a small room with plain furnishings—a bed, an old-fashioned dresser, a little desk with a wooden chair. Nothing looked familiar. Everything was so basic and traditional; it could be the nineteen forties or fifties. Her chest tightened. Maybe she was locked in. If she couldn't get out the door, maybe she could escape through the window. Frantically looking around the strange little room, she saw a flat-screen television. This was enough to bring her mentally into the present. Her breathing started to become more regular, and she felt her heart rate begin to slow. With effort, she managed to step out of her dream.

The talking macaques had been right. Susan wondered if she would have realized this if the earthquake had not distracted her. Maybe she did have some answers, but she didn't have all.

CHAPTER 29

THE NEXT DAY, she went into another large lecture hall and sat in the back row near the door. When the lecture started, Susan pretended to be taking notes. Unfortunately, it looked like taking notes with a pen and a notepad was a thing of the past. Most of the students were using laptops and other electronic devices, and it did not look like many were taking notes. A few were working a crossword puzzle from the student newspaper. If Susan wanted to attend more classes, she'd at least have to get a copy of the paper.

Susan had never needed corrective lenses until she was in her mid-forties and began using reading glasses. That no longer was a problem—surely a side effect of the GI-80. But she was glad she'd purchased the clear glasses. In addition to helping change her appearance, they made her look more studious and less attractive, although, even with the glasses, she could tell she was attracting attention from male students.

After sitting through two lectures, Susan hurried out of the classroom. The last thing she wanted was to be noticed, and she didn't want to have to think up more phony answers to questions. She walked to the edge of campus and crossed the street, returning to the restaurant Steven and Jeff had shown her yesterday.

By the time she got her food, she could not find a single unoccupied table. Standing near the counter with her tray, she looked around and saw two girls at a table that had an extra chair. When

Susan asked if she might sit with them, the two smiled and said of course. One of them complimented Susan's shoes, and the other leaned over to look at her footwear. Susan had selected well; both girls wanted to know where she'd purchased them. Introducing themselves as Courtney and Katie, they told Susan they were in Delta Delta Lambda. Susan had to smile when she heard this. This was the house Jess had said was known as Visa Visa MasterCard. Susan told the girls her name was Morgan.

When Katie asked Susan if she was dating anyone, Susan replied briefly that she was but things were not going well. This elicited a high level of sympathy from both girls; then the conversation took a strange turn. Courtney began giving Susan advice about dating and relationships. Susan could only assume this was a result of her vague comment about her nonexistent problems with her nonexistent boyfriend. It was apparent that Courtney had had several boyfriends in the past and a relationship with another boy that she'd ended recently. When she was done relating her experiences to Susan's supposed situation, Katie said something that left her shocked and deeply distressed.

"Morgan, I know how upsetting all of this can be. You know, teen romances never last. Believe me, you can find someone better."

Susan could not believe what she had just heard. She even felt her mouth open in utter surprise. How could they possibly think she was that young? Seeing the look on Susan's face, Courtney said, "Katie, look how you've upset her. Morgan, Katie was only trying to be helpful."

Susan could not reply. She looked down for what she thought would be only a moment and found that she could not look up again. She could hardly believe this was happening.

Courtney and Katie began talking even more, trying to correct what they thought had upset Susan. When she was able to look at them again, Susan found she was still at a loss for words. Finally, she said haltingly, "I—I just never looked at things…that way."

If things had been unreal until then, they were about to get stranger. Katie and Courtney suddenly put their arms around Susan and hugged her. Still shaken, Susan found the sudden display of affection unsettling. They gave her their names and cell phone numbers and asked her to please stop by their sorority house over the weekend. Susan thanked them but said she couldn't make any promises; she just didn't know what her plans were.

Once they left, Susan took her tray back to the counter and asked if she could take the uneaten food with her. She did not see anyone following her, but as a precaution, she walked several blocks out of her way and then circled back to the guest house. That gave her time to think about what had just happened. Was it possible that she looked that young? She had not looked at herself closely since she'd been in the store restroom on Tuesday. What did it matter, anyway? Tomorrow she could call Russ, and after that, things would start returning to normal.

She would ride a BART train to a public area a distance from the campus and make the call, she planned. When Russ told her things were resolved, she could get back on a BART train and go straight to his office, an easy walk from the Montgomery Street BART station. Russ could get some money for her, and she could take BART back to the Oakland airport, get her car out of the lot, and go home. Maybe instead of going home, she would go to Bunny's house. She'd ask Russell to lend her a cell phone or buy her a disposable phone to use until she got a new one. She would probably need some identification before she could replace her phone. Just in case Russ told her not to come to the office and to meet him someplace else, she'd take a transit map with her, though it was doubtful she'd need it.

Back at the Faculty Club, Susan was in no hurry to look in a mirror. Instead of going up to her room, she went to the business center to spend some time in the virtual world. Lately, the virtual world seemed more genuine and familiar than her current reality.

CHAPTER 30

THE NEXT DAY after breakfast, Susan packed her Cal tote with her few possessions. The weather was cool, so she put on both of her sweaters. Last night when she'd returned to her room, she had taken a good look at herself in the full-length mirror on the back of the bathroom door. She could see why Katie might have thought she was so youthful; standing naked in front of the mirror, she couldn't tell if her body looked as young as her face. She needed more than self-observation for a good evaluation.

Susan looked around the room to make sure she hadn't left anything. She had more than enough coins for a call on a public phone from anywhere in the Bay Area to San Francisco. She didn't want to get stuck in commute traffic after she made her call, in case she had to take a bus, so it was best to wait a bit before leaving.

It occurred to her that she could wipe down the room to avoid leaving fingerprints. That's what actors do in movies when they are being pursued. Thinking it a good, if overly dramatic, idea, she used one of the small bathroom towels to methodically wipe everything clean, even the bathroom and shower floors, and took the plastic liner from the wastebasket to throw away in a public trash can. Then she wiped off her room key and left it on the little desk. Just before walking out the door, she put her Cal tote bag inside her shopping bag as one extra precaution. That done, she left the Faculty Club through the rear stairwell and walked to the BART station. She took the first train, which was headed east toward Pleasanton/Dublin. Her transit options from there were very good.

Coming out of the station in San Leandro, she saw a public telephone across the street, under an overhang and partially enclosed on two sides. Thinking that was the best public phone she was likely to find, she dialed Russell's office and asked to speak to Mr. Harris.

"May I say who is calling?" asked the receptionist.

"Please tell him it's his Choga instructor."

Susan had been waiting four days to speak with Russell. She was desperately lonely and worried, not only about herself but about Bunny. Apprehensive about her business and anxious to be back in her normal surroundings, she had pinned all her hopes on Russ.

"Thank you for taking the time to telephone me," Russ said, speaking slowly and deliberately. "I am sorry to say it is impossible for me to make it to Choga class today. Right now, I am experiencing tremendous difficulties with a particular case. The situation is dangerously complicated. There is opposition from the government, both federal and state. Other interests are also aligned against this—religious factions, animal rights activists, as well as the medical establishment. In addition, at least one business rival is involved. I cannot say for sure, but if you look at the ABCs of this, everything points to corporate surveillance and espionage. I have an idea of how things can be resolved, but I need time to work on it. I hope you can understand."

Susan felt her chest tighten again. "I do understand. When do you think you can make it?"

She could hear Russ sigh before he replied, "I'm not sure how long it will take. I will be tied up for at least a week."

Susan thought quickly. "What about next Friday? Do you think you can make a Choga class then?"

It took a moment before he answered. "A week from today? Yes, that should work."

Susan took a deep breath. "I will be in class next Friday. I will certainly see you then."

She waited to hear if Russ would say anything more. Every moment she stayed on the telephone, she was at risk. Russell's voice softened as he spoke his last words. "I wish it could have been sooner. Goodbye."

As she hung up the receiver, Susan heard her coins drop inside the phone's metal coin box. She had forgotten that sound. Did the pay phone at the airport make that sound? She didn't recall hearing it. The jangling of the coins struck a note of finality. She was completely alone, cut off from the one person she had thought could help her.

Tears clouded her vision. She couldn't continue like this for another week. More than anything, Susan wanted to be sitting on the floral couch with her mother's arms around her. She wanted to tell Bunny that she had been right after all. That day she had been so cranky, she had been PMSing.

It didn't matter what her attorney said—she should give herself up and take her chances. She had enough coins to call Russ back. She'd ask him to find her a good criminal defense lawyer. She didn't kill Gary. There was some explanation for his death. A defense lawyer would be able to use this to get the charges dismissed or, at the very least, get her released on bail. Why hadn't Russell suggested this? Why did she have to remain a fugitive for another week?

Taking her shirt out of her tote bag, she wiped her eyes. As she did so, Susan's emotions changed abruptly.

She couldn't return to the BART station. If her call had been traced, someone could arrive at any moment. She had no idea how soon the next train would arrive, and standing on the platform, she would be easy to identify and apprehend. Using her shirt, she wiped down the telephone to remove any fingerprints. Frantically looking around, she saw an approaching Alameda County Transit bus. She had no idea where it was headed, but when the doors opened, she got on, paid her fare, requested a transfer, and took a seat near the back exit.

Sitting on the bus, Susan forced herself to think systematically.

She was in deep trouble, that was for sure. Russ had said that the federal government was involved, and the state government as well. What were his exact words? He was *experiencing tremendous difficulties* with a *dangerously complicated situation. There is opposition from the government, both federal and state.* Why would GI-80 be something they would care about?

Russ had used the word *dangerous.* This was most certainly deliberate on his part. That she was in danger made sense to her. Somehow, she had known this since Tuesday, ever since she ran out of her lab after striking Gary. She had taken extreme precautions—getting rid of identifying items, changing her appearance, wiping away fingerprints. Susan was surprised to realize she'd been relying on feelings and instincts. As a scientist, she had been trained to rely on evidence to the exclusion of all else.

Susan had been on the run for four days and hadn't slept more than a few hours at a time since Monday night. Making emotionally based decisions was exhausting, and now she needed to stay hidden for another seven days. She couldn't do this for another week—but what choice did she have? Finding a criminal defense attorney and giving herself up was not an option. What she needed was a plan, and all she could do was to keep moving until she came up with one.

Amazingly, in a conversation less than two minutes long, Russell had given her a great deal of information. He'd also raised many questions. It was doubtful the government would be interested in GI-80's cosmetic effects. What if GI-80 really had age-reversing or anti-aging capabilities? Susan had no idea how long the effects of her therapeutic would last; they could be long-term or only temporary, providing just a fleeting age reversal. Why hadn't Russell said more? Was he so sure that she could figure this out on her own?

As the bus rolled along, Susan began to connect the dots. Clearly, even the possibility of an anti-aging drug had the potential to cause problems. Social Security and Medicare would be directly affected—good reasons for the federal government to oppose this therapeutic.

The federal government also provided pensions. Similarly, state governments had enormous problems with unfunded-pension liabilities. This looming disaster was a daily drumbeat in the news. Susan had heard recently that many states and even local governments had problems with pension and healthcare costs for retirees.

Pensions, Social Security, and Medicare were likely the main factors, but there could be others. Inheritance taxes were currently at low levels, but they did contribute revenue, and there had been talk of increasing these rates. In California, property taxes were assessed based on the purchase price. In some cases, these assessments could be transferred from one property to another; it was only when someone died that property taxes were raised. The State of California and perhaps other state governments would have good reason to oppose GI-80, since it could dramatically affect not only their expenditures but also their revenues.

At the next stop that appeared to be a hub, Susan got off the bus. Seeing another bus nearby, she looked at the route name and number, which gave her an idea where the bus was going. She handed the driver her transfer and took a seat.

Figuring out this much was an accomplishment, but it didn't change her situation. She'd need every bit of her intellect and concentration to stay hidden for another week. Over thirty percent of her journey was complete, but her situation had gotten worse. She had less than twenty dollars left, and she had just made a big mistake.

Susan realized that she might have been caught on a surveillance camera at the San Leandro BART station. She had made the call to Russ's office from a phone close to the station, and it was possible that someone checking surveillance footage from the station could find out what she looked like. She didn't know if BART stations had such cameras installed; she should have done an Internet search before leaving the Faculty Club.

And she could have been picked up on satellite surveillance. She had seen an article not long ago about satellite tasking and re-tasking to select certain areas for view. This had never been her field of interest or expertise, and she had only briefly scanned the piece. She regretted it now but could never have imagined that she might be tracked by the government. She wondered how long it took to re-task these satellites. Had her call to Russell's office lasted long enough for the government to have gotten a satellite into position? Since she didn't have enough information, she would have to assume that she had been spotted. The bus could certainly be tracked from space.

Getting off the bus near the Union City BART station, she saw a coffee shop. Hurrying across the street, she went in and headed to the restroom. Here, Susan removed both of her sweaters, her pants and her shirt, and put on her dress. She took out her Cal tote and turned it inside out, so the logo would not be visible. Then she put her sweaters and the rest of her clothing in the bag. She wondered how detailed an overhead view would be. She had heard that satellite cameras could read license plates and even a newspaper headline. Was that true, she wondered, or disinformation deliberately spread? If it was true and she had been caught on surveillance equipment, whoever viewed it could see her shoes. Removing her flats with the gold medallions, she put on her rubber flip-flops. Then she removed her fake eyeglasses and put them, along with her shoes, in the tote bag and discarded the shopping bag in the trash.

Leaving the restroom, she walked out to the food service area and waited. After a short while, a stocky young man came in. Susan watched as he approached the counter. Before he could order, Susan walked up to him and smiled slightly.

"I need a favor," she told him quietly, "and I am embarrassed to ask."

The fellow looked at her and then looked around. She had spoken so softly, he was not sure she was speaking to him. When he looked back at her, Susan asked, "Are you going to the BART station when you leave here?"

The young man said with a smile, "I was planning on it."

She lowered her voice to a whisper. "I have a seizure disorder and sunlight bothers me. I think it is particularly bad today, and I don't want to fall while crossing the street. I am so embarrassed to be talking about this. Could you help me walk over to the BART station?"

"I'd be happy to help you. I can take you now and come back for my coffee."

"I'm not in any rush," Susan said. The lies were coming easier. She did not want him returning to the coffee shop after they had crossed to the BART station. "Please go ahead and get your coffee."

While he was ordering, Susan put her hair up in a ponytail and tucked the ends under the elastic holder to look like a bun. She wrapped one of her scarves around her hips and tied it like a sarong. From the air, she hoped it would look like a long skirt. She wrapped the other scarf around her head. She put on her sunglasses, though they were barely visible because of her head covering. She was glad that she hadn't worn them earlier, while she was making her phone call.

When he had his drink in hand, Susan asked her new friend if he could steady her when they went outside. "Once I get into the BART station, I'll be fine. I just have to get out of the sunlight."

The young man put his arm around her shoulder, and Susan wrapped her arm around his waist. Susan hoped they would look like lovers from the air. Once they got into the BART station, she said, "I am so grateful. You've done your good deed for the day. Thank you so much."

The young man seemed disappointed that his job was finished. "No problem. Do you need anything else? No? Glad I could be of help."

After buying her ticket, she had very little money left. The only thing she had to help her survive for a week was her brain. On second thought, she also had her new good looks. Scratch that, she thought to herself with a wry smile; she had her brain and her old good looks.

CHAPTER 31

SUSAN CHANGED TRAINS and directions frequently. At one station before boarding a new train, she put the scarves in her tote bag, then put her shirt on over her dress. If she were caught on camera, she hoped this would make it harder to identify her. Susan guessed that the surveillance satellite would be less effective without daylight and hoped that by the time it got dark, she would have a plan in place. She had to secure a place to sleep, money, food, different clothing, and, if possible, another pair of shoes. A hat would be good, too. If she were able to get these things without being detected, she had a chance to make it until Friday, when all she needed to do was to come up with a plan to get to Russ's office.

When it grew dark, Susan rode the train back to Berkeley, exiting two stops away from the campus. As she walked indirectly toward the campus, she checked behind her frequently but did not see anyone following her. A block from the soup restaurant, she saw a policeman walking toward her. She assumed the local police would be on the lookout for her, and as he drew closer, Susan could see he was studying her.

Fortunately, she was near the pedestrian entrance to a multi-story public parking structure. Susan raced to the stairwell door, ran up two flights of stairs, and exited into the parking area. Crouching behind parked cars until she was behind a pillar, she noticed she did not feel out of breath. She was very alert but not panicked.

Crossing to the opposite stairwell, she took the stairs down to the street level on the other side of the parking lot and walked quickly to the soup restaurant. This time, she wanted to run into Steven, Jeff, or one of the sorority girls she had met there. She had not eaten since breakfast and was very hungry. A bowl of soup and a sandwich were exactly what she craved, but she did not have enough money left for even one item and had only two stamps on her loyalty card. And none of her new friends was there.

At the first corner store she came to, Susan used the rest of her money to buy a candy bar. It was Friday night, and the streets around campus were filled with young people. After twenty-five minutes, she arrived at her destination, walked up the stairs, and rang the doorbell. When no one answered, she rang the bell again.

Through the glass panel on the door, Susan saw a young girl come down the stairs, wearing an oversize T-shirt and pants that looked like pajama bottoms. Her long blond hair was held back with a black velvet headband. "Can I help you?"

"Is Katie here?" Susan asked.

"Katie? On Friday night?"

"How about Courtney?"

The girl shook her head.

This was not good. But Mandy had said it was impossible to tell if your luck is good or bad. With that in mind, Susan decided to push against her luck. She had one more question. "How come you're here on a Friday night?"

Apparently, this was a funny question. "I'm taking O-Chem, or more accurately, I am flunking O-Chem and trying to pull a passing grade on my exam on Monday. Whatever score I get, it won't be enough. I'm still going to fail the course, and it's too late to drop it."

Silently thanking Mandy, Susan smiled her first genuine smile in three days. She stuck out her hand and said, "I'm so pleased to meet you. You can call me Morgan. I'm your guardian angel."

The girl looked at Susan wide-eyed, then extended her hand. "I'm Arielle."

CHAPTER 32

SUSAN WORKED LATE into the night tutoring Arielle on the basics of organic chemistry. Fortunately, late-night studying seemed to give Arielle an appetite, and when they took a break, the two went down to the kitchen for a snack. Her stomach growling, Susan devoured two cheese sandwiches and two glasses of milk. Even as they ate, she continued to explain the basics of "O-Chem." She did not want to have a personal conversation with this girl if she could avoid it. She'd much rather talk about science than make up lies she would have to remember to avoid contradicting herself.

When both were too tired to continue, Arielle insisted that Susan sleep in the guest room and loaned her a pair of pajamas. Susan had never visited a sorority house before and was surprised to hear it had a guest room.

Taking out her hair extensions, Susan marveled at the rapidity with which her situation had changed. Her stomach was full and, at least for tonight, she had a good place to sleep. No, she had a great place to sleep. The cozy room had a comfortable double bed with clean white sheets and a warm, colorful quilt. There were clean towels on the white-painted dresser and even an extra blanket in the closet. The window had a secure lock. Most important, no one knew she was here except Arielle.

Susan wanted to think more about her situation. There was still a lot to figure out, but once in bed, she immediately fell asleep.

David's arms were outstretched. Susan was so happy to see him. It had been so long since she'd heard him speak. It was wonderful to hear him again. "I need you to help me. Susan, you can come back. You are the one who can do this."

Susan wanted to help her father, but she didn't understand what he needed. She reached out her arms to touch him, and as she did, David faded away. Susan looked around. She wasn't alone. Bunny was standing in the shadows; Susan could hear her voice but could not reach her. Calling her mother over and over again, she realized Bunny could not hear her.

Susan woke up crying. This time, she knew where she was, but her dream was more real to her than the guest room. As a scientist, Susan did not give dreams any significance. She tried to reason her way out of the distress that consumed her, yet she could not shake the feelings from her dream. Susan felt something important had been communicated to her. Her father needed her to do something for him.

She lay in bed worrying about her mother and herself. Unable to go back to sleep, Susan thought about her conversation with Russ. He had said that besides the federal and state governments, other interests were opposed to her research. That religious groups would be against it was no surprise. Conservative religious organizations had consistently opposed advances in biotechnology. Had Russell wanted her to infer that they could be physically dangerous? From the way he had phrased it, Susan concluded the answer was probably yes. If not, why would he have mentioned it in a conversation he was trying so hard to keep brief? Could religious fanatics have been behind Gary's murder?

Russ had said that animal rights groups presented an immediate threat, too. Just as with the religious opposition, he did not need to tell her these groups were against her research unless he'd been trying to warn her.

He had also told her the medical establishment was opposed. This was odd. Susan remembered Dr. Klein's repeated and rather shrill phone calls asking if she had retaken her blood test. Susan wished she could discuss this with her attorney. Actually, she wished she could talk about her situation with anyone.

Russ had communicated a great deal in very few words. Clearly, she was not simply wanted for questioning about Gary's murder. If that were the case, she could come back and, if necessary, post bail. Even O.J. Simpson hadn't been convicted of murder. And how would a murder conviction help the government or any of the groups opposed to her research? Others could produce GI-80 if Susan were locked away in prison. And the newspaper articles about Gary's death had been so short and lacking in detail.

As Susan thought about it, the pieces began to fit together. She realized what the government and the rest of her *opposition* were after. She understood what they intended to do. The government and all the groups Russ had mentioned needed GI-80 not to exist. So long as she was alive, the drug could be re-created and brought to market. Even putting her in prison could not stop this. The only possible solution was for her to cease to exist. Now she fully understood what Russ had been trying to communicate.

She had to stay hidden for a week. The task seemed overwhelming, but if there'd been a way to turn herself in safely, Russ would have arranged it. How had he put it? *The situation is dangerously complicated.* He had been trying to tell her that once she was in police custody, the government could find a way to kill her and say she'd died of accidental causes.

Susan remembered a Russian in London who had been poisoned with a radioactive substance slipped into his tea. Could the U.S. government do something like this? She hoped she would never find out. But surely, if the government wanted her dead, it could use one of the groups opposed to her work, or kill her and claim a religious fanatic or an animal rights lunatic had done it.

To give up meant certain death. No, that wasn't an option. Bunny hadn't given up when David died. She owed it to Bunny to see this through. At least now she had a better idea of what she was up against.

CHAPTER 33

THE NEXT MORNING, Susan had a chance to look around the sorority house, which was more like a home than a dormitory. Downstairs, it had a traditional living room, with a formal sitting area that looked as if it had been decorated in the 1950s, a small, casual lounge area with a television, and a large dining room, where she ate a late breakfast with Arielle and a few of the other girls. After a good breakfast, Susan insisted that they resume studying. Amazed at Susan's knowledge, Arielle repeatedly asked her how she knew so much about chemistry.

Susan tried to evade the question, but Arielle continued to express her astonishment at her breadth of knowledge. Finally, Susan said to her in a serious tone, "Arielle, I want to tell you the truth. Last night I lied to you. I am not really your guardian angel. I am Delta Delta Lambda's resident genius."

Both laughed long and hard, and for a brief moment, Susan actually felt lighthearted.

She was in the dining room having an afternoon snack and a study break when Katie and Courtney came back to the house. By that time, Susan was set up: Other girls needed tutoring, and although she had not asked for money, they were planning to pay her. They didn't call this place Visa Visa MasterCard for nothing.

When asked about her boyfriend, Susan looked down at the

floor, trying to determine how to reply. Deciding the less said, the better, "I just left," she told them.

That was enough for Katie and Courtney. The two began filling in the backstory without any additional information. They told her they totally understood and agreed with her decision, then busied themselves thinking of ways to help. Maybe Susan could go with them tonight when they met their dates. Susan declined gracefully, claiming Arielle still needed her help.

By evening, it was agreed on by all that Susan would stay in the guest room for at least two more nights, though Katie and Courtney assured her she could stay longer if she wanted to. Arielle gave Susan the cash she had on hand to pay for some of her tutoring and promised to get more from the ATM.

Still concerned that the shoe medallions might show up on a surveillance camera and lead someone to the sorority house, Susan went out later that day to buy new flats and a pair of athletic shoes as well as two pairs of socks. Her excursion went well. She gave a wide berth to the police officers she saw and nobody seemed to notice her.

Dinner at the sorority house was surprisingly good. She was the only one who ate bread—in fact, several slices—with her meal. Susan supposed that most college girls watched their carbohydrates to keep their calorie count down. She had so many other problems at present that gaining weight did not even make it onto her radar. She was grateful to have a full stomach and glad that she didn't have to go out again that day.

Susan planned to spend Saturday night helping Arielle and anyone else who might need her assistance. Courtney and Katie stopped by Arielle's room to say goodbye; Susan suspected they would not be back until Sunday.

Arielle's roommate was gone for the weekend. Sitting in her quiet room talking about the basics of organic chemistry was the best experience Susan had had all week. It was almost impossible to believe that just seven days earlier, she had been watching a baseball game with Russell.

Maybe someone from the government, not FAN, had broken into her lab initially. But that was unlikely; no one could have known the capability of GI-80 then. Susan and her staffers had observed only that the animals dosed with GI-80 had been unusually active—nothing that would be of interest to the government. It must have been radical animal rights activists that broke the back door and took all the lab animals. Or could it have been Avery?

It had been clever of Russ to use the phrase ABC to inform her that Avery Biogenetics Corporation had been monitoring her work. Susan wondered if his telephone line had been tapped, and if the person monitoring the call realized what her attorney had been telling her. Yes, the phone most probably had been tapped, and no, it would have been difficult to decipher the reference. Susan thought it unlikely that the German management team had heard anyone use this acronym. Few on the old team were left, and the ones still around didn't seem to be doing much talking these days.

Interrupting Susan's thoughts, Arielle asked with a big smile, "How do you think I'm doing, Morgan? Be honest."

"You're doing great, Arielle," Susan was able to answer truthfully. "You're going to do well on Monday. I think you understand the material. How did you do on the practice test?"

Now Arielle was beaming. "I did so well that…" she paused dramatically, "we don't have to study anymore tonight. We can P-A-R-T-Y."

Arielle was correct; she did understand her organic chemistry material now. Susan was dubious about going to a college party, though. She could borrow a book or some magazines or, better yet, a computer.

"I don't know, Arielle. I think I'll just stay here. Maybe you can't tell, but I am pretty shy, and I'm not good in social situations."

Arielle was not deterred. "All the more reason you should go. Look, we've worked hard all day. Let's go have some fun! All the fraternities have parties on Saturday night. Let's stop by one or two—it'll do us both good. There's more to life than studying. I'll text Katie and Courtney and see if we can meet up with them."

Susan had not been able to stop thinking about her mother and father. How she wished she could think of some way to contact Bunny. She could not recall ever being out of touch with her mother for this long. Her mother needed her and she needed her mother. In her dream, it had been her father who needed her. She had absolutely no interest in attending a fraternity party, and agreed to go only because she did not want to stand out any more than she already did. Bunny would be worried, but she had her friends to help her and would certainly be okay for a few days. Susan had to make it to safety for her mother's sake as much as her own. Staying safe was her job now—staying safe and crafting a plan.

Arielle lent her a tight-fitting, stretchy black dress with silver metallic trim and a pair of five-inch heels. As if that wasn't enough, she provided silver bracelets that she claimed matched Susan's earrings and completed the ensemble. The dress was shorter and more form-fitting than anything she had ever worn. Susan hoped she could walk in the shoes and worried about sitting down without displaying her undergarments. Showing her panties was one thing, but falling and breaking an ankle or a leg was another; even a sprain could be disastrous. She couldn't risk doing anything that would require medical assistance.

When she put the outfit on, she felt ridiculous. She wanted to change into her own clothes, but Arielle wouldn't hear of it. She assured Susan that she looked terrific and insisted she not wear her glasses.

Once Susan's outfit was selected and confirmed, Arielle got dressed. She wore a short bright pink skirt, a tight black off-the-shoulder sweater, and thigh-high black leather boots with very high heels. Looking in the mirror, she seemed pleased at what she saw. Susan thought Arielle looked even more outlandish and trashy than she did. She wondered if Arielle's parents knew their daughter went out dressed like that.

Unlike schools where the fraternities and sororities are at separate ends of the campus, the Greeks were clustered together at UC Berkeley. Susan and Arielle had only to cross the street, and they would have their choice of parties.

As they walked, Arielle told her the image each house had on campus. Kappa Theta, Jess's sorority, was a good house, Arielle said; she had almost rushed there. Zeta Kappa Pi, Steven and Jeff's fraternity, had a lot of parties, but most of the guys were not very good-looking. Delta Delta Lambda girls did not date boys from that house. Too bad for you, Steven and Jeff, Susan thought. She did not need to ask how people saw Delta Delta Lambda.

The street was filled with young people, walking and milling around, and Susan and Arielle were attracting attention from the people they passed. Susan was sorry that she had agreed to go out and especially regretted her clothes. Maybe she could stay at a party for just a short while and then find an excuse to leave.

The next house was Alpha Kappa Phi. Arielle said they should either go there or to Beta Sigma Chi. They were the top fraternities on campus and each threw good parties. "What do you think? We can go to Alpha Kappa and maybe stop at Beta Sig on the way back."

Remembering the results of her Internet search, Susan asked if they could go to Beta Sigma Chi first.

"Good choice. We'll go there first. If they ask you questions, you can just say you're thinking of rushing Delta Delta and came to visit. That's true, isn't it? You are considering becoming a Delta, aren't you?"

Susan nodded. She understood now what rushing meant but felt fatigued from constantly lying. At the Beta Sig house, the door was open, and a young man standing outside invited them in. Arielle showed her student ID, and after considerable discussion was able to get Susan in without one. They walked into a large, dimly lit room, its walls covered with school flags and other memorabilia.

Some people were sitting around talking, but most were dancing to loud music. The place was packed.

Susan stuck close to Arielle, who began talking to some boys who seemed as interested in Susan as in her friend. One left and returned with beer. Arielle took a glass, and when he held out the other one to Susan, she said she would wait and maybe have some later. She really wanted a drink, but beer was not what she had in mind. On second thought, she realized, beer was probably as good as it would get, and a little might relax her. She didn't want to draw attention to herself, and not drinking at a fraternity party would accomplish exactly that.

Susan motioned to the boy that she wanted the glass after all. She hoped that a little beer would not interact significantly with the GI-80. She had had some wine with Russ last Saturday night and had not been aware of any negative interactions. She really could not drink much, since she needed to stay conscious of her surroundings. She couldn't sit in the short dress and certainly didn't want to try dancing in such high heels.

Sipping her beer, Susan tried to hear what the people around her were saying, which was difficult, since the music was so loud. She wondered if GI-80 had any effect on reversing hearing loss—something else to be researched if she lived long enough to bring the drug to human trials. Her nerves could not take much more of this. These thoughts, combined with the loud music, were too much for her. Apparently, GI-80 did not have the ability to reverse musical taste, she thought wryly.

Leaving Arielle, she walked around to see if she could find a way to make the time she had to remain at the party more tolerable. As she did, Susan thought about her situation. She could stay at the sorority house until Monday or Tuesday and possibly longer. She might even be able to stay until Friday, when she planned to meet Russ. But there would be more girls at the sorority house once the weekend was over. More girls would mean more talk. Already, several were aware that Susan knew a lot about science and math, and once they went back to class, they might mention the young genius in their guest room. No, it would be better if she left on Monday when classes started. It would be safer for the girls, too.

She was relieved to find the music was not so loud in the hallway. The walls were covered with pictures of past and current members of Beta Sigma Chi; judging from the number of photos, the fraternity had been around for quite a few years. Before she reached the back of the house, a young man blocked her way.

"Who goes here? No one goes into the kitchen without permission. And if you want to get by, you'll have to give me a kiss."

Susan saw he was drunk or high or, more likely, both. High as he was, he might not remember their conversation. She had heard that some classes were videotaped and shown on the Internet. She did not want to attend one of those. Probably only the professor was filmed, but a student asking a question might be as well, and she could be caught on tape. Susan thought of asking the boy if he knew which classes were webcast, but just then, a better idea occurred to her.

Giving him what she hoped was a bright, winning smile, Susan said, "You're the president of Beta Sig, aren't you?" She tried to sound impressed. She had no idea who the president of the fraternity was.

The remark distracted the fellow blocking her way. "Hell, no. I'm not the president."

"You'll have to prove it," Susan responded in what she hoped was a teasing way.

"Okay. Come over here," he said, leading Susan to the pictures of the current fraternity brothers. "That's the president right there." He pointed to a young man in one of the portraits. "Do I look like him?"

She could play this one out. Looking from the picture to the inebriated boy and back again, she replied, "Oh, I am so sorry. You are so much better-looking than he is. I hope I haven't hurt your feelings."

Her new acquaintance was smiling happily at her. Susan smiled back. "I didn't know your fraternity was so big. Are all these, um, brothers here tonight?"

Just as she had hoped, her new friend began telling her who was at the party and who was not. Some had already left and a few were upstairs.

If the FBI or police found out that she had come to this party, she did not want anyone to remember that she had asked about anyone in particular. By then, Susan had learned that her inebriated friend's name was Bret.

"Bret, where's the president? Is he here?"

Her question was enough to elicit information on the where-abouts of many of the frat members. Susan indicated another of his brothers.

"He's almost as cute as you. Is he here tonight?"

Her friend happily obliged with details concerning the boy she was asking about.

"What about him?" Susan pointed to another picture, the only one she was interested in.

"That's the T-Man. He's not here tonight. I don't think he'll be coming. He moved out of the house this year."

"Oh, why? Didn't he like living here? It seems like such a great place," Susan said.

"Oh, yeah, it's a great place, all right. But T-Man got a car, and there's no parking here. He found an apartment on Telegraph Avenue with parking and even a Subway right in the building."

Figuring the more questions she asked about random people, the less likely Bret was to remember anything specific, she went on to ask if this guy was a player or if that one had a girlfriend. All the talking must have given him an appetite, because all of a sudden, he asked, "Hey, are you hungry? Want to go see what there is to eat around here?"

Edging past a couple locked in a passionate embrace, oblivi-ous of the people around them, she followed Bret to the kitchen.

Maybe some food would make him more coherent and she could question him about the webcasts. When Arielle was ready to leave, she found Susan on a stool next to the kitchen counter and the still-high resident of Beta Sigma Chi with one arm around her and the other on the counter in front of her. Bret still had not gotten a kiss, although Susan had been flirting mightily in hopes of learning something useful. They had been talking less than half an hour, but it felt much longer. She couldn't wait to get away from Bret and out of the fraternity house.

"Sorry. My friend's leaving now. I'll catch up with you later," she told him, using a phrase she'd heard someone use earlier. Walking back to the sorority house, Susan felt extremely glad that she wasn't a real college girl. A couple of hours of high heels, blaring music, beer, and mindless conversation were more than enough for her.

CHAPTER 34

LYING IN BED, Susan continued thinking about her conversation with Russell. He would not have said ABC if he didn't have reason to suspect that Avery Biogenetics had been monitoring her research. The only way that Avery, or anyone else, for that matter, could have gained information was to have a spy on her staff. It could be Wolf, Mandy, Kevin, or Jess. Susan had occasionally employed other people part-time, but they would not have had exposure to her proprietary research, and Avery had no need to spy on their contract work. Anyway, no one else had worked for her since she'd started investigating GI-80.

Methodically, Susan thought about each of her staffers. Wolf had been on site almost immediately after Gary was killed. Was it possible that he could betray her like that? She pictured Wolf's face and shook her head from side to side. She had to think this through logically, put all the facts together. Who else could she rule out?

Jess was busy with her social life, sorority, and athlete boyfriends. She came from a wealthy family and had excellent career prospects. She had de facto acceptance into the doctoral program; when she finished, she would have her choice of research positions. No, Susan corrected herself, Jess didn't have to wait until she completed her PhD. She had excellent prospects now. Susan had been lucky to get Jess to come to Glass Biotech. There was no reason for Jess, who was just starting her career, to sell inside information to another biotech firm.

With her looks, Jess could be in Hollywood, but her heart was in science. All things considered, Jess was the least likely to be the spy. Yet Susan was aware that when people are physically attractive, something called the halo effect causes all types of good qualities to be attributed to them. She hoped she was thinking clearly and not being misled by Jess's appearance.

Reflecting further, Susan felt Jess's erratic schedule eliminated her. Because of her other commitments, she worked less than the rest of the staffers. If she were the spy, there would be big holes in the information she could deliver. Everything pointed to eliminating Jess. Still, until Susan had proof, no one could be ruled out.

Could it be Kevin? Kevin was an unusual fellow, all right. He could quantify anything. Could he put a price on loyalty?

She began running through her experiences with Kevin; things she had heard him say in conversation ran through her mind. It was almost as if she were watching a movie, with scenes of Kevin passing through her head in fast-forward. Kevin lived by playing the odds. He spent his free time gambling online and was known to be successful. Laboratory research itself was a gamble, since it involves looking for a long-shot response. Being on the take was the direct opposite of this.

And Kevin was by nature an anarchist. He often left work early on Fridays for his rides with Critical Mass. His participation was a key part of his identity. This did not correspond with a spy's profile: A spy would stick around if there was marketable information to be obtained. But what if he wasn't leaving early to ride with Critical Mass? Could he be meeting with Avery instead?

That didn't make sense. Kevin was always trying to get his coworkers to ride with him. Susan thought he was not likely to be the turncoat. Even under her current circumstances, she found herself smiling when she thought about him. He was an appealing, quirky little guy. She had the feeling she could count on him; but was she right?

She did not think it likely that Kevin or Jess were spies. That left Wolf and Mandy. Ostensibly, the facts pointed to Wolf. He had returned to the lab and had been there when the FBI and police were investigating Gary's murder. Russ had said Wolf told the FBI that Susan had given everyone the afternoon off so that she could be alone in the lab. Had he really said that? Could Russ be lying? No, how could Russ have known about the afternoon off? And how could he possibly have known Wolf's real name?

Wolf had not wanted the day off. In fact, Susan had been prompted to buy lunch for everyone primarily because he was so unhappy about his home life with Mother Wolf around. He would have had no way of knowing that she would recover so quickly and come into the office.

What if he had assumed she would not come in to work that day and returned after lunch to do some surveillance? And once in the building, he'd come upon Gary and killed him? This didn't make sense, either. Why would Wolf kill Gary? Susan could think of no possible explanation. Wolf had more access to the lab than anyone other than Susan herself. And there was no surveillance for him to do on Tuesday while she was home sick. The only lab work in progress was Avery's work. No GI-80 had been formulated.

How had it happened that she had been so ill, anyway, and then suddenly felt well enough to go to work? Monday night, she had been so sick, she barely made it from her front door to her bedroom. In less than twenty-four hours, she.... It was as if she... had a youthful immune system, which kicked into high gear quickly to fight off whatever had invaded her system. So GI-80 did activate an immune response. This would indicate that aging itself is tied somehow to the immune system and can be reversed. Without further research, of course, it was impossible to prove this connection. It could be that the involvement of the immune system was tangential. GI-80 might work in another way, reversing the aging of many organs, those in the immune system only a few of them.

Susan had inadvertently unlocked one of the biggest mysteries of the human condition. She'd made one of the greatest scientific discoveries in history. At the same time, she was running and hiding to save her life, while her research was in a health club locker protected by a five-dollar combination lock. If she were killed, this discovery could be lost forever.

It was overwhelming. She couldn't bear to look at the big picture. The only way she could cope with her situation was to look at each of the details, one by one. Susan closed her eyes and tried to focus.

Out of the blue, Susan knew who the spy was and knew it with certainty. Was it really that obvious? ABC's spy was an American Born Chinese. Mandy was selling information to Avery Biogenetics. Thinking back to the day after the earthquake, when she had returned to the lab from Russell's office and witnessed the GI-80 animals acting so strangely, she recalled ruining her shoe in a puddle of automotive fluid. Her shoe was proof that Mandy had been in the parking lot earlier.

Later, when she had driven over to Avery, the management had already been informed that GI-80 was showing promise, because Mandy had been there, parking her car in the rear of the building and entering through the back entrance. That was the same day Mandy had purchased pastries for everyone. Kevin, God bless him, had pointed out how expensive they were.

With her parents controlling and pressuring her at every step, Mandy would be easy to buy, and Avery had the money to do it. Yes, it was Mandy who was selling secrets. Like the other staffers, she had keys to the lab and knew the codes for both the old and new alarm systems. She could have given them to someone at Avery. How very convenient for them.

Could Wolf be involved as well? Wolf liked Mandy; Susan could see that. Were they dating? Could they be involved in this together? Her instincts told her that Wolf was loyal and trustworthy. But she needed to be careful. Her feelings had not served her well in the past.

Chapter 35

WHEN SUSAN AWAKENED on Sunday morning, she was surprised that she'd been able to sleep as well as she had. Her dreams were still troubled, but it seemed she was learning how to wake herself up before they completely terrified her, and then get back to sleep without lying awake for hours. Lying in bed this morning, she was aware that she had the rudiments of a plan. In fact, after awaking from a bad dream, she had worked out some details before falling back asleep. If everything went as planned, she could get to Russell's office on Friday. If things went awry, she would have problems, for sure, but she had time to work on back-up scenarios.

While Arielle had been taking a practice test the previous day, Susan had used her laptop to view local news sites, but she hadn't found any recent articles on Gary's murder. She would have liked to do a specific search about the murder but was afraid it might be tracked somehow to the computer.

After a late breakfast, Susan and Arielle walked to the library. Arielle planned to study by herself and ask questions as needed. Susan would tutor another girl in advanced calculus right before dinner, and she had loaned Susan her university ID card, which would enable her to enter the large library, or what Arielle called the "main stacks."

During the short walk to the main part of the campus, Susan saw Jess immediately ahead of them. She noticed that she did not feel panic or agitation. Calmly, she walked as slowly as possible to increase the distance between them. Her main concern was that Jess might know Arielle and stop to chat. She tried to think what to do if that happened, but fortunately, Jess appeared engaged by her companion. For some reason, however, Jess turned around twice. The first time, Susan bent down and pretended to retie her shoelace. By the second time this occurred, several people were between them.

She thought it unlikely that Jess would recognize her, but she was relieved that she didn't have to find out. She certainly didn't want to be put in a situation where she had to talk to her. Bunny had known her voice immediately, and Russell had recognized it as recently as two days ago.

In the library, Susan asked her companion, "Arielle, where are you going to be? I want to use a computer with Internet access and look at online databases for journal articles. Where can I do that?"

Arielle told her where the student-accessible computers were. Since almost everyone came to the library with a device of some sort, shared-use computers were in little demand, she said. Susan found she needed a user name and password to access the Internet from the library's computers; fortunately, she still had the user name and password that she'd been given at the Faculty Club, and they worked.

She went to some random websites that would not be noticed— shopping sites, movie listings, and historical searches. Only after that did she look for what she was really seeking. When she finally located the correct website, she opened a calculator tool and ran various calculations on a spreadsheet. She reviewed her figures to make sure the math was correct—there was no room for error— then evaluated her formula once again. The equation had to be challenging enough to make it very difficult to interpret and solve; and it had to have only one solution.

Once satisfied, Susan hurriedly typed out an email message but did not send it. Rereading what she had written, she thought that sending it would be either the smartest or stupidest thing she had done since leaving her laboratory. Silently praying it was the former, she hit the Send button.

The next morning, after an early breakfast of granola, banana, and milk, she left the Delta Delta Lambda sorority house. As she said goodbye to the few girls who were awake, Susan wished she could have remained until it was time to meet Russ in San Francisco. Her stay had gone far better than she could have imagined. But who knew what would happen if she were located there? The people who were after her would not want to leave any witnesses. She might have stayed too long already.

This time, she was wearing clothing given to her by her grateful students: a blue-and-gold University of California, Berkeley sweat-shirt and a pair of jeans. So many students walked around in these sweatshirts that the campus and nearby streets looked like a dark blue lake. It would be hard to track her from the air or even on the ground in this outfit. Most of the students wore either flip-flops or white athletic shoes with white laces, like Susan. She was even car-rying a plain black nylon duffel bag, a gift from one of the girls she had tutored, who had an extra one. It still had the tags on it.

It was really too bad that she could not stay longer at the soror-ity house. She wanted to hear how Arielle did on her chemistry mid-term. She could call her in a week, when grades would be posted—that is, if she was still alive. Susan waited for the anxiety she was expecting to overwhelm her. It didn't come. Yesterday, when she had seen Jess ahead of her, and now, remembering the danger she was in, she did not become apprehensive. Nor did she panic. Susan found this very interesting. Was it possible she was becoming accustomed to living in such danger?

She certainly was not unconcerned. Her thoughts about dying within the week were sobering. Still, she had been successfully on the run for six days. She had a full stomach, more than three hundred dollars from her tutoring, the rudiments of a plan, and only five more days before she planned to meet her attorney. Was it possible the worst was behind her?

Susan couldn't shake the feeling that she was overlooking something. What could it be?

As she walked around Berkeley, once again taking a circuitous route to her destination, she prayed that Russell could come through for her. She was putting a lot of faith in him. He had not let her down, but circumstances were different now. What if his plans to help her did not materialize? What if he gave up or did not even try? No, Russ would not have told her to wait until Friday if he didn't plan on trying to help her. And what alternative did she have?

Other than hearing it from Russ, she had no confirmation that the FBI was involved. What if this was something he had fabricated to get her to hide out? The newspapers had said nothing about the FBI. Could Russ be working with ABC, or some other faction? This was a murder case, after all. Hiding out for so long instead of turning herself in did make her look guilty and, in all probability, dangerous. Had Russ put her on a more perilous path?

Susan realized she had made an unconscious decision to trust him when they were at dinner and the ballgame. Russ was the one she had called when she'd seen she was in a bad situation, and she had followed his advice. She only hoped her intuition was steering her in the right direction. Judging character had never been her best skill.

If she only had someone she trusted to talk to, but there was no one she could confide in. She felt so alone. She consciously tried not to think about her mother by pushing all thoughts of Bunny to the back of her mind and focusing on her current situation. Would she ever be back in her quiet, comfortable life?

She had planned to arrive at this spot right after the first breakfast service at the sorority house, and she was on schedule. She walked around the building to look for other exits and then crossed the street to watch it from the opposite corner. If a car came out of the garage or someone walked out the main entrance, she could see it from there. If this did not work out, she would contact Jeff or Steven, the fraternity boys she'd met after her first class on campus, and see if they could help her find a place to stay, at least for one night.

Almost immediately, the door to the front entrance opened and two Asian American girls walked down the stairs and headed up the avenue. A little while later, a short fellow came out and walked in the same direction.

Susan moved back onto the sidewalk and leaned on the building behind her. After another fifteen or twenty minutes, the door opened again, and a tall brown-haired man began walking at a rapid pace toward the campus. Still on the opposite side of the street, Susan had to jog to keep up with him, her duffel bag bumping into her hip. She was glad she was wearing the athletic shoes instead of her flats.

She followed him into a classroom building and to one of the larger lecture halls. She would not be noticed if she sat in on this class; then again, what if he left early for some reason? Sitting on the grass across from the building, she waited for the student she had just followed to come out.

After fifty minutes, students started leaving the building. The fellow she was waiting for headed toward the main stacks and entered the library café, where he got in the line for food. Susan got in line, too, with two people between them. She ordered a cold drink and a salad, then saw that he was sitting at a table near the windows. She had been hoping all the tables would be filled so that she could ask to share his. Since this was not the case, she took her food to a nearby table.

Now that she was this close, she could see how nice-looking he was, with dark brown eyes and wavy hair and a tan. She thought he was at least six-foot-one. Now if she could only think of something to say. Lamenting her poor social skills, she racked her brain.

If she dropped her notebook or duffel bag, maybe he would pick it up and she could start a conversation. Susan took her notebook and pen out of the duffel bag and placed them at the edge of the table; all she needed to do was to give the notebook a little push.

But before she could move, he spoke to her. "Excuse me, can you watch my things? I forgot to get something."

She was too taken aback to do more than nod her head.

When he returned, he was carrying two brownies. "Here's one for you," he said. "Thanks for watching my stuff."

Susan smiled and thanked him. For a while, they ate in silence, as she tried to come up with something to say to him. Eventually, he looked up and said to her, "Let me introduce myself. My name is—"

Before he could finish, she interrupted him. "I know what your name is."

CHAPTER 36

Now HE WAS the one taken by surprise.

"It's Tyler."

"That's right. Do I know you?" he asked.

Susan smiled and waited. She wanted her answer to have maximum impact. She had only one chance to do this right.

"Well, you don't know me now, I guess. But you did." Again, she paused. "You went to the Montessori school in San Rafael, didn't you?"

She searched her brain for the name of his preschool teacher. She was sure that Rosa had mentioned it more than once. She should have thought about this while she was waiting for him to come out of class. The information was in her brain, though, and she tried to retrieve it. "Our teacher was…Gail and another woman…."

"Jody. Gail and Jody were our teachers," Tyler said. "I can't believe you remember that, and that you recognized me. That's incredible. How were you able to do that?"

Susan gave him her best smile. "Easy, because you haven't changed a bit."

Tyler laughed heartily, and Susan tried to laugh along with him. She hoped that she sounded genuine and lighthearted. She had never been good at acting, and her heart was anything but light. Her situation was oppressive, and it saddened her to see the little boy she had known all grown up. Looking at him now, she felt a sense of loss.

Tyler had been an adorable sandy blond child, with big brown eyes. Probably because of his life with a very troubled mother, he had, the few times Susan had been with him, always seemed overly serious for a boy his age. Seeing him now only emphasized how much time had passed. Looking at him made her lonely for Rosa.

And meeting Tyler made her feel even more lost and alone. Apart from a few hours at the sorority house when she'd been tutoring, Susan had been consumed by anxiety every waking minute for a week. Even her sleep was filled with the danger and uncertainty she faced. Most of her nights had been spent lying awake in the dark, running past and future scenarios through her mind until she'd been able to fall asleep again.

But she must be improving her ability to dissemble, since it appeared Tyler was buying her little performance. Susan told him her name was Morgan.

"I remember being so sad when you moved away. And I remember when your grandmother came to class and brought Kelly."

Tyler was astounded. "I can't believe you remember all that. Kelly was great, wasn't he? I loved that dog. It's amazing you remember his name. When he came to class, he jumped on the children, he was so excited. Some of them started crying, and they never let him come back."

Things were going better than she had hoped when she'd come up with this plan. Scientist that she was, she should have realized that the problem with plans often has to do with the fact that objects in motion tend to stay in motion.

Tyler had a class after lunch, and they made plans to meet again when it was over. While he was in class, Susan went into another classroom in the same building. She had learned from Arielle that only the larger classrooms had videotape equipment. With that in mind, she went into a medium-size class and took out her notebook and pen.

While the professor was talking, she thought more about her immediate situation. Other than the two police officers on Telegraph Avenue last week, she had not had any close encounters. Was she overlooking something? She didn't want to leave Berkeley if she could avoid it. She still had four nights to go and hoped that Tyler could find her a safe place to stay.

But she worried about being seen with Tyler. She promised herself that if she felt anyone was getting close, she would leave him immediately; she only hoped this would be enough to keep him safe. Looking around the classroom, she did not notice anyone watching her, and she had not seen anyone who appeared to be following her.

When the professor started asking questions about the assigned material, Susan regretted sitting in on the class, but he never called on her. Afterward, she met up with Tyler. Not wanting to be out more than absolutely necessary, she told him she was tired and asked if he knew someplace they could just sit and talk.

"We could go back to my apartment. I have a roommate, Kyle. But he's out of town. He's on a dig."

"A dig?"

As they walked to his apartment, Tyler told her, "Kyle's considering going for a PhD in archeology. He wants to see if he really likes that type of work before committing to graduate school. At the moment, he's in Turkey on a work/study program."

"Have you heard from him? Does he like it?" Susan asked, trying to make small talk but grateful his roommate was so far away. The fewer people she spoke with, the safer they were.

"Well, he emailed and said it's the most boring thing he's ever done. All day, he sifts through dirt under the burning sun. The food's horrible, and everyone goes to bed at seven at night," Tyler said, laughing.

Susan asked how he'd ended up at UC Berkeley. Tyler talked at length about his life and his family. She had heard about him over the years from Rosa. Now she was getting to know the adult he had grown up to be.

Tyler's apartment was on the second floor of the modern stucco building. He had a car in the garage, he told her. The building was on a slope, so the garage was a partial basement. She already knew the garage was the reason he had moved into this building. The car was a gift from his grandparents, he added. Susan, of course, knew he was talking about Rosa and Ray.

The front door opened into a combination living room, dining room, and kitchen. A bedroom and a bathroom were just off the living room. Tyler took two cans of soda from the refrigerator and handed one to Susan, apologizing for being out of beer. Normally, she never drank soda, but right now, she had more on her mind than counting calories. Anyway, it seemed to her that she was noticeably thinner. She could not be sure, since she had been avoiding mirrors and had not weighed herself in several days.

Susan sat down on the futon couch and opened the can, and Tyler joined her. The only other places to sit were two wooden chairs next to a small table. It felt good to be in a home, even if it was just a student apartment, and to be sitting with someone who wasn't a complete stranger.

Against the wall opposite the couch was a television. Tyler explained that it belonged to Kyle, and the poor fellow missed it terribly. From what Susan could tell, the conversation was going well. When it reached a point where it seemed appropriate, she came out with what she most wanted to know.

"Tyler, would you know someplace I could stay for a few nights, any girls that might have space for me? I have some money and can pay."

She had been planning to tell Tyler that she'd gotten into an argument with her roommate, because the roommate had borrowed her clothing without asking. Though the quarrel was frivolous, she wanted to cool off before going back. This sounded less menacing than the real story—that she was wanted for questioning in the death of her ex-husband, who'd been found bludgeoned, with a slashed carotid artery, at the business she owned. And to be completely accurate, the people looking for her didn't want to question her.

Tyler didn't have any questions, either. "You can stay here if you like. And call me Ty. Everyone does. Only my family still calls me Tyler."

Susan knew that at least one of his fraternity brothers called him the T-Man. Saying nothing about this, she replied, "I appreciate the offer, Ty, but I was hoping you might know some girls I could stay with."

She had not planned on staying with a man, even one as young as Tyler. Staying here would not be as comfortable as the sorority house. She didn't even have a nightgown.

"Don't get me wrong. I'd like the company."

Maybe he was as comforted by her presence as she was by his. Could he be lonely, too? Perhaps he wasn't used to living alone. Still, this was not part of her plan.

"Ty, that is really nice of you, but I'm not sure it would be the best thing. I am not the most sociable person, and I don't want you to get the wrong idea."

"There's something different about you, Morgan. You're very serious. In fact, you are the most serious girl I have ever met. I don't think I have the wrong idea."

His reply caused Susan to reconsider. Maybe staying with Tyler could work. He hadn't asked any questions about her situation and didn't seem the least bit curious about it. And Tyler might be less likely to mention that a girl was staying at his apartment than some girls would. From the look of the apartment, it didn't appear he had many guests drop by.

Susan said, "Okay. What idea do you have?"

"That you are looking for a place to stay and nothing more. I promise this is just a place to stay," he said. Abruptly, his tone changed. "Come on, Morgan, you have to trust me," he went on in a tone of mock surprise. "We've known each other since preschool!"

Both of them laughed at this comment. Her acting skills were getting better.

"All right. I am going to trust you," Susan said in a serious voice, "but if I am going to stay here, I should tell you two things. I have a problem as well as a confession to make."

CHAPTER 37

SUSAN COULD SEE that she had shocked him. It took him a moment to speak. "Okay. I'm ready. What is it?"

"What do you want to hear first, the problem or the confession?" she asked in a way that she hoped was playful enough.

"The problem," replied Tyler.

"Okay," Susan said. "If I am going to stay here, my problem is that I don't have any pajamas."

Tyler rolled his eyes and looked at the ceiling. "Problem solved. I will lend you a T-shirt."

"What if it's not long enough?" she asked teasingly, although she was actually concerned about this.

"I am so tall, it will come down to your knees. And if that's not enough, I will lend you a pair of boxers to wear under it."

Susan nodded. "Problem solved."

"Now let's hear the confession."

"The confession is," said Susan, pushing her hair back with both hands, "this is not my real hair. If I am going to stay here, I want you to know that it comes off at night."

Tyler looked at her. "That's huge, really huge—I never would have guessed. You're totally bald!"

"No, I'm not!" Susan protested. "My hair is just not this long."

"Gotcha!" Tyler said.

They laughed, and though she was just pretending to be carefree, she felt her heart lighten a little.

After a while, Susan told Tyler that she would cook dinner for him as a thank-you for letting her stay. She looked in the compact kitchen and saw what pots and utensils were available. It would be much better if they ate in the apartment; the less she went out in public, the safer they both were. She made a shopping list with enough food for at least three days, hopefully longer.

She was surprised at the quantity of cookware, cutlery, and utensils they had. She assumed most young men ate only microwaveable food or takeout. When she asked Tyler about this, he told her that Kyle was obsessed with food and did some cooking. His grandparents had recently moved out of state, he added, and had cleaned out their house. Kyle had been thrilled when they drove over and picked all this stuff up.

Susan and Tyler joked about how it might be impossible for a food enthusiast to endure the deprivations an archeologist would face on a dig. They agreed that when he returned from Turkey, Kyle would have to find a new career path.

"Maybe he should be a restaurant reviewer," Susan suggested.

"He is already a big Yelper," Tyler told her.

Susan had no idea what a Yelper was but did not want to ask. She handed Tyler the list and tried to give him enough cash to pay for the groceries. When he refused, she attempted to convince him to split the cost.

"That's not fair. I eat more than you do, and you're doing the cooking," he protested.

"You don't know that you eat more. Anyway, you're not charging me to stay here, so at least let me pay for my food," she insisted.

Tyler finally agreed, took some cash from her, and went out with the list, which included several bottles of wine. Susan hoped that he would come back with something decent; if not, she would use whatever he bought to cook with. She'd also asked him to pick up some reading material for her. She didn't care what he selected.

That night, at the little round table in the living room, Susan could tell that Tyler was enjoying his meal. She'd only made a simple pasta but had added a lot of ingredients to the bottled sauce, and the bread he'd brought home was delicious. The wine he had chosen was adequate.

After dinner, Tyler gave her a key to the apartment and set up an extra desktop computer. When he was done studying, he sat on the futon couch to watch television. He patted the cushion next to him, and when Susan sat down, he asked what she would like to watch.

"Show me what you like. I'd like to see something new." She didn't mention that anything they watched was probably new to her. Tyler selected an engaging drama set in the 1950s and a comedy newscast. He was surprised that she had not seen them and gave her some background on each. Susan had consumed two glasses of wine with her dinner and felt more relaxed. It was unlikely anything could give her real peace under her current circumstances. Still, it was the best she had felt since tutoring at the sorority house. As the evening wore on, Susan realized it was the best she'd felt in a week.

Tyler kept his promise and gave her a white T-shirt and a pair of gray-and-white-checked boxers. It was her choice, he explained; she could sleep on the futon or in Kyle's bed. Susan deliberated for just a moment before opting for the bed. She was too old to be sleeping on a couch.

She was conscious of Tyler lying in the next bed. He was such a nice young man, and she knew how much he meant to his family. She owed it to Rosa to make sure nothing happened to him. She hoped she was doing the right thing. Could the FBI link her to Rosa and then make the connection to Tyler? Susan didn't think so; Tyler was Rosa's step-grandson and had a different last name. Susan was glad, now, that she hadn't had any contact with Rosa since she had moved to Idaho. The FBI would check her phone records—how long did they keep those records, anyway? Rosa had been so busy getting ready to move that over the last few months, they'd only seen each other at the gym. Even well before then, most of their contact had been at FitMarin.

Susan wondered how her friend was doing. She certainly could not call her now. Why had Rosa not contacted her? Susan missed her terribly. Could something be wrong with Rosa or Ray? She didn't want to ask Tyler. Maybe he would talk more about his grandparents tomorrow and she could get some news. Before she fell asleep, Susan promised herself once again that she would leave at any sign that she was being followed.

Chapter 38

Early the next morning, Tyler left for swim practice and would not be back until after lunch. Susan learned he had practice every day that week; fortunately, no meets were scheduled. She didn't know how she could have gracefully refused to attend, but such a public event would have been risky for both of them.

While Tyler was gone, she planned to do some cooking, and some thinking. She was beginning to understand what she was up against and how her adversaries were organized. Russ had artfully delineated the forces against her—the federal and state governments, animal rights activists, the religious right, the medical establishment, and at least one biotech firm, Avery. All but one had made sense to her. As Susan organized the ingredients for the first recipe, she suddenly understood more.

What if Dr. Klein had alerted someone in the government that one of her patients, a research scientist, had discovered something that had anti-aging effects? Even if she had said it was just a possibility, the government might be forced into action: With unfunded pensions and entitlement programs like Medicare, public budgets could not afford to have more people living longer. The government paid the majority of the funding for many of the medical establishment's programs. If that funding was jeopardized by her research, it might work with the government, or even alone, to make sure Susan was stopped before the research could progress.

But Susan had not figured out what GI-80 could do until this past Tuesday. It wasn't until she'd learned that her photographs were the only things stolen from her mother's apartment that things began coming together for her. This, and Dr. Klein's increasingly bizarre behavior, had given her the clues she'd needed to start making sense of what was happening. But both Mr. Black Car's stalking her and her gym locker being broken into had occurred before Susan knew what she had discovered with GI-80.

Furthermore, one menopausal woman with a hormone surge was unlikely to trigger a massive response from anyone. Certain drugs and even some foods can trigger hormonal reactions; some cosmetics and packaging contain substances that can have a hormonal effect. Could any of these materials be enough to reverse menopause? And how could Dr. Klein have put this together so quickly? Susan couldn't think of any explanation for that.

Russ had said that the religious right and the more fanatic animal rights activists were involved. Susan had already been well aware that animal rights people could be dangerous; the police had even told her about their threats. That they and the religious right would be opposed to her research went without saying, unless Russ had been trying to communicate something else. What was the word he had used? *Aligned.* Animal rights groups, religious factions, at least one biotech company, and the medical establishment were aligned with the government.

Susan understood how the medical establishment was in league with the government, but how did these other two groups line up?

Standing in Tyler's apartment, the answer to this question came to her. Their involvement was actually straightforward. The animal rights extremists would disrupt her research to protect the lab animals; and religious fanatics would try to stop the research completely. It was well known that the government had informants within these organizations, whom they could use to plant information. Using these groups, the government could put an end to research it opposed.

But the initial break-in, when her lab animals were taken, could have been engineered by Avery Biogenetics. Could it be responsible for the break-in on Halleck Street as well? Could Avery have tipped off the animal rights fanatics? That would be less risky than commissioning the robbery themselves.

If the experiments at Glass Biotech were successful, it could mean that some research Avery had completed would be worthless. Taking all the animals had set back her research, but it was more likely the animals had been taken so that Avery could biopsy their tissue, hoping to discover what residue they could find from the therapeutic they had been administered. Depending on how a biologic was metabolized, this was sometimes possible. Since GI-80 effects were systemic, she thought it was unlikely that Avery had gotten anything useful.

Almost all pharmaceutical companies would be affected by her research. If GI-80 did actually reverse the aging process, these companies would sell a lot less of their highest-volume and most profitable products. High blood pressure, type 2 diabetes, and high cholesterol might be eliminated, and seniors would no longer lead *medicalized* lives.

Susan was a scientist by temperament as well as training. Ordinarily, conspiracy theories did not hold much allure for her. Was she thinking clearly now? Or was it possible that she was delusional, a mental side effect of the GI-80? If she were deluded, however, Russell—who had been the one to lay out the opposition in their phone call—was as well, and he had not taken any GI-80. If it was safe to return, Russ would not have told her he needed more time.

Susan still didn't know how Gary fit into all of this. Was he Mr. Black Car? Someone must have given Gary the new alarm codes. That pointed to him working for or at least having contact with Avery. Like Mandy, Gary would be easy to buy, and he would come cheap. He had long been resentful and felt cheated when her payout had come in after the divorce. Was Avery using her ex-husband to spy on her?

Susan couldn't recall ever attending a company event with Gary, and not many employees were left from her tenure there. And who had killed Gary, and why? She might never know the answers to all these questions. But they were all in it together—Avery, the government, and the medical community—and they were using the crazed animal rights groups and religious fanatics to do their dirty work.

Had one of these extremists been sent to the lab to kill Gary, or her? Or to kill both of them and make it look like a murder/suicide? Hitting Gary with the bat had ruined that scenario. Gary's killer would have to have known the codes for the alarm. He or she must have deactivated it, murdered Gary, and then reset it before leaving—that's why she hadn't heard it go off when she drove out of the parking lot. If she hadn't run out as quickly as she did, she would be dead now, too. She was sure of it.

Chapter 39

The only time Susan went out of the apartment that day was to climb the stairs to the roof. It had a covered deck with a large sitting area; if she crouched down, she could look out through the slats in the railing without being seen from above or from adjacent buildings. She did not see anyone watching the building from a nearby rooftop or street, although someone with a telescope or special equipment might be able to detect her presence behind the railing. It was always possible that she had been tracked or followed.

Susan went up to the roof deck several times that day but never noted anything unusual. If someone suspected she was here, there was no reason to wait before trying to apprehend her. Still, the feeling that she was overlooking something continued to trouble her.

When Tyler returned from class, she was surprised at how glad she was to see him. When he was in the apartment, she did not feel as lonely.

After dinner, she appreciated the quiet in the apartment as he studied. When he was done, they sat on the futon couch watching TV. Susan found she was interested to see what programs young people were watching. Focusing on these shows, she was able to escape her circumstances for a while.

The next morning, after Tyler left, she went up to the roof deck again. She had almost two hundred and fifty dollars left and could pay for two nights' accommodation, but she didn't have a credit

card or an ID, which made finding paid accommodations complicated. And she couldn't think of a safer place. No, she would stay
put for the time being.

She worried that Tyler would think it odd that she was hanging
around the apartment all day, so she concocted a story about going
to class and doing some shopping on Telegraph Avenue. She would
have to look online for class names and times. Maybe she would just
tell him that she had visited a friend on campus. Susan hated having
to spend her time thinking up all these lies.

Back in the apartment, she began cleaning the kitchen. The
work went so quickly, she decided to clean the entire apartment. It
was so small, it wouldn't take long to make everything immaculate.

She was considering asking Tyler for a ride that night. Maybe
if she cleaned everything, he would feel an obligation to drive her.
On the other hand, he might not even notice. Some men don't pay
attention to details like housekeeping; Gary had been one. Thinking
of Gary, Susan realized she still did not feel any sorrow that he was
dead. She was only sorry that she was involved and that it had complicated her life.

Not wanting to think any more about her ex-husband, she
turned her attention to the task at hand. She cleaned the bathroom,
vacuumed the floors, and wiped off all the surfaces, light switches,
and door knobs in the tiny apartment. The only task left was cleaning the mirrors. Susan had been dreading this and had left it for last.

She cleaned the bathroom mirror, barely glancing at herself, and
then had to face the full-length mirror affixed to a wall in the living
room, near the bathroom door. When she finished, she stepped
back to look for streaks or spots and saw her face and body reflected
in the glass. She remembered what Katie and Courtney had said
about teen romances. Could she really look that young?

Peering closely at her face, she did not see any wrinkles, fine
lines, or discolorations. Had she looked like this when she was
twenty? She had not spent as much time primping as other girls.
When she was in high school, Bunny had always pestered her to

dress up more and wear more makeup. Bunny loved cosmetics and wanted her daughter to be a "glamour girl," as she used to put it. What mother wants her high-school-age daughter to wear more makeup?

Thinking of her mother made Susan smile. Her smile faded quickly as she wondered if she would ever see her again.

Wondering how much her body had changed, she pulled off her shirt and leggings and slipped out of her panties and bra. Her stomach was flat and her breasts were not sagging. Her scientific nature taking control now, Susan turned her back toward the mirror and tried to look over her shoulder. From what she could see, the back view was as good as the front. Her butt was picture-perfect. Cosmetic surgeons would not be fans of GI-80.

Maybe that was not a joke after all. Could that be the medical establishment Russ had referred to in listing the opposition? *Opposition* was not the correct term, however. A more accurate word was *enemies*.

Just then, Susan heard someone put a key in the front door and open the lock. The mirror was less than fifteen feet from the door. Susan had used the interior bolt when she came down from the roof, and whoever was outside began knocking loudly.

CHAPTER 40

SUSAN'S HEART WAS pounding so hard, she thought she could hear it. She didn't know what to do. Should she put some clothing on or try to see who was at the door? Could it be the FBI, or some fanatic tipped off about her location? She didn't think Tyler would be back so soon, or banging on the door like that.

She grabbed her clothing and held it in front of her as she went to the door. The peep hole was too high, but the table and chairs were near the front window; she could stand on one of the chairs and look through. Moving closer to the window, Susan noticed a gap of about half an inch between the blind and the window jamb. The blinds were not custom-made, and someone had installed a stock size that did not fit perfectly.

Through the blinds, she saw a woman in a blue dress. She could not see her face, only that her dress went past her ankles. She stood very still, gripping her clothing, and after a few minutes, the woman walked away. When she did not return, Susan quickly got dressed, her heart still pounding. She didn't think the woman was an agent or an assassin, but who was she? Why did she have a key to Tyler's apartment? Susan wished she could go take a look from the roof deck but didn't dare leave the apartment.

An hour later, she heard another key in the door. Peering through the edge of the blind, she saw Tyler, his hand raised and ready to knock. Susan slid the bolt and opened the door.

"Tyler, I am so happy to see you," she told him once he was inside and the door safely locked.

Tyler gave her a beautiful smile.

"A woman tried to get in today. She scared the daylights out of me. I was completely undressed and she was banging on the door. I think she had a key."

Before Susan had a chance to describe the woman, Tyler erupted. "That was Shithead. I hate that woman. She's the manager here. She doesn't do a damn thing. Walks around in a blue dress, right? Her kids cry all the time, and she leaves their scooters and big wheels in the garage. You can't even back your car out without running over them.

"Good thing you were here and had the bolt on. She just walks in when she feels like it and looks around. Jackass!" Susan had not seen Tyler so agitated. "Last month, two guys from upstairs took all her kids' toys that were lying around the garage and threw them in the dumpster right before the trash pickup. Shithead went door to door searching apartments to see if anyone had the toys stashed away. It's illegal, but she doesn't care. She says she's not from here, so the laws don't pertain to her. I hate that woman," he repeated.

Susan looked at him wide-eyed and said, "Ty, your enemy is my enemy."

Just as they started laughing, Susan realized she had not created a story to account for her day.

"Don't you want to know why I was naked when she came by?"

Tyler looked at her and grinned. "Shoot."

"Well, I was cleaning. Do you notice any improvement?" she asked playfully.

Tyler looked around and said, "Everything looks great. But I think you need to take all your clothes off again, because I see some spots over there that you missed."

Susan felt so relieved and elated that Shithead had not been looking for her, Tyler's comment struck her as very funny and silly.

Tyler leaned over and put his arms around her. "Morgan, really, thank you for cleaning the place up. It looks great." He gave her a kiss on the cheek.

"Do you have a lot of studying to do tonight?" Susan asked.

"Some. Why?"

"I need to go someplace and was hoping you could drive me. It should take less than an hour."

She could take a bus—she'd already researched the transit route online—but it would be safer if he drove her. She didn't dare take a taxi.

"No problem. I'll be glad to take you. Is there anything good to eat here?"

"I'll make you a snack, but can you do the laundry before dinner? I don't want to run into Shithead if I go to the laundry room. We don't have to leave until after eight."

Susan heated up a large slice of baguette with roasted peppers and melted cheese and showered while he ate. She fixed her hair, extensions and all, and put on makeup. Bunny would have been so pleased and proud to see how nice she looked.

By eight-thirty, they were ready to leave. Tyler's studying was done, the laundry folded and put away, and the small kitchen cleaned up. Susan was wearing her blouse over her jeans and carrying one of her sweaters in case she got cold. She'd selected the one she hadn't worn on Friday, just in case she'd been picked up on a surveillance camera.

She was feeling agitated and sick to her stomach but tried to act composed. While she was showering, Susan had revised her plan, adding a stop before returning to the apartment. If someone followed them, she might be able to spot him there; she didn't know where they would stop, but she would think of something. If someone wanted to intercept her, it would probably be when they made that stop. Tyler would be in less danger in a public place.

Susan had no idea if she would be successful tonight. If she did not achieve what she intended, she would have to do things more directly or come up with a different approach. Mentally, she was already working on this.

Tyler's parking space was so narrow that he had to back the car out before she could get in. Oddly, he had not asked her where they were going. But then, he hadn't asked how she had spent her day. He closed the garage door with his remote and turned the car onto the street. As they moved along, Susan looked in the side-view mirror. When she put the visor down, there was a mirror there as well. If she leaned to the right, she could see directly behind the car.

Susan had Tyler make several turns onto smaller streets. Her message could have been intercepted and deciphered by the FBI and a couple of agents could be waiting for her, though it was possible they would not recognize her.

She planned to ask Tyler to remain in his car and promise that if she did not return in ten minutes, he would leave without her. With her destination in sight, she revised the procedure.

"Pull over and turn off the engine, please." Tyler parked the car and shut off the lights and the engine. It had occurred to Susan that she would be more difficult to recognize if she appeared to be part of a couple. Sitting in the dark, she turned to her friend. "Tyler, I have to find someone. I don't know if the person I'm looking for will be there, and I need a favor. Can you act like we're together?"

"Morgan, I have news for you. We are together," Tyler told her softly, his words breaking the serious tone of the conversation.

As they walked up to their destination, Susan could see a number of people standing around. When Tyler saw the sign on the building, he said, "Do you know what this place is?"

Susan did not reply. Instead, she did something Tyler had never expected.

Chapter 41

Susan pulled Tyler toward her and kissed him on the mouth. If he was surprised, he did not show it. He returned her embrace, kissed her back, and held her tightly. Susan had recognized one of the people milling around on the lawn. Standing alone watching the crowd, in street clothes, was Officer Morales.

When she pulled away, she whispered, "I know exactly what this place is."

The air smelled of burning marijuana. When Susan looked for Officer Morales, she saw him on the porch of the building. After a moment at the door, he went inside. She wondered if he was off duty or was working in plain clothes. Could he be looking for underage drinkers or marijuana smokers or had he been sent to find someone in particular?

"Why do you want to go to a biker bar?" Tyler asked.

Before she could answer, he tightened his arms around her and kissed her. Agitated and nervous, Susan was surprised to feel a wave of passion run through her body. She responded to his kiss with genuine ardor. Finally, she pulled back, ending the kiss and focusing on her surroundings.

Young people were congregated on the lawn outside the bar. Others were standing in the parking lot. Even more were on the porch under the neon Round Up sign. The parking lot and the street in front of the bar were filled with cars and motorcycles. Bicycles were chained to bike racks near the porch as well as to the porch posts and railings.

Susan hoped the person she wanted was outside and not in the bar, where Officer Morales was. There was no direct light, only the light reflected from the porch and windows. She looked around and thought she recognized the man she was meeting. His build and height looked right—he was a lot shorter than Tyler and not much taller than Susan—but she could not make out his coloring in the diffuse, dim light.

Pulling Tyler by the arm, she walked toward the man, then stopped when she was close enough to touch him. The fellow's back was to her now, so she couldn't be sure it was him. When Susan reached out and put her hand on his arm, the young man turned. At first, neither said anything as they stood looking at each other.

Then the man nodded. He stopped studying her eyes and began looking her over, his expression registering his surprise. "I almost didn't recognize you!" he exclaimed, grinning broadly. "You are so hot!"

This was not what Susan was expecting, and she suddenly felt shy, especially with Tyler standing there with his arm around her shoulder. She looked down but looked back up at the man almost immediately.

"I wasn't sure you would get my message, and if you did get it, that you would figure it out," she said softly.

Still smiling, he replied, "It was the greatest message ever! When it came up on Two Plus Two, I knew it was from you. Macaques don't usually send messages on poker websites. What a great formula! I had fun with that, too. It took me thirty-nine minutes and twenty-two seconds to solve."

The message she had sent ostensibly came from *Gina's friend, Gigi.* Susan knew this would get Kevin's attention and signal that she had sent it. The message itself had been a numeric formula; she had used an exponential number for the number of hours from the beginning of the year to set the meeting time. The meeting place, the Round Up, was part of the formula and shown as a double negative: *square down.*

"You don't know how happy I am to see you. Will you do something for me?"

Kevin replied immediately, "Of course. I want to do anything I can to help."

Susan put her face next to his and whispered in his ear. Kevin gave her a disbelieving look. "*That's* what you want me to do?"

Susan nodded. Kevin smiled and said, "Okay," drawing out the word so it sounded like *Ohh-kayy.*

"That's not all." She whispered in his ear again. Kevin sucked in his cheeks and nodded, his eyes shining in the dim light. "You got it."

"Just one more thing," Susan said, whispering her last request.

"Oh, no, not that. Not in front of everyone."

"Suck it up, Kevin," she told him sternly. "And you can't tell *anyone* about this. Will you promise?"

"I promise." He leaned over and whispered, "Meet me right next to the sculpture, southeast corner. Allow plenty of time."

"Thank you. Thank you so much, Kevin. I have some money if you need—"

"No, I'm good. See you there."

Kevin stretched out his arms and gave her a big hug, and she hugged him back. Then he turned around and walked into the bar.

"Let's go," Susan said. She put out her hand for Tyler's, and hand in hand, they walked back to the car. As she glanced around, she did not notice anyone watching them.

When they were back in the car, Tyler said, "What, no more kisses?"

Susan laughed. "I have a better idea. Let's go get some groceries. I'll cook for you tomorrow."

"I think I liked the first idea better, but it looks like I'll have to settle for idea two. Groceries it is."

She hoped Tyler wouldn't want to go out drinking or clubbing first. She wanted to avoid being out in public more than necessary, and from what she'd seen in the mirror today, she might well be carded. She did not want to try to explain to Tyler why she had no identification. She'd already acted weird enough.

The stop she had selected was a supermarket that was not located between the Round Up and Tyler's apartment but on the north side of Berkeley. When she didn't spot any car lights behind them, she allowed herself to think her plan might work.

Susan remembered Rosa telling her that pot roast was Tyler's favorite meal. Of course, Tyler was probably seven years old at the time, but she hoped he still felt that way. She would be gone on Friday, and at least she could leave him some good food.

The market had a vast liquor section, and when they had everything they needed, they went down the liquor aisle to select some wine. She wanted to buy at least three bottles, two to drink and one for cooking. As they were putting the third bottle in the cart, she heard someone call out, "Hey, Brittany!"

It was Justin, the night clerk at the Faculty Club. Trying to think of something—anything—to say, Susan found her mind was completely blank. The only thing she could do was to smile at him.

"Hey, how are you doing?"

"I'm fine. How are you? Nice to see you again," she said, trying to keep the conversation as formal and impersonal as possible. She did not introduce Tyler. Anxious to leave but wanting to do it gracefully, she looked at Tyler. "Is there anything else we need?"

Tyler shook his head. Turning back to Justin, she said, "Nice to see you. We've got to go."

"Brittany," Justin said before they could walk away, "I need to talk to you."

Susan was aghast. What could he possibly have to tell her? Hadn't he said enough already? "I'll meet you in the checkout line," she told Tyler.

Tyler face had registered his surprise when Justin had called her Brittany. Up to now he had asked her very few questions, but that surely was about to change. She was worried now–what could she possibly say to allay his concerns? She hated that she would have to come up with more lies.

"Brittany," Justin said intensely, "after you left the Faculty Club, some people came looking for you. It was strange, because they didn't know what you looked like and wanted us to describe you. I was the only one who remembered seeing you, and I only remembered because you were so cute."

He blushed, embarrassed by his remark.

"I didn't trust them. As I said, it was strange. They talked to the general manager, and I think they looked for fingerprints in your room. There were three of them, and they all looked as though they were trying to dress casually but didn't know how. All three were wearing black belts with white shirts tucked into their pants, and their pants were belted high up. They gave me the creeps.

"Anyway, I told them a girl had been there, all right, a fat blond with bad skin. I said that she'd been driving me crazy trying to get me to explain how to use the computer, like she'd never used a computer before. I said I was trying to study and she would not leave me alone." Justin gave her a shy, proud smile. "I did good, didn't I?"

Susan smiled back at him, nodding emphatically. "Thank you, Justin. You did great." Suddenly overcome with the desire to hug this boy, she reached out, wrapped him in her arms, and gave him a tight squeeze. Normally so reserved, she was as surprised by her action as Justin. Giving him one last smile, she rushed off to find Tyler.

When she got to the checkout line, Tyler was preparing to pay the cashier. Susan insisted on paying half the bill. After they put the groceries in the trunk and got in the car, Tyler asked the question she'd been expecting. "Morgan, what is going on?"

CHAPTER 42

SUSAN SAT WITHOUT speaking for a few moments. Tyler waited patiently.

"Ty," she said at last, "we both know I am smart enough to make up a story you would find believable to explain what happened just now. I am not going to do that. But I am not going to tell you what's going on, either. I can't. If it were in your best interest to know the truth, I would certainly tell you. I trust you enough to tell you."

Now Tyler was silent, and Susan was hoping he was thinking about what she had tried to say. "Do you trust me?" she asked.

After a moment, he replied, "Yes, I do. I don't know you, but I trust you. I can tell there's something genuine about you. As I said before, you are a very serious girl."

The little boy she had known had grown into a fine person. "Ty, you can leave me here if you want to. Really, I have enough money. Do you want to go back without me?"

Tyler shook his head, put the key in the ignition, and started the motor. Susan looked in the side mirror and scanned the parking lot.

"You've made the right decision. Wait until you see what I'm going to cook for your dinner tomorrow," she said, trying to sound more upbeat. "And by the way, please don't head directly back to your apartment. Take a long way and make sure no one is following us."

"Morgan—or Brittany, I don't know—in your case, a little trust needs to go a long way."

By the time they got back to the apartment and were putting away the groceries, they shared the opinion that they hadn't been followed. Tyler opened a bottle of wine and poured two glasses.

"Come sit down. What do you want to watch?"

"It's your choice," Susan replied, sitting next to him. "Thank you so much for all your help, especially tonight."

She felt so relieved being back inside his apartment. The wine, along with Tyler's presence and demeanor, had a calming effect on her. She believed Kevin would try his best to do what she'd asked. Even if he didn't succeed, she could work on crafting an alternative plan the next day, while Tyler was at swim practice and class.

"You're welcome. It wasn't all that hard," said Tyler, flipping through the channels, "except, of course, for kissing outside that bar. That was tough. I said I would drive you, but I never signed up for that!"

Susan was surprised to see Tyler looking so relaxed.

"Yeah? How come you started kissing me back? Don't expect me to feel sorry for you!"

"Well, I don't really know why I kissed you back. It must have been some stupid guy thing. What'd you think?"

Not to be outdone, she teased him back. "I have no idea, because I'm not a guy. I didn't think about it then, and I'm not thinking about it now, either. So there!" This was new for Susan.

"The hell you're not! I bet you haven't thought about anything else," Tyler said softly, and he gently pulled her toward him.

His comment struck her as funny, and Susan lifted her chin to laugh. As she did, her cheek rubbed against his face. Tyler had shaved before they left the apartment, and his skin felt smooth and warm. She closed her eyes, and a wave of desire swept over her. In an instant, Tyler's arms were around her and she felt his muscular body pressed against hers. He put his hand to her face and turned her head toward him.

Susan could not recall desire or passion ever coming upon her so quickly. When she felt his lips on hers, she responded with an open mouth. Wrapping her arms around his neck, she ran the side of her face down his and kissed his neck. Tyler put his hand near her waist and reached up under her clothing. His touch on her skin felt wonderful. She heard him murmur against her hair, "Morgan, Morgan." With her eyes closed, she drifted off. At that moment, she really was Morgan.

Tyler leaned forward and, in a single motion, pulled off his sweater along with the jersey underneath. Susan stared at his bare chest. He had a beautiful body, very muscular and lean. She could see no hair on his chest, and the muscles beneath his skin were clearly defined.

As she sat staring, Tyler stood and unbuttoned his trousers. Once again, he needed just one motion to remove his pants, so she had no idea if he'd been wearing underwear. He was so young and gorgeous. Susan wondered if she had ever known anyone this good-looking. Perhaps in a movie, but never standing in front of her. There was no question what she was going to do. Right or wrong, things were in motion, and she was being swept along.

Reaching down, Tyler took her arm, pulling her to a standing position. Susan pushed her long hair back and reached up to touch his face. When he pulled her sweater and shirt over her head, he removed both garments at once. The fellow was a master at getting clothes off quickly, Susan thought vaguely. Maybe swimmers learn how to do that.

Pulling off her jeans, she was glad she was wearing the white lace bra and panties she had bought. She hoped she looked almost as good to him as he did to her. It seemed she did. He began running his hands up and down her shoulders, and then down her back and buttocks.

"You have a beautiful body," he said. "I never imagined you would look this good without your clothes." Maybe neither of them had much imagination.

As he continued holding her tightly and stroking her body, the physical sensation was luxurious. He even smelled wonderful. Susan put her arms around him and felt the smooth, strong muscles in his back and shoulders.

Tyler did not seem to be in any rush. He sat down on the sofa and pulled her next to him. He unhooked her bra, pulled the straps off her shoulders, and tossed it toward the television. For the first time, Susan noticed the television was still on. When he saw her breasts exposed for the first time, he bent his head to kiss them, and Susan heard him murmur something.

A moment later, he reached down and removed her panties. Susan watched them as they, too, flew toward the television. She had no idea where they landed. When Tyler pushed her back on the sofa and got on top of her, she began breathing harder with excited anticipation. Tyler whispered into her hair, "Do I have to use something or are you protected?"

Susan found it impossible to focus enough to comprehend what he was saying. "I'm sorry, what?" Before he finished asking a second time, she grasped what he wanted to know. "I never thought about it."

Tyler put a hand on either side of her shoulders and pushed himself up and away from her.

"You never thought about it?" He sat up. The mood had changed.

"No."

She was fifty-three years old, for heaven's sake. Susan put her hands against her mouth. "Oh, Tyler, I am so sorry. I got swept away. I don't know what I was thinking. I can't do this. It's not fair to you."

"Fair to me? I'll use something. Don't worry about it."

"No, I shouldn't. This isn't right."

"What's not right?" he asked. "A minute ago…."

"I'm sorry."

Susan collected her clothing and walked into the bedroom. When she returned to the living room in her jeans, shirt, and sweater, Tyler had his clothing on as well and was watching TV. She walked to him and put out her hand, and he reached up and took it.

"I still really like you," he said. "But you *are* a strange girl."

Susan nodded. "I would agree with that."

CHAPTER 43

By then, Susan knew the training lanes in the university pool were available several times a day but that Tyler preferred the morning swim. She was still in his roommate's bed when he left the next morning, musing about what had happened, or almost happened, the night before. She wondered what he would think if he found out how strange she really was.

Two more days, and she could try to get to Russ. She wondered briefly if it was possible things were not as bad as he had indicated. Her encounter with Justin disproved that. He'd indicated that three government agents were looking for her. That was a lot of manpower. What could have led them to the Faculty Club? The fact that they were there when she had not used any credit cards or cell phones must mean that the search was extensive. But they had not found her, at least not yet.

She had wanted to try to get into a laboratory on campus today, but that was not an option now. Even leaving the apartment might be too much of a risk. Compelled to make sure it was still safe here, Susan dressed quickly and went up to the roof deck to look around. As she climbed the stairs, she hoped she would not run into Shithead or, for that matter, anyone else. She did her usual surveillance and looked around before exiting the stairwell.

Once back in the apartment, Susan started cooking, finding any instructions needed on the Internet. Tyler would have some good leftovers to remember her by.

She wondered if he was what the college students called a player. Once Bret had brought the subject up, Susan had followed his lead and asked about some of his fraternity brothers. Now she wished she had asked about Tyler. He was expert at removing clothing, that was for sure. Susan could not take off her own clothes as easily as he did. She concluded that that fact alone defined Tyler as a player.

She, on the other hand, had always been the good girl, always doing the right thing, not that that would help her in the present circumstances. Getting to San Francisco and Russell's office was a long shot, and the odds of Russ being able to protect her for any length of time were longer still. Susan gave her plan to reach him a one-in-ten chance of succeeding. She calculated the odds of Russ finding a way to keep her safe at one in twenty. Combined, the odds against her survival were one in two hundred—not a bet she wanted to take. Still, what choice did she have?

She wondered if Kevin ever played odds as long as these. When she'd seen him in the dim light outside the Round Up, it was as if he were an illusion. She wished that she could talk to him. She continually worried that GI-80 could be affecting her brain. Was it possible that Kevin *had* been an illusion? Could all this be the aftermath of the fever she'd had a week ago? She shook that thought off. No, that wasn't possible; Tyler had seen Kevin, too. He had definitely been there—that much, Susan was sure of.

Focusing on the tasks at hand instead of all this speculation, she finished her cooking and cleaned up the kitchen. She hoped Tyler loved pot roast as much as he had as a child. With the roast in the oven, the aroma spread through the small apartment. She would have liked to let in some air but did not want to do that while alone. The windows off the bedroom opened to a catwalk with stairs leading to the floors above and down to the ground level. The windows in the front room opened to the walkway connecting all the apartments on that floor.

Susan stepped into the shower and then, in tribute to Bunny, fixed her hair and makeup and dressed up as much as possible with her limited wardrobe. When she was done, she looked at her reflection in the tall mirror.

"You are a strange girl," she said aloud. "But then, you always were."

After taking the pot roast out of the oven, she sat on the sofa and turned on the television set. Since staying with Tyler, she had viewed more TV programs than she had in her life. Whatever happened after the next forty-eight hours, it wouldn't include watching television—that one thing was certain.

The combined aromas from the pot roast and the other things she had cooked was becoming exceedingly unpleasant. If someone wanted to get to her, he or they could as easily break down the door as climb through a window. Susan opened the bedroom window, then did the same in the living room and kitchen area to get some cross ventilation. She tilted the slats in the blinds up so that the air could flow through but no one could see in.

Conditions in the apartment began to improve rapidly. She sat in front of the television again but could find nothing that interested her. Maybe for her, watching television was enjoyable only when she did it with Tyler.

Going to the computer, she looked for the *New York Times* online and found some articles of interest. What she really wanted to do was to go to some scientific websites, but she couldn't risk looking at anything unusual or specific to scientists; better to stay with general-interest sites. She skimmed local newspaper web pages and did not find anything more about Gary's murder. Lost in the virtual world, Susan was abruptly brought back to the real world when she heard shouting outside. It was Tyler, and he was screaming!

CHAPTER 44

"I DON'T KNOW what you want, but get away from me!"

Fear gripped Susan. They were here for her, and they were going to hurt Tyler. Someone would certainly be waiting if she tried to leave by the back way. She didn't know what to do. All she could think was that she didn't want any harm to come to Tyler.

Then she heard his voice again, shouting, "I don't know where the hell your kids' toys are, and I don't fucking care!"

Susan stood with her mouth open, ready to cry with shock and relief. Through the gap in the blind, she saw Tyler walking to the apartment with his back to Shithead and his fists clenched, the veins in his arm bulging. Shithead was following him, mumbling something over and over again.

He turned around and continued swearing, his voice growing even louder. Susan saw a door open and a man come onto the walkway; he was not as tall as Tyler but much stockier. She wondered if she should go out and try to help. At least with her there, it would be two against two.

The neighbor walked over to Tyler. "What is she doing now?" he asked. Turning to Shithead, he said, calmly but in a very loud voice, enunciating every syllable, "You know, lady, you're crazy. If you bother anyone here anymore with your shit, I'm going to call the police and tell them you are crazy and dangerous. You know what they'll do then? They'll take your children away from you. Got it? Then you won't have to worry about their stupid toys anymore!"

Susan saw Shithead's eyes widen and her expression change. Facing the two men, she walked backward until Susan lost sight of her. Tyler shook hands with the fellow. Susan heard the neighbor say, "Anytime, pal."

Poor Tyler, she thought with some regret. Friday, she would be gone and there would be no one to protect his apartment while he was out. She unbolted the door so that Tyler could let himself in and quickly started closing the windows so no one could hear what they said. Tyler did not look as if he was in the mood for conversation. His face was red and his jaw was clenched. He bolted the door behind him and walked into the bedroom without saying a word.

When he did not come out immediately, Susan went back to the computer and continued reading. Now she understood why he got so agitated when he spoke about the manager. She hoped the neighbor's threat would be enough to keep Shithead away from him.

After some twenty minutes, Tyler came out of the bedroom and smiled at her, looking his usual relaxed self.

"Something smells good. What is it?" he asked.

"Pot roast." Susan wanted to say something about what had happened on the walkway but couldn't find the right words.

"For now or for later?"

"For whenever you want. It tastes even better reheated…. Um, Tyler, I am leaving on Friday." When the words finally came, she found she had more she wanted to say to him.

"Is it because of what happened out there?"

"Oh, no. I was proud of the way you handled that. Some men don't stand up to women when they need to. Do you want to know something? When I saw your neighbor come out of his apartment, I didn't know if he was going to help you, so I was going to come back you up."

"That would have been funny. What exactly did you plan to do?"

"I have no idea, but I thought that at least with me there, it would be a fair fight."

Tyler smiled broadly, then his smile faded. "Do you really have to leave?"

Susan nodded. "There's something I want to tell you," she said, resisting the urge to look down. She didn't want to do that any longer. She'd spent enough of her life feeling shy and awkward.

Forcing herself to look in his eyes, she said, "Ty, about last night…I have something I need to say. I think that for us to…" she hesitated, "to be intimate would be the wrong thing to do. It would not be fair to you, and I do want to be fair to you. But I want to be intimate with you more than anything I can think of."

Tyler opened his mouth in surprise. "Are you saying you want to have sex? Is that what you are saying?"

He was so beautiful. She nodded as she replied simply, "Yes."

It seemed to Susan as if the conversation was progressing in slow motion. Tyler just stood looking at her. Finally, he said, "Morgan, I have to tell *you* something."

Perhaps after last night, he didn't want to be involved with her. Maybe he wanted to tell her that he had a girlfriend. It was unlikely she was in Berkeley, since no girls had called or been by since she'd been at the apartment. Maybe the girlfriend was in Idaho, as if it mattered where she was. Susan hoped he did have a girlfriend, or better yet, lots of girlfriends.

What a sweet man he was. Tyler had grown up to be such a beautiful person. Susan thought she knew what was going to happen next, but she was completely unprepared for what he had to say.

"I'm in love with you, Morgan."

Hearing these words, Susan felt her legs could not support her. Fortunately, she was near the little dining table, and she leaned on it before sinking into a chair. This was the last thing she'd expected. She remembered how annoyed she'd been when Bunny said that things happen when you least expect it.

Susan had proven herself a master at figuring things out. She'd worked out who was spying for ABC. She'd figured out how to evade her enemies for more than a week, and she'd found a way to contact Kevin with a message only he would understand. Now she was presented with something for which she had no aptitude at all. Her reasoning power was really all she had. She had to think this through and do it quickly.

But her ability to focus and to analyze was not clicking into gear. "You can't be in love with me," she said. "You don't know me. Lately, I don't even know myself. I do think we care about each other."

Tyler was looking at her with an odd expression. Feeling she had to explain herself more coherently, she continued, "Ty, the only person I love is my mother. I think I'm a momma's girl."

Even as the words came out of her mouth, she realized how inane they were. How could someone so brilliant in biology and chemistry be such an idiot in social situations?

"I'm relieved to hear that," Tyler told her. "I thought you might have a boyfriend." His body language and tone of voice gave evidence that he was reassured and not put off by her stupid comments.

Susan seemed unable to stop talking. "A boyfriend? How would I have a boyfriend?"

Tyler had the most dazzling teeth and beautiful smile. Susan couldn't help smiling back.

That was all the encouragement he needed. In just two steps, he crossed the room and pulled her up from the chair. He wrapped her in his arms and began kissing her, first on her mouth and then on her neck and chest. Any focus she'd had was completely lost. All she was able to do was to rely on Tyler to keep moving forward. He must have had more concentration than she did, because in a single motion he lifted her up and, while kissing her throat, carried her into the bedroom. As he carried her, she felt his body pressed against hers.

After placing her on his bed, he removed his clothes, the sunlight shining through the window blind illuminating his face and body. In the natural light, he looked even more stunning than he had in the lamplight. With Tyler's help, Susan's clothes came off. Once removed, they miraculously disappeared.

Tyler was touching her all over her body. Susan did not want to close her eyes, but she couldn't keep them open. He was on top of her now, and she wasn't able to hold a thought for more than a second or two. When he came, she felt her body respond. The sensation she experienced came in a series of waves that washed over her whole body. The feeling went all the way to her toes.

She had no idea how much time had passed. When Susan looked at Tyler, she was sure she had never seen anyone so handsome. She wanted to say something but didn't know what would be appropriate. What came out surprised her as much as it did Tyler.

"That was the greatest experience of my life."

Tyler looked at her. "Mine, too."

"But I've lived longer than you have," Susan blurted out.

The sound of his laugh and his radiant smile were transporting.

"How much longer, two weeks? You knew me in preschool, strange girl. You can't be that much older. Anyway, none of that matters to me."

Tyler pulled her toward him. He held her tightly and kissed her neck.

"I am a very strange girl," Susan reminded him.

"Thanks for telling me. I never would have figured that out," he said with a smile.

"What do you mean that none of it matters to you?"

Tyler looked at her. He was so beautiful. "Morgan, I see the kind of person you are. The rest doesn't matter. You know what I want, don't you?"

At that moment, she wanted nothing other than what she had. She wanted to stay where she was, with her body next to Tyler's. She certainly didn't want to think about Friday.

"I haven't a clue. What do you want?"

"What I want..." he hesitated for effect, "is...pot roast."

"So they're right when they say that the way to a man's heart is through his stomach," she said, relieved, trying to poke him in the midsection.

"Uh, there are other ways, too."

"I'll try to remember that."

"Don't worry, I'll remind you."

"Are you always such a funny guy?" Susan asked him.

"Always," he told her, lightly kissing the top of her head.

Susan felt his shoulder against the side of her face. She was not anxious for this moment to end.

CHAPTER 45

Susan had insisted that Tyler maintain his regular schedule; the more normally he behaved, the safer it would be for both of them. As she lay in bed after he left for swim practice, the sun poured in through the window, signaling that it was going to be a beautiful day. She felt frustrated, though, that she still had no idea how GI-80 functioned. Even if she could access a lab now, there wasn't enough time left to do any research.

She had designed the therapeutic to boost the immune system, and it seemed likely it did. But how did this affect aging? No current theory of immunology could account for it. Was it possible that GI-80 functioned outside the active immune system? What if humans had a parallel immune system, which was dormant but capable of preventing or reversing aging if activated? What could be the trigger?

If GI-80 could alter a set of immunoglobulin molecules that was not generally activated, it could potentially have this effect. But which molecules?

Could it be the IgE antibodies? These antibodies were not well understood. Current speculation was that when the human species evolved, our bodies came into contact with all sorts of viruses, bacteria, and parasites. In response, humans developed the IgE antibodies, which specialize in combating parasites. These antibodies no longer serve this function in today's developed, largely parasite-free world. Unable to do so, they cause the majority of allergies and some other autoimmune diseases, according to one theory. If their original function was to repair parasite-caused damage at the cellular level, what if, when activated, these antibodies repair not only damage caused by parasites but all, or almost all, cellular damage?

Since what we call aging is largely cellular damage, repairing this damage would look like age reversal! Of course, this would have to be verified by research, but Susan felt sure she had figured out how GI-80 worked. What an accomplishment to discern this merely by thinking about it. When had she become so intuitive?

The magnitude of her discovery was overwhelming. And so far, the knowledge was hers alone.

CHAPTER 46

SITTING IN THE car, Susan ran through the details again. Had she missed anything? Even if she had, could she do anything about it now?

She looked at Tyler as he drove, as handsome in profile as when she looked at him straight on. If today were to be her last, she had definitely enjoyed it. She and Tyler had spent time together earlier. Susan smiled just thinking about it.

After he'd left for morning practice, she'd gone up to the roof deck and done her regular inspection of the surrounding area, grateful she had made it this far. She had vacuumed the apartment and put in a new vacuum bag, then wiped down everything in the apartment, as she'd done at the Faculty Club and in the guest room in the sorority house which now seemed like years ago.

She dressed in her jeans, athletic shoes, T-shirt, and two sweaters. Although she did not need to wear makeup, at the last minute she decided to put some on. A face full of makeup would make her look different from the way she had two weeks earlier. She thought about how pleased and happy Bunny would be to see her wearing all these cosmetics. Then she realized her mother would be overjoyed to see her no matter how she looked. She didn't want to consider the odds against their being together again. The plan she had was the best she could do with her limited resources.

She put on her silver earrings and clear glasses and packed the rest of her belongings in her tote bag. Some things that might be useful to Tyler or his roommate, like her blow dryer and scissors, she carefully wiped off and put under the bathroom sink. When she realized there might be a way to trace these items to her, she put them in her tote bag and left nothing behind.

She was glad the apartment was so small. It had been easy to wipe everything down. She didn't think that she had forgotten anything. She had even wiped the railing in the stairwell leading to the roof, and she had dropped the vacuum bag in a trash can two miles from the apartment.

Tyler had offered to drive her to San Francisco today. Susan found it surprising—and fortunate—that he accepted that she had to leave unquestioningly, as he had accepted everything else. Though her original idea was to take public transportation, she realized that going by car would be safer for her. She didn't think he would be in additional danger if he drove her. She prayed she was right about this.

When they drove through the Bay Bridge toll plaza, Susan ducked, just in case there were cameras. She thought of the Chinese proverb about the impossibility of assessing luck. While she had come to agree with the saying, she did feel she'd been fortunate to have found Tyler. Certainly, the time she'd spent with him had been extraordinary.

And he had certainly enjoyed her pot roast. Susan smiled when she thought of him sitting on the futon with her, eating his second and then third helping as they watched television. She was proud of herself for remembering what Rosa had told her so long ago about Tyler's favorite food. Her mind was definitely her greatest asset. Incredibly, with no other resources, she had survived unimpeded for eleven days.

Of course, her intellect was also responsible for getting her into this situation: If she had not been so clever, so focused and observant, she would never have been able to create GI-80. Without her, all the problems that GI-80 could create would disappear.

Was she as smart as she thought she was? Could this plan of hers really work? And if it did, would Russ be able to do his part?

"Pull over there," Susan instructed as they approached a short side street near the San Francisco Embarcadero. "You can shut the engine off if you want."

Tyler turned the key in the ignition, and for a moment they just sat there, looking at each other.

"When you get home, wipe down this car. I didn't touch anything today, but I rode in it before and may have left fingerprints."

Tyler nodded, then took her hands in his and kissed them. "This is serious, isn't it?"

"Yes, very. Thank you so much. You'll never know what you've done for me."

"Will I see you again?"

"I don't know," Susan replied sadly. They sat quietly again until she said, "I need to ask another favor, and I want to tell you something, even though I know you probably won't believe me.

"If you don't hear from me in three months, will you tell your grandmother Rosa something for me? You will need to do this in person. Do not tell her on the telephone or with any type of mail. Please tell her that you met her best friend and that our time together was wonderful."

"You want me to tell my grandmother we had sex? You're right, I don't believe you!"

"Oh, that's not the part you won't believe. That's the favor."

"Sorry, I don't think I can do that."

"Will you at least tell her goodbye from me?"

Tyler nodded.

"Ty, here's the part you won't believe. Please never repeat this to anyone, not even Rosa. I just want you to understand." Susan paused. "I am a scientist and I made a discovery, a dangerous discovery. If anyone connects you to me, play dumb. Don't let anyone know that I know Rosa. Tell them you can't keep track of all the girls you hook up with. If someone asks if anyone stayed with you, read them the riot act about Shithead—tell them she is ruining your sex life. Tell them that you can't have any girls come over, let alone stay over. You could even say that you had a chance to have two girls stay with you while your roommate was gone, and because Shithead keeps entering your apartment unannounced, you missed your big chance. Act like you're a player and just interested in getting some action. Will you do that for me?"

Susan saw the corners of his mouth turn up in the beginning of a smile as he nodded.

"I have to go now," she said.

Tyler reached over and pulled her toward him. When he put his arms around her and kissed her, she kissed him back, feeling overwhelming sadness.

"Goodbye, Ty."

"I love you. You know that, don't you?"

"Yes, I know. I love you, too." She took her tote bag and got out. By the time she shut the car door, tears were rolling down her cheeks.

Susan was so heartsick, she felt physically ill, but she had no time to stop. Hurrying down the street, she kept an eye out for what she was seeking. She prayed that she had not endangered Tyler further with the things she'd just told him. No, he was safe. She had not told him that much, and now she was away from him. Harming him would be pointless. If anyone connected them, she hoped they would realize that. And if they did, she hoped they would care.

Further down the street, she saw a woman sitting on the sidewalk, wrapped in a blanket, her head buried in her crossed arms. Susan thought she looked as though she might be sleeping sitting up. She had a paper plate on the ground in front of her, and an old gray dog was lying at her side.

Her heart went out to this woman, sitting on the street each day with only a dog for company. She reached into her pants pocket for her wallet and put two twenty-dollar bills on the plate. Maybe this gesture would bring her luck, and if so, the right kind. If things didn't work out today, Susan figured, she wouldn't need the money, anyway. Then, on impulse, she set the tote bag filled with all her possessions—cosmetics, clothing, notepad, dryer, scissors—next to the plate. The homeless woman looked up at Susan, her face registering recognition. Sticking one foot out from her blanket, she pointed to the athletic shoe Susan had given her. Could it really have been just eleven days ago?

CHAPTER 47

As she rounded the corner, Susan stopped abruptly. The plaza and the entire area around it was jammed with people and bicycles—Critical Mass in all its glory. Accurately estimating the number of people was impossible. There had to be thousands of bikers, perhaps even tens of thousands. She had never imagined it could be so massive.

And something else was unexpected. A third of the riders were wearing face paint or costumes. Halloween was three days away, and these riders were obviously celebrating early. If she could not get to Russell today, Susan thought, she could meet him in a costume on Halloween, enlisting the aid of a random biker to help her with an outfit and a place to stay. Relying on Kevin or Tyler a second time would be too dangerous for everyone.

A number of the female riders had on fishnet hose and very short pants or, in some cases, no pants at all, just the fishnet stockings and a skimpy top. One woman actually wore a pair of fishnet tights and no top. Susan marveled at her audacity—and even more, at her body's ability to thermoregulate. Several bikers were dressed in superhero costumes. The atmosphere could not have been more contradictory to her mood.

Kevin had told her to meet him on the southeast side of Vaillancourt Fountain, and Susan wove through the mass of bikes and bikers to reach it. The fountain and sculpture were jarring and ugly, giant concrete blocks that looked like haphazardly placed wild fingers angrily pointing to the sky. The structure had been the source of ongoing controversy and discord in the community, the perfect background for the anarchists who made up Critical Mass.

In all her mental rehearsals, she had never doubted that Kevin would be here. Maybe she was too early, or could it be he was late? As she wended her way through the crowd, Susan grew increasingly worried. What if he didn't come? What if he had been detained after they'd met at the Round Up?

She was sure that Kevin had said the southeast side of the fountain. Susan felt a nervous flutter rise up her chest and into the lower part of her throat. There were so many bikers; he could be here and unable to find her. Maybe another biker could help her get to Russell. Frantically, she looked around. Time was growing short. If the group left at five-thirty, the ride would start in less than ten minutes. Maybe Critical Mass tended not to leave on time. They were anarchists, after all. But hadn't Kevin specifically told her to leave plenty of time?

All around her, bikers were putting on their helmets. She saw the young man next to her slipping on a pair of fingerless gloves. They would be starting shortly, and she couldn't move far from the fountain's edge to look for Kevin. If she did, he would never find her. She felt herself starting to panic. She had promised herself that no matter what happened, she would not do that.

She heard someone whistle and yell something she could not distinguish. She turned around but couldn't see where the sound had come from; there were just too many people. Another whistle came from somewhere in the crowd, and at least this time, she was looking in the right direction. It was Kevin, walking his bicycle straight toward her. Susan rushed over to him.

"I was just confirming the route. The ride is set."

"I didn't see you. I was so upset!" The relief she felt was palpable.

"You were upset?" Kevin said. "What about me, walking around with a girl's bike? I had to bring this thing over on BART."

The smile Susan gave him was radiant. "Sorry. I've never ridden a boy's bike. Didn't I say you had to suck it up?"

Kevin smiled back. Apparently, he thought this was funny, too.

"I bet no one even noticed. This *is* San Francisco," Susan added.

Kevin pushed the bicycle over for her to hold, then took the helmet off the handlebars and put it on her head.

"Fasten it. That's right. The strap needs to be tighter. Here, let me help you."

Once her helmet was fastened and adjusted, Kevin told her, "Everything is set. I made a couple of changes to the plan."

"What changes?"

The plan was very simple; she couldn't think of anything that could be altered without messing it up.

"Don't worry. I did everything you asked. I just arranged for some added help at the door if you need it."

"What help?" Susan asked nervously.

"Don't worry about it. If you don't need it, you'll never know about it, and if you need it, you'll have it."

Susan was not pleased to hear about improvised changes. Kevin didn't know exactly what she was planning, so how could he provide additional help? Before she could ask for more information, he began telling her something else.

"There is another small change. I did not tell anybody; I promised you I wouldn't. I did say today's ride was a really big one and he should come along."

Susan had no idea what Kevin was talking about. Last-minute changes were very risky. Why would he improvise? The smell of marijuana was wafting through the plaza. Some of the riders were already high. Could Kevin be stoned as well?

CHAPTER 48

KEVIN OBVIOUSLY THOUGHT something was amusing. Grinning at her, he pointed to the biker directly in front of her, a tall rider with his helmet strapped on, ready to ride. Only when she saw his sharp-toothed smile did Susan realize who it was. "Wolf!"

Susan could feel herself smiling so widely that her face actually hurt.

"Hey, Kevin didn't tell me what was up, only that someone would look different. I didn't even see you until he whistled for you. I don't have to work these days, you know, so I finally came along on a ride. I've missed you. We've all missed you. You're looking good."

"I've got to hurry," Kevin said. Then he turned to Wolf. "Stay near her. Help her if she needs it. Hold the bike when she gets off." Once he started moving through the crowd of cyclists, Susan quickly lost sight of him.

Even with the two bikes between them, Wolf's arms were so long that he was able to reach out and give her a big hug. She tried to hug him back but was just able to awkwardly squeeze his arms. Susan looked into his face and found she had no words to express her joy. She had unconsciously believed that she would never see him again.

Everyone around them was ready to go. Susan could see the ride's leader and knew she was close to the front. He raised a hand high over his head and made two forward motions with his arm. He shouted something, but she could not hear what he said.

It was decades since she had last ridden a bicycle, but after a few unsteady pumps on the pedals she found her balance and rhythm. What they always say about never forgetting how to ride a bicycle was evidently true. She rode along easily keeping pace with Critical Mass. As the throng of riders surged forward, she was swept up in the excitement of being part of this immense group. When she had ridden a bicycle in the past, it had generally been pleasurable. Today riding as part of such a large group was exhilarating and thrilling. Susan was overcome with a feeling of joy and elation that was transporting. Riding with Critical Mass had only been a way of getting to Russell's office without being intercepted. She had never expected the ride itself to be so amazing.

At her immediate left and keeping the same pace, Wolf, she was sure, was experiencing the same elation. As if acknowledging her thoughts, he burst into song, his deep and resonant baritone filling the air around them.

The bikers of Critical Mass did not stop at traffic lights or stop signs, yield to pedestrians, or observe driving lanes. As she peddled, Susan was aware of altercations breaking out; she could hear swearing and shouting. But since she was toward the front of the ride, she could not see what was happening to cause the commotion. Critical Mass controlled the road and no other traffic could pass in either direction.

The ride leader signaled to the right, and Critical Mass turned onto Sansome Street. Susan's heart was racing and she was breathing quickly. She knew that she was almost at her destination. As they approached Russell's office building, she could see two men standing outside the building's entrance on the sidewalk. As she rode closer, she could see they wore identical black suits, sunglasses, and what looked like earpieces. Susan had a plan to get past the doorman, but she hadn't planned for this. The police or FBI had either intercepted and understood her Choga message or had been routinely watching Russell's office. She had no way to get around two men who would be armed and prepared to stop her. She could continue riding with

Critical Mass and attempt to reach Russ another time, maybe on Halloween when she could be in costume.

Just then, the Critical Mass leader gestured four times consecutively, a motion Susan had not seen him make earlier, and four cyclists rode off the street and onto the sidewalk. She saw Kevin was also outside on the sidewalk. As the four bikers approached, he backed up against the building to avoid the bicycles coming his way. The cyclists rode past the entrance doors, then stopped and got off their bikes. To her amazement, Susan saw they were blocking the two dark-suited men to enable her to enter the building.

Thinking quickly, she made her decision. The door to the office building would still be guarded on Halloween. She had to try now. She stopped riding and quickly took off her helmet. After Wolf took both the helmet and bicycle from her, she sprinted toward the building. Kevin was inside the lobby now, right by the entrance. As he held the front door open behind him so Susan could enter, he was talking loudly to Gus, the building guard.

"Hey, homie, you need to leave some TP in that stairwell. Pretty inconsiderate of you," Kevin yelled taunting Gus.

Susan could not hear what Gus replied but saw him start chasing Kevin out the door and onto the sidewalk. Gus was shouting at the top of his lungs at Kevin, who was running full speed toward Wolf and the girl's bike. Susan saw the door to the stairwell was open. As she raced into the building, she heard one of the men shout, "There, it's her!"

Another man's voice cried out, "The son of a bitch just peed on my shoes!"

Almost at the stairwell now, she heard another voice taunting, "It's a disability, dude. It's called urinary incontinence, and it's protected under the ADA. My friends here have it, too. It comes from spending too much time on a bike seat."

Susan heard shouting and swearing but had no time to look back at what was happening behind her. She started running up the four flights of stairs to Russell's office. Soon she heard footsteps on the stairs behind her. She didn't know how far behind; she just kept climbing the stairs as fast as she could.

When she reached the fifth floor, she pulled the stairwell door open and ran out into the hallway. Russ's office was at the far end. Racing down the hallway, she heard footsteps pounding behind her. She was running so fast, she surprised herself. The door to the law firm was only a few yards away. If the door was unlocked, her odds would greatly improve.

CHAPTER 49

SUSAN DASHED THE last few yards toward the office door. From the thundering footsteps at the other end of the hallway, she was sure that both men were chasing her. Russ would have made sure the door to the law firm was unlocked. If more men were waiting inside, she could only hope that he could protect her. What choice did she have?

When she put her hand on the doorknob, it turned immediately and she hurried into the reception area, shutting it behind her and breathing hard. Everything looked in perfect order but eerily empty, until Susan saw Russ in the doorway to the hall that led to the attorneys' offices. He was wearing dark suit pants, a white shirt, and a tie but no jacket, which struck her as odd. She had always envisioned him in a suit if she made it to his office.

"I'm sorry. The office is closed," he said.

She had never heard him speak so coldly. Even on the telephone, as he'd been choosing his words so carefully, Susan had felt a warmth and concern that she'd believed genuine. It felt as if she'd been punched in the stomach. How could she have been so wrong?

She heard footsteps pounding down the hall. In a moment, it would be over. She'd blindly misplaced her trust. There was nothing to do but say just as coldly, "You really turned out to be a disappointment, Russ."

She hated herself as much as she despised him at that moment.

She had thought she'd been so clever with her plan to get here. Russ looked surprised—no, stunned. How did he think she would feel? She might as well tell him off, since she'd be dead once the men came through the door.

"Susan," Russell said in astonishment, "is that you?"

It had never crossed her mind that Russ would not recognize her. Kevin and Wolf had been able to identify her, and Susan had grown accustomed to her appearance. That Russell had failed to make this connection came as a complete surprise.

"Yes, of course it's me," she said, relief flooding through her.

Russell crossed the reception area and pulled Susan to the side with one hand while locking the door with the other.

"If they want to come in, they'll have to break the door down, and I assure you, they won't do that," he said with what sounded like a sigh of relief. "Come with me."

As they walked down the inner hall, someone was trying to turn the outer doorknob and then began banging on the door. Russell gave no indication that he'd heard or cared. Once in his office, he closed the door and just looked at her.

"This is incredible. You said you'd had a breakthrough, but I never imagined this. I have never been so worried or stressed before."

"I wasn't particularly relaxed, either."

"Susan, I am so sorry. I wish there had been another way. It felt horrible cutting off all contact, knowing you were alone in such a dangerous situation. I couldn't do anything for you except leave you out there by yourself while I tried to find a solution. I kept telling myself that if anyone could survive this, it would be you. Please understand that any help I could have tried to offer would only have led them to you. You had to do what you could to stay safe and get back here, and I had to do my part."

Susan had never seen him so talkative.

"Seeing you, I finally understand. I knew the government was opposed to your research and prepared to prevent it from continuing, but until now, I really didn't comprehend why. I was followed everywhere I went. This building has been under constant surveillance. Agents from the FBI have been outside at the front and back entrances this whole time. If you look out the window, you can see them."

For some reason, Susan saw a glimmer of humor in that. "No, I think they're out in the hall now."

Russell attempted a smile. "I tried to tell you on the telephone who else is involved. These people are willing to do anything to stop you."

His somber tone made Susan nervous. "So this is hopeless?"

She had miscalculated badly, then. The odds were not twenty to one; they were insurmountable. This realization came with a tidal wave of sadness and regret. Maybe if she had stayed on the run, she could have had a life of some kind. Was Russ in danger as well?

"That's the reason I needed you to give me time. It took awhile, but I was able to connect with a group powerful enough to stand up against all this. I only had to show them why it was in their self-interest to help you."

Before she could ask any more questions, he took his suit jacket from the back of his chair and put it on. "Let's go."

He opened his office door and motioned for Susan, then took her arm. In her earlier visit to his new firm, she had only gone as far as his private office. Why were they walking through the office suite? And why hadn't the agents broken through the main door?

Halfway down the hall, Russell opened another door and gestured for Susan to enter before him. Filling most of the wood-paneled conference room was a massive wood table surrounded by oversize camel-colored leather chairs. Seated around the table were seven men Susan did not recognize.

As the two entered the room, the men stood up. All were middle-aged and wearing unusually well-tailored suits. Six of the men were Caucasian and one was Asian. All looked surprised.

"Gentlemen, this is the woman I was telling you about. I would like to present Dr. Susan Glasser."

Russell was smiling and appeared calm. One by one, he intro-
duced the seven men: Mr. Ashio Nakayama, Mr. François Bregard,
Mr. Peter Davis, Mr. Hartmuth Moehring, Mr. Guiseppe Ferdilino,
Mr. Allister Whitley, and Mr. John Cole. Each told Susan what a
great pleasure it was to meet her. She still had no idea who these
men were.

Once the formal introductions were complete, Russell said,
"Let us all take our seats. Dr. Glasser has had a long day and trav-
eled a difficult road to get here."

As the men smiled at this remark, Susan took the chair nearest
Russell. She prided herself on her ability to classify people based
on their appearance, but who these men might be was completely inscrutable.

"Gentlemen," Russell went on, "on the table in front of you
are the documents I've prepared. I presume you have had adequate
time to review them. Please sign and date each copy, indicating the
agreement and commitment of your respective companies. Your signature should be on the line above your printed name. After you
have signed all nine copies, Dr. Glasser will sign them. There will be
an original for each of you to retain."

Turning to Susan, he said, "Dr. Glasser, these men are prepared
to help you continue your research. Collectively, they pledge to pay
Glass Biotech two hundred thousand dollars per month to ensure
that you have the funding you need. In addition, they will provide
the resources and funds necessary to guarantee your personal security. In return, you promise to fulfill three conditions.

"First, you commit to continue your research, moving to
human trials as quickly as possible. Second, you agree to provide
regular updates on the progress of your investigations. And third,
you consent to wait a minimum of twelve months after they have
been informed in writing of the results of your human trials before
informing anyone about the nature, progress, or results of your
research. This limitation is intended to include the entire scientific
community, any government entities, all business interests, and the

media. This agreement is binding for four months and renewable under the same terms at their sole discretion. This contract can be altered only through the written consent of all parties."

Susan was completely baffled. Who were these men, and what kind of agreement was this? The men were obviously important. The people chasing her had not forced their way into the office. But how could they guarantee her safety, and why were they offering so much funding with what appeared to be no strings attached?

CHAPTER 50

THE MYSTERY MEN immediately began signing the documents and passing them to one another. Susan noticed that each man used his own pen. There were no pens on the table and her attorney did not offer to provide any. For some reason, this struck her as one more oddity in a strange situation.

Susan must have looked uncertain, because Russ spoke up addressing not only her but the men in the conference room. "Dr. Glasser, I can see you have questions. I still have not told you who these men are. Collectively, they represent the largest insurance companies in the world: Japan Post Insurance Company, Axa, American International Group, Allianz, MetLife, Zurich Insurance Group, and ING."

Allister Whitley spoke first. "Dr. Glasser, please do not be surprised that you have not heard of us prior to now. I would be surprised if you had. We endeavor to keep a low profile, and it's unusual for anyone outside the highest levels of our industry to contact us. Few people outside this room even know our organization exists. Together, we form a trade organization created to enable large insurers to work together to further our collective interests, without, of course, violating any anti-trust legislation."

His last comment must have been humorous, because he and the other six men smiled broadly.

Ashio Nakayama nodded to Russ. "Mr. Harris approached the

head of my company in Tokyo about your breakthrough. Once my CEO became aware of the implications of your findings, he contacted me, and I contacted the other members of our association. After hearing what Mr. Harris had to say, we agreed to offer you our support. We have flown here to deliver this promise of assistance and collaboration in person."

"You see, Dr. Glasser," Russ explained, "your research has the potential to immensely increase their assets."

Susan was still puzzled. What could her research do for the insurance companies?

Russell continued, "If your research proves successful, it has the potential to reduce their liabilities for life and possibly even health insurance payouts. Premiums already collected for these policies amount to massive reserves. The value to their collective organizations could be trillions of dollars. A small investment in your company and your safety has the potential to bring them enormous financial rewards."

Susan stood up. As she did, all the men started to rise.

"Gentlemen, please, remain seated," she requested. She could see the surprise on the face of each man as she spoke. She looked so young and was dressed so casually, but she had the bearing of a poised and confident woman. The disparity between her appearance and her demeanor had to be striking.

"Thank you for coming today. I appreciate the time you've taken and the effort you have all made to be here, as well as your very generous offer of assistance. I look forward to a successful and profitable future for us all. I accept your offer, with the conditions outlined by my attorney and friend Mr. Harris, with gratitude."

When she mentioned his name, Susan smiled at Russell.

"I do have one request." Again, the men looked at Susan in surprise. "A few of my, shall I say, associates who helped me arrive safely today had an unfortunate encounter with the men who attempted to block my way. I would request that you provide them the highest-caliber legal assistance, should they require it."

The men nodded and, as Susan sat down, continued signing and dating their contracts.

"How did you ever think of this?" she asked Russ. "And how did you find them?"

"I'll tell you later. We have a lot to talk about."

Once the paperwork was signed and quickly checked over by Russell, the seven insurance executives asked Susan to pose for photos with them. Susan made them promise to return to take more pictures when she was properly attired. When they'd finished, one of the men explained that their limousines, which had been delayed, had arrived. There had been a major traffic disruption earlier, undoubtedly caused by Critical Mass. A security team to provide protection for both Russ and Susan had also arrived.

They said their goodbyes in the reception area, the security team by the front door. Russell was grinning and his eyes were shining. He was clearly proud of himself.

"Russ, you did it! You came through! I cannot believe that I ever doubted you. I don't think anyone else could have done what you did." If possible, Russ's smile grew even broader. "How did you ever think of this?"

Russell just kept smiling. He certainly had something to smile about, but she still had problems.

"Russ, I'm going to need a criminal lawyer. I'm still wanted for questioning in Gary's murder. Is there any more information about who the killer was?"

"As a matter of fact, there is," Russ replied, still smiling. "Let's go back to my office." As they walked, he went on, "It seems that your ex-husband was a busy guy. He was working for Avery Biogenetics, getting information on you."

"But Gary didn't have any information on me. I hadn't seen him in years."

Again motioning her to walk into his office before him, Russell glanced at his watch.

"Avery didn't know that. I would guess that he approached

them initially, trying to get some money. At any rate, he was an easy person to make use of. Gary Keller had been beating the bushes for funds. He'd been attempting to extort money from his former business partners. Trust me, no prosecutor would try to make the case that you were the most likely one to kill him. Many people had better reasons to want to see him dead.

"And Avery will want to see this investigation stopped. Their involvement is very deep. A formal legal-discovery process would prove extremely embarrassing, at the very least. Avery likely provided Gary with the codes to your alarm. I checked the time you called me from your car when you ran out of the lab. It was a full eight minutes before your alarm was activated. According to your security-monitoring company, the delay on the alarm is only two minutes.

"When I saw that differential, I knew this was not a coincidence or just about killing Gary. There were easier ways to do that. It was about involving you. Having you both turn up dead would have provided an excellent opportunity to get rid of Gary, who might have been difficult to silence, and eliminate you without a lot of questions asked. When that plan failed, they used the situation they had to implicate you. They created the grounds for considering you dangerous. Then once they found you, they could have justified killing you, and destroying the threat your research posed.

"Now that you're back safely, the government will want this to go away. Once your formula is secure, you personally are no longer of any interest. And I'll bet the investigation into Gary's death comes up with evidence that he was the victim of an attempted robbery at your business."

Susan had never felt such overwhelming relief. "But there's something else I couldn't figure out. The government would have had to know about the effects of GI-80 before I did. How is that possible? I didn't figure out what was going on until Tuesday, the day Gary died. Someone else had to know well before I did."

"That's correct. It seems the government was tipped off by

two doctors in North Coast Medical Group, Denise Klein and Philip Horzman."

"North Coast Medical Group—that's the network I use. Denise Klein is my gynecologist, and yes, that makes sense. She'd seen my bloodwork and could have known something early on. But I don't think what she knew from that could have been enough to trigger a government response. And who is Philip Horzman? I've never heard of him."

Russell opened a manila folder on top of his desk. The first pictures he showed her were of Denise Klein. Some were apparently surveillance photos, showing Dr. Klein near her car, walking, entering a building. Others were more formal shots.

"Yes, that's my doctor, Denise Klein," Susan confirmed.

Russ handed her some other photos. "This is Dr. Philip Horzman," he told her, pointing to a distinguished gray-haired man talking to Dr. Klein. "Philip Horzman has a cosmetic-surgery practice. I was informed he became suspicious that someone in the Bay Area appeared to be getting noticeably younger. The observed effects exceeded those achievable by cosmetic procedures. He put out an inquiry, asking if any other medical professionals had seen any evidence of this, and elicited a response from Dr. Klein. They connected early on. Klein told him her suspicions about a patient, and they were able to connect the dots. One or both then tipped off the government."

"But what about doctor-patient confidentiality?"

"Turns out your Dr. Klein has religious scruples about tampering with God's order for the world. She's a fundamentalist. God's laws supersede man-made regulations."

Susan looked at the photographs again. She had never visited a cosmetic surgeon and did not recognize the man in the pictures. Russ handed her a professional biography of Philip Horzman, providing details of his life from early childhood in California's Central Valley through his current practice in Novato. Scanning the document, Susan could see nothing that pointed to where they could have crossed paths. She was even more certain that she had never met this man and had no idea how he could know about GI-80.

The folder held surveillance photos of Dr. Horzman, too. Susan stopped at one showing him at a restaurant with a woman.

"Russ, I know this woman! Why do you have her picture?"

Looking at the photograph, Russ replied, "That's Andrea Horzman, Philip's current wife."

Andrea Horzman! Was that her name? So it was BB who'd first realized what GI-80 could do. Body Beautiful turned out to be a veritable body of knowledge.

"This all makes complete sense now. Andrea Horzman goes to my gym. She was the first one to notice my physical changes. From something she said, I realize she must have discussed this with her husband. I remember her saying that people wanted to know what I had done. I thought she was talking about me pouring water on an electric heater."

"Why would you pour water on an electric heater?"

"It's a long story. You had to be there," Susan told him as she put the photographs back in the folder. "Before you explained their business, do you know who I thought those seven men were? They were wearing such expensive suits, I thought they were the Mafia."

Russ threw his head back and roared with laughter. Feeling lighthearted, Susan laughed with him. As she did, she noticed how beautiful his smile was. He really was a very appealing man.

Still laughing, Russ took out his cell phone. "I had no idea what time you would arrive today. I was hoping to celebrate wrapping this up. Now it's gotten too late. I need to make one call." He put his finger to his lips.

So he had a girlfriend. Susan wondered how he'd had time to meet someone so quickly, especially when he had been so occupied with this investigation. Still smiling, Russ pushed a button on his phone. "Hi…yes, everything's just fine, but I'm running late—too late for dinner tonight. No, I'll pick you up tomorrow, six o'clock exactly. I promise. Yes, of course. I'll put her on the phone now, Bunny."

Acknowledgments - Afterword

I HOPE YOU enjoyed reading my novel as much as I enjoyed writing it. I would like to thank the people who helped, encouraged me, and believed in my book throughout this process: my dear husband and two daughters; my science consultant, Colleen Carlston; my editor, Pamela Feinsilber; and my proofreader, Lisa Matthews. I would also like to express my appreciation to Michael Coffee for allowing me to visit his company's research laboratory.

The science and historical references in the novel are true. However, since GI-80 has not yet been created, the biochemical reactions to this powerful biologic are, alas, imaginary.

You can email A. M. Matthews with comments or questions at PiggybackPress@hotmail.com or visit Book *Body of Knowledge* on Facebook at fb.me/BookBodyofKnowledge.

ABOUT THE AUTHOR

 A. M. Matthews lives in the San Francisco Bay Area with her husband and the family dog. Born and raised in Miami Beach she comes from a family of writers – some well-known, some not known at all. A. M. Matthews has always enjoyed creating and telling stories and is highly regarded for these abilities. After raising her children and a career in management, consulting and teaching, she decided to devote her time and energy to writing. Body of Knowledge is her first novel – it is the book she always wanted to read. Currently, she is working on a second novel, also science fiction set in the biotechnology industry. You can contact her with comments or questions at PiggybackPress@hotmail.com.

www.ingramcontent.com/pod-product-compliance
Lightning Source LLC
Chambersburg PA
CBHW060634260626
47161CB00008B/2882